For Myself Alone

A Jane Austen Inspired Novel

By Shannon Winslow

For My Dear Parents

Harold & Doris

Soli Deo Gloria

Preface

Like many of you, presumably, I adore the work of Jane Austen. Her subtle stories of love triumphant and her witty, elegant prose suit my taste exactly. They have influenced my own writing more than anything else.

When I began this novel, my goal was to create, not a sequel or tie-in this time, but a new story – one I imagined Miss Austen might have written next. I didn't have in mind any direct reference to her work, only a nod to her style. With her words so deeply entrenched in my mind, however, I often found myself thinking of and alluding to various passages from her books as I went along.

Rather than fight the temptation to borrow some of her expertly turned phrases, I decided to go with it. After all, I couldn't hope to improve on the master. So, if you are a Jane Austen aficionado, you will no doubt recognize a quoted line here and there (a list of which you will find in the appendix). I had a wonderful time tucking these little jewels in between the pages. Hopefully you will find just as much fun discovering them as you read. I trust you will accept this as I intend it – as a tribute to Jane and to her fans. Enjoy!

Respectfully,
Shannon Winslow

Let other pens dwell on guilt and misery. I quit such odious subjects as soon as I can, impatient to restore every body, not greatly in fault themselves, to tolerable comfort, and to have done with all the rest. – Jane Austen

Prologue

Through the first two decades of her existence, Josephine Walker led a singularly uneventful and ordinary life that gave little hint of what was to come. She had done nothing in that period to significantly distinguish herself from her contemporaries by way of either excessively good or prodigiously bad behavior. So it was, therefore, a matter of considerable surprise to those who best knew her when, at the promising age of one-and-twenty, she became the concentrated focus of so much local speculation and gossip.

The inhabitants of a place so unaccustomed to serious scandal could not reasonably be expected to ignore an exceptional bit of news when it came their way. Tongues wagged tirelessly as accounts of "the trouble in Bath" made the rounds. Where or how it began not one of the residents of Wallerton, in Hampshire, could testify with any security. What is not in dispute, however, is that Mrs. Oddbody was overheard dishing out a fine portion of the story to her neighbor in the street one day.

"My dear Mrs. Givens, have you heard about Miss Walker? She is just returned from Bath, you know, and in quite a state of agitation. There is big trouble brewing with that young man of hers; depend upon it. I expect it is the corrupt atmosphere that worked the mischief. The things that go on in that town... Well, let me tell you, it is quite shocking! I daresay many a respectable young woman has lost her character in that heathen place."

Mrs. Givens, being of an unselfish nature, shared the somewhat-altered morsel with her husband. "Miss Walker has completely lost her character, Mr. Givens. I have just had it from Mrs. Oddbody, a most reliable source. Evidently, she began cavorting with a very unsavory element in town, keeping company with some strange man. Now she has brought a great calamity down upon her head."

Mr. Givens, in turn, generously passed the tidbit on to his brother-in-law Mr. Pigeon, adding his own considered opinion to the report. "It will lead to legal action, I shouldn't wonder. It shows a careless disregard for the credit of her family to involve herself with a man of obscurity. Then, as they say, 'The apple does not fall far from the tree.' Was there not rumor of some trouble of that kind with the mother years ago?"

Mr. Pigeon recapitulated the account to his wife. "They say the mother is to blame. But mark my words, Agatha, it is the money at the heart of the matter," he concluded with irrefutable sagacity. "By heaven! A woman should never be trusted with money. No doubt it has completely gone to her head. She would have done much better never to have been given it in the first place. Bad judgment on the part of the uncle; bad judgment indeed."

"Unfortunate as the event may be," summarized Mrs. Pigeon for her brood of three fledgling girls, "we may draw this useful lesson from Miss Walker's plight. A lady cannot be too much guarded in her behavior towards the undeserving of the other sex. No matter who is to blame, it is the woman who gets the worst of it when things go wrong. We must take care that nothing of the kind will ever befall any of you, my pets."

Miss Walker's name was on everybody's lips. The more her story was exaggerated and embellished by repetition, the better it suited the assorted purposes of those who told it. To the charitable, she became an object of pity; to the hard-hearted, a source of cruel diversion; and to every teacher of morality, an example conveniently close to hand. Various versions of the tale, containing various proportions of truth to fiction, spread throughout the village at lightening speed. No one could agree upon the particulars, but about one idea all opinions united. This misstep was sure to damage the lady's standing in the community and be the ruination of her chances of ever making a respectable match.

Part One

1

Josephine Walker

I know that in the grand scheme of things the misadventures of one country girl amount to no more than a drop in the great watery deep. However, in the infinitely smaller scope of that particular young lady's imagination, the very same drop may prove enough to thoroughly drench her. I am one such girl, just come in from a soaking rain.

With my hand still damp, metaphorically speaking, I take up my diary from its traditional resting spot on the bedside table. I stroke the pebbled surface of the embossed red leather binding and trace the name engraved on the cover in gilt lettering: Josephine Walker. The book was a present for my seventeenth birthday, a parting gift of sorts from my hapless governess. In it I have diligently documented, without embellishment, the meager fare of which my life has consisted for the four years since. Putting pen to paper always gives me comfort, although the stories I write for children are on the whole, I trust, far more entertaining than the entries in my diary.

Judging from the stillness of the house, even the last of the servants has retired. Only the great clock in the hall and a distant discontented dog keep me company through the watches of the night. The relief of sleep escapes me. My restless mind continues pacing to and fro, retracing the turbulent events of the past few weeks. How glad I am to be home at Fairfield again; vain was my wish to leave it in the first place. How much misery might I have been spared had I never gone to Bath? I craved adventure then. Now the peace of privacy and the company of my closest friends are all I yearn for.

By the flickering candlelight, I revisit a simpler past as set down in the foremost part of the volume in my hand. As I leaf through, my eye catches upon a date with a small star carefully drawn beside it. A significant day: my first grown-up ball, I remember, smiling. A dozen other entries of similar import are denoted by the same fanciful symbol, marking bits and pieces of my innocent youth.

As I continue turning forward in time, my diary falls open to the twenty-seventh day of April, the current year – a day which earned not just one star, but an entire constellation. With equal agitation of an entirely different sort, I likewise opened to a fresh page in my diary that night. I remember taking inordinate care writing the date, adorning the capital "A" with as many scrolls and flourishes as I could devise. I was in no hurry. At last I had something truly worth recording for posterity. Yet in my excitement, I hardly knew where to begin. Nothing in my past had prepared me for the circumstances in which I found myself.

I grew up here on our small estate on the outskirts of Wallerton, in Hampshire, and my childhood was in most ways quite unremarkable. Although, looking back, I must admit my conduct was often far from exemplary. Being more interested in playing cricket with my brothers than learning my music and French lessons, I daresay I gave my poor governess a very difficult time.

Nevertheless, to her great credit and my parents' supreme relief, Miss Ainsworth somehow managed to equip me with all the basic skills society considers essential for a lady of my station. Thus, I can play and sing passably, hold my own in trite conversation, pour tea without disaster, and do every kind of needlework imaginable. Still, although the word is often very liberally applied, no discriminating person would be tempted to call me truly accomplished.

With my genteel education complete and a decent dowry laid by, I was deemed "finished" and ready to make my way in life. Yet, when I came out into society – my debut upon the larger world – the world was generally unimpressed. Oh, my height does give my figure a certain degree of elegance, and my hazel eyes are often complimented, but I believe the consensus at the time was that my looks did not much exceed the average. The young men of my acquaintance were apparently of the same opinion, since I noticed they withstood my modest beauty with remarkable ease.

Had I been born male, my agile mind might have been judged my most valuable asset. Though as it is, this particular quality has not always served me to advantage, especially in my relations with the opposite sex. To my dismay, I have discovered that most gentlemen do not wish their prowess in the intellectual realm challenged, especially by anyone female. I remember once reading that a woman, if she have the misfortune to know anything, should conceal it as well as she can. Perhaps I should have taken this advice to heart, for I believe my wit has proved a bit too sharp for some. Having once been cut by it, many a man has declined to be put at peril of it again.

Mr. Walter Summeride, a man of a more courageous constitution, did like me well enough to ask my father's permission to pay his addresses earlier this year. He is doubtless a very good sort of man but, alas, entirely lacking the qualities most likely to engage a lady's affection. Being little disposed to marry at the time, I was, therefore, unmoved by so slight a temptation. I found it impossible to return his regard, his discriminating taste and my father's decided recommendation notwithstanding.

"I insist that you consider this proposal, Josephine," Papa advised me on the occasion. "Marriage is your only honorable option, as you well know. Mr. Summeride would be a respectable match for you. A curate's income is not large, to be sure, but he has excellent prospects for a better situation, what with your uncle taking such an interest in his career. And think how pleasant it would be to settle in Millwalk parish."

He paused, staring down at me from his position of authority with a look of studied grimness. "You must take into account that, as a young lady of small fortune... and limited claims of any other sort... you have little reason to hope for anything better. The facts are these: you are now twenty years of age and have no other prospects in view. If you do not marry, you must go out as a governess or be a burden to your family the rest of your life."

Before I could make my choice between the unhappy alternatives thus so eloquently laid before me – being Mrs. Summeride for all eternity or staring the ignominy of spinsterhood in the eye – fate intervened.

My dear uncle, my father's elder brother, died suddenly. Apoplexy, the doctor said. On the twenty-seventh day of April, my family and I traveled to Millwalk, his country estate, gathering there with a dozen other people (including the amorous curate) to hear the contents of the will. In a solemn, steady voice, a bespectacled solicitor read out the smaller legacies – for the distant relations, the household's perennial servants, and so forth – before moving on to the major bequests, the part which most concerned my family.

We took the news calmly enough when the man announced that my eldest brother Frederick had been given the estate proper. Next, he said Tom, my other brother, would receive the valuable living provided by the rectory. I smiled serenely. All this unfolded exactly as any competent observer would expect; since Mr. Joseph Walker died childless, his nephews were the obvious beneficiaries. But not one of us anticipated the will's final entry:

"To my beloved niece and namesake, Josephine Walker, I hereby bequeath the sum of twenty thousand pounds, which is invested in the funds at five percent, and which shall be administered by her father, Mr. Harold Walker, until she reaches her majority – upon her twenty-first birthday or upon her marriage, whichever of these events should occur first."

I am certain I must have gasped, and I remember it took a curious amount of self-control to keep my jaw from dropping slack in disbelief. I was suddenly made a woman of independent means! That my uncle should have remembered me with some mark of his affection came as no surprise. That he should have chosen such a generously pecuniary way of doing so astonished me exceedingly.

Which of the other competing emotions that next tumbled over me claimed the greater share, I truly cannot say. However, when I glanced across the room at the unappealing Mr. Summeride, I felt only profound relief.

2

A Ball

I had seen enough of the world to know that money, in sufficient quantities, had the power to make people behave very foolishly – those who possessed it as well as those around them. I could not control the folly of others, yet I fervently hoped to avoid making a ninny of *myself* over my unexpected good fortune. In this resolve I was materially assisted by the fact that the funds were not immediately available to me. Any plans for embarking upon a reckless bout of spending would have to wait at least until my next birthday. Hence, my style of life did not change at once, nor did my dependence upon my father's pleasure.

For better or for worse, other effects of my inheritance manifested themselves without any delay. As my new-found virtue – my large personal fortune – became known, my status among my peers and betters underwent a dramatic alteration. People of fashion were suddenly disposed to think me "tolerably handsome" after all, and now my wit earned me the credit of being "clever" and "amusing." In short, my faults and deficiencies quickly diminished into insignificance, and my society was soon industriously sought by some of the very same young men who were so recently too squeamish to bear it.

I confess I enjoyed the attention at first, but it was an inferior pleasure and, like cloth of poor quality, quickly wore thin.

"Who will be your next partner, Jo?" asked my closest friend, Agnes Pittman, during the supper break at a ball not many months after these events transpired. "I imagine your dance card is full again tonight. You are quite the most popular young lady in Wallerton these days."

"Yes, my card is full, as, I would warrant, is yours. Mr. Freddy Hopkins is next on my list," I said, absently picking at the cold ham on my plate.

"Oh, yes. Freddy is an excellent dancer, and I think he has taken quite a shine to you, my dear. I have more than once heard him sing your praises up to the stars."

"Empty flattery. Six months ago he gave me no notice at all, so how can I suppose that his interest is sincere now?"

"Oh, his interest is sincere, all right!"

"I stand corrected. I should have said that his interest in *me* is suspect. I make no doubt his interest in my money is quite genuine indeed."

"Now, Josephine, you cannot truly be surprised by his behavior. You are no simpleton; you understand how the game is played."

"Yes, although I am not at all certain I wish to play it," I said, rising from the table.

Agnes likewise abandoned the remains of her supper and followed me back in the direction of the ballroom. "What? Do you find men so very unappealing?"

"On the contrary. Some of them I like uncommonly well."

"So, then?"

"Then let them behave like rational creatures instead of hungry wolves. I would respect them all the more for it.

"Really, Josephine, how you carry on!"

"And do stop calling me that. You sound exactly like my father when he is cross with me about something."

"Just as you wish then, *Jo*. But I do not understand why you insist on being so difficult to please. Enjoy your new power over men and make the most of your advantage. That is my advice." She paused to return the admiring look of a passing gentleman. "I doubt you will hear Pamela Hurst complaining when men run after her because of her beauty. Why should you object when they chase you for your money? As long as it achieves the desired result, what is the difference if a girl's fortune is in her face and figure or in the funds?"

"When you put it like that, I suppose there is no difference between the two; both are equally artificial."

"There now, have I not set your mind at ease? It is all a matter of how you look at the thing," Agnes concluded with satisfaction.

I had to smile at her manner of reasoning. From it, I could see there was nothing to be gained by debating the point any further. "Yes, of course," I answered lightly, setting aside my peevishness. After all, nothing should be allowed to interfere with the pure enjoyment of a ball. If the circumstances were somewhat ridiculous, so much the better, for then the more easily might I find humor in them.

Agnes and I parted ways as the music from the string and woodwind ensemble at the top of the room resumed. An eager Mr. Hopkins arrived to claim my hand, leading me out onto the polished wood floor. As we went about our business, I was not surprised to discover him quite unequal to the task of sustaining his share in the conversation. I admit it; my mind soon wandered from my partner and my eyes did likewise. I began by absently surveying the room. Yet before long, without any conscious design, my perusal took a more specific turn. I scanned over the heads of the crowd for a tall, fair-haired man with a friendly countenance and a familiar form. Where was Arthur? I had seen him earlier, so I knew he must be somewhere about.

Arthur Evensong would have been a much more pleasing partner for me. *He* was no flatterer. He instead paid me the higher compliment of treating me as an equal. I had by no means any special claim upon Arthur. In fact, everyone in Wallerton acknowledged him to be Agnes's rightful property, the parents of the two having long since settled the matter and the couple themselves showing every inclination toward the match. Yet Agnes would not have begrudged me a share of his attention, and I would have been grateful for it at that moment. For, if he had chosen to do so, it would have been in Arthur's power to keep the wolves at bay.

As it was, I felt the greedy creatures closing in, circling and weaving all about me on the dance floor as if I were a plump rabbit, ready for the taking. Still, picturing the unsuspecting Mr. Hopkins and the others festooned with large, pointed ears and bushy tails poking out from under their cutaway coats gave me considerable amusement. I eyed my partner and thought, "Yes, we may have some sport together – the hunter and the hunted – but this is one rabbit who has no intention of being caught, at least not yet... and not by the likes of you."

Mr. Hopkins was succeeded by several others of similar bent before I found myself unexpectedly at liberty. John Franklin, having sprained his foot, was obliged to forfeit his turn. Since the last thing I wanted at that juncture was to attract a replacement partner, I quietly eased myself away from the group of dancers, melted through the crowd of onlookers, and did my best to disappear into my surroundings. I had nearly made good my escape into the next room when a man addressed me from behind.

"Jo… "

I started, momentarily cringing at the sound of my own name. Just as quickly, I relaxed again and turned round when I realized the warm baritone voice belonged to Arthur Evensong.

"Why do you steal away into the parlor, Miss Walker?" he continued with a spark of amusement. "You truly have the look of a fugitive, skulking about in dark holes and corners. Have you committed a dreadful social *faux pas* or are you hiding from someone particularly annoying? Which is it?"

"The latter is a more accurate surmise," I answered with a laugh. "I finally have a dance free and I am determined to keep it that way."

"What a pity, for I would have gladly asked you."

"And there is no one here with whom I would rather dance, old friend. Will you not stay and talk with me instead? Let us sit down; my feet are grievously in need of rest."

Entering the deserted parlor, Arthur led the way to seats at its farthest reaches where it was comparatively quiet. A minimum of candles had been deployed there, and the dimness gave a soothing relief from the relative brilliance of the ballroom.

"Oh, what a pleasant reprieve this is!" said I, stretching my feet out in front of me.

"I am surprised to hear you speak so. I thought surely you must be enjoying yourself this evening, for you have never been in want of a partner. Of that much, I am certain. Is it not every young woman's idea of bliss to be the belle of the ball?"

"Oh, I love to dance. The livelier the music, the better I like it. Still, I am tired… and a little disappointed with the quality of the company. I would much rather spend the evening with you and Tom, but I suppose that would not do. I cannot dance with my own brother, and Agnes would never spare you so long. Although in truth, you do seem to be neglecting her tonight, even without my interference. I have only seen you dance with her twice. You accuse me of skulking? I suspect, Mr. Evensong, it is you who has been hiding. Good heavens!" I said, feigning shock. "Surely it cannot be Agnes that you are avoiding."

This taunt had the anticipated effect; a great blush, starting from Arthur's crisp, white cravat, suffused scarlet to the tops of his ears.

"Well, you have done it again, Jo. My face is burning. I hope you are satisfied."

"Now, do not be cross, Arthur. I count it as a marvelous, almost magical, thing, the way you color at the slightest provocation. I have found it quite irresistible ever since we were children, as you well know."

"I suppose I am only annoyed because I have no means to retaliate. You seem peculiarly immune to the frailty yourself, which is a shame. It certainly would become you much better than it does me." The irritation in his countenance faded along with the redness. "As for Agnes, she would have me standing up with her for every dance if she could, which would be highly improper since, despite what everybody may think, we are not formally engaged."

"Ah, so you would spare her reputation. How chivalrous of you, sir."

"She may dance with whomever she pleases, and she must grant me the same freedom of choice, my preference being to remain mostly in the background."

"Well, in this case, I am glad you *were* waiting in the background and that I stumbled upon you. At least I can have you to myself for these few minutes. I never see you anymore, Arthur. Why have you stopped coming to the house?"

"It is not by my own inclination that I stay away," he said in a more solemn tone. "Your father has made it clear... well... We all understand that your circumstances are entirely different now. Others must command your attention at present."

"Many things have changed, yes, but some things never should. I shall always remember my true friends and I hope they will do the same for me. You cannot believe me so weak as to lose my sense and forget my loyalties over money."

"It is not just the money, though, is it? The attention and the expectations accompanying your inheritance are powerful forces. They cannot help but alter you."

"To my mind, it is not my behavior that is altered! It is yours and everybody else's." I took a deep breath before continuing. "Now Arthur, I must return to the dance. Will you not shake hands with me before I go, and say you are still my friend?"

He took my hand and met my gaze with his startlingly blue eyes. "Of course I am your friend, Jo, now and always. Nothing shall ever change that."

3
Papa's Indisposition

"My dear, you simply must tell me all about last night's ball," my mother insisted after breakfast the next morning. The two of us had moved to the sitting room and taken up our needlework. "I did ask Tom earlier, but it was of little use. Men are generally hopeless when it comes to such things in any case. I depend entirely upon you for a full account. Are there any new romances afoot, any intriguing alliances taking shape? Tell me all about your partners and which girl had the prettiest gown."

"I barely noticed what anybody wore, Mama. As for the affair itself, I cannot imagine that there is anything extraordinary to tell. It was just what you would expect and have seen a dozen times before: the usual people were there; the standard dances performed; and the supper edible, but not overly fine. We all had a delightful time, and nobody got overly inebriated or taken into custody."

"What kind of a reply is that, child? I declare, your report is no better than your brother's after all. If I had been able to go myself, I would not need to trouble you for descriptions. But I could hardly leave your father with his health in such a poor state."

Effectively chastened, I apologized for my impertinence at once and answered all Mama's questions, supplying the colorful little details of which she is particularly fond. Since being out in company is one of the chief pleasures of her life, missing the festivities of the previous night had been a true sacrifice. This she had dutifully borne in consequence of Papa's troublesome indisposition: gout, the curse of many a well-to-do gentleman.

"I see Papa did not come down to breakfast again," said I. "Is he quite unwell?"

"He is not in bed, but he keeps to his room this morning," Mama replied.

"Can Mr. Trask do nothing more for him then?"

"The draughts he prescribes give little relief, and your father has thus far resisted the other recommendations – moderating his diet and taking the waters at Bath. I do not know how much longer we can go on like this, however. He is in a great deal of pain."

"Then he simply must go to Bath. The hot mineral springs are said to be highly therapeutic. Do they not have the credit for Mr. Tupper's cure a year or two ago?"

"Yes! You are correct, my dear. I had quite forgotten. I shall have to remind your father of Mr. Tupper's enthusiasm for the place. And perhaps you could put in a word for Bath as well, Jo. Together we may be able to persuade him to take medical advice in spite of himself."

"Oh, I do hope so... for his health's sake."

Yet, in truth, it was more than my father's gouty legs that I imagined would benefit from a change of situation. A removal to Bath would be no hardship for me either, I believed. I found it a very compelling prospect to trade the society of Wallerton, which had lately become so irksome, for a completely fresh arena, one wholly unspoilt by prior knowledge of my circumstances.

Once again I mused over the paradox of my inheritance. Whilst it gave me a degree of independence that I had heretofore no right to expect, it had also made me its bondservant. Although with silken cords, I was tied to the thing nonetheless and could not escape the unpleasant effects it secondarily created, at least not in my own county. Elsewhere, with any luck, no one would know about my fortune unless I chose to tell them.

My mind was soon made up on the subject. Father simply must be convinced to submit to a season in Bath for his own good... and for mine. Any scruple I might have felt over attempting to influence him in such a matter I successfully crushed with the weightier notion that the goal – his recovered health – justified whatever means I had to employ. When, a few days later, I found him alone in his library, sitting with his legs propped up on cushions, I took my chance. I came in and perched upon the edge of his desk as I had been in the habit of doing from when I was a girl of six or seven.

"How are you feeling today, Papa?" I asked. "I have been so worried about you."

"Very poorly. Very poorly, indeed," he growled. "I suppose I should not grumble, though. After all, as your mother would probably point out, compared to what some people suffer, my complaint must be considered quite trivial. Still, it is enough for me, I admit."

"Is there nothing you could take to give you present relief? A glass of wine; shall I get you one?"

"No, no. Stay where you are. According to Mr. Trask, too much wine is part of my problem. I swear he would see me bereft of that and of every other pleasure."

"So, he recommends some alteration in your diet, then? Is there anything else you can do?"

"Well, he did suggest that taking the waters in Bath might be of use, though I put no stock in the advice."

"Why is that? I thought you had a high regard for Mr. Trask's medical opinions. I am sure I have often heard you say so."

"Oh, I think he is quite a clever fellow. And when he is giving his orders to somebody else, it is all very well. But I reserve the right to decide what is best for me. Can you honestly picture me lazing about in Bath, Josephine? I should feel quite ridiculous bathing with strangers and imbibing those dubious waters. Besides, it would be a very costly undertaking. I can hardly justify such an extravagance."

I frowned and looked away as if deep in thought.

This presently prompted Papa to ask, "What is the matter? Said I something amiss?"

Shaking my head, I replied, "Never mind. I know you must do what you think is right."

"Come now, child. There *is* something troubling you. I can always tell. Out with it."

"It is only that… well… I have seen how concerned Mama is about your health. I really think it is taking a toll on her nerves to see you suffer as you do. If there is anything that can be done to make you well, I believe it would be a kindness, as much to her as for yourself, to see that it is done."

"So you think I should relent and go to Bath, do you? For your mother's sake?"

"For her sake as well as for your own, I wish you would consider it."

Father leaned back in his chair, folded his arms over his chest, and shook his head, a satirical grin playing across his face. "I do not know if I have ever before witnessed so much selfless compassion in one family," he said with biting sarcasm. "In an amazing coincidence, your mama has also recommended that I

16

decide in favor of Bath, as kindness to *you*. Now confess, Josephine. The two of you are in league together, are you not?"

"Really, Papa, I have no idea what you mean..."

"Oh, I think you have. You are simply surprised to be found out. Well, never mind," he said in a softened tone, reaching for my hand. "I choose to flatter myself that you both have my best interests at heart. If we are to go to Bath, however, will you have the goodness to allow me at least the pretense that it was by my own choosing?"

"Certainly, Papa. You shall have all the credit for it." I gave him my most winning smile and left him to his thoughts and his books, confident that the campaign was all but won. I expected he would make a temporary show of stubbornness in compliment to his pride. Then, with any luck, he'd come round.

And indeed, after leaving us in suspense for a full week, my father announced that he would allow himself to be taken to Bath after all. For this proof of his good judgment, Mama and I rewarded him with a liberal show of praise and affection.

So we were to go to Bath! With great difficulty, I kept my outward enthusiasm in check, reminding myself that this trip was not primarily intended as a holiday for me. Still, I could not contain my inner exhilaration over the promise of so much novelty. My head teamed with images of what the place would be like, the sort of people we might meet, and how I should behave to best advantage. For the most part, my good sense held sway, preventing a headlong plunge into unbridled optimism over what lay in store for me there. Occasionally, I did set loose my fancy, freeing my imagination to roam where it would. And it would ramble into some very pretty places.

4

Farewell Party

It was mid-September, and Fairfield hummed with a vast deal of activity as the place prepared to give up all its principal occupants at once. In addition to the three of us bound for Bath, Tom and Frederick would be leaving as well – Frederick to take possession of his uncle's properties, and Tom to Oxford to begin Michaelmas term. So, it amounted to a mass desertion of the manor house, which was to last some weeks.

As with any event of similar magnitude, my sociable mother instinctively felt the need to mark the occasion in some appropriate style. Accordingly, at the breakfast table one day she ventured, "Did you know, Mr. Walker, that we are not the only ones about to quit Wallerton? The Brownings will soon set off on a tour of the continent, and several of the young men are due to return to university. With all this leave-taking about to commence, it struck me that it really would be a kind convenience if everybody could be gathered at the same time and in the same place to say their good-byes. Would not you agree?"

"So you think we ought to host a party of some sort, no doubt."

"Precisely."

"But why should we expect people to come and celebrate our pilgrimage to Bath for the cure? It is tantamount to asking our friends to attend an official observance in honor of my gout," he complained.

"Stuff and nonsense! Really, Mr. Walker, where did you get such a notion? No one in their right mind will think anything of the kind. We always give a little soiree in the fall. Everybody knows that. This year we have just had to move up the date a little, that is all."

I believe husbands and wives generally understand when opposition will be in vain. Papa's objections soon gave way, and the plan went forward for a supper and card party at Fairfield to be held a few days before our departure.

My mother was in her full glory as the preparations began. Resembling a general marshalling the troops for an important military campaign, she assessed the task before her, organized the servants, and set everyone to work toward the goal of perfect readiness. Serving as her assistant and understudy, I could not help but catch her excitement as we counted the days until the event.

The night at last arrived and so did our guests. Except for a Mr. Evans – a cousin of the Bickfords visiting from Surrey – everybody knew one another, so no formal ceremony and few introductions were necessary. Agnes soon gravitated to my side, favoring me with an embrace and a kiss as was the custom between us. She looked especially well. The plaits and curls of her golden hair adorned her head in an elaborate arrangement, and the sapphire muslin she wore mirrored and, in turn, enhanced the color of her eyes. Her fair face struggled to express an intense blend of emotions, lending her the additional appeal of a sympathetic heroine, a damsel in distress.

"Why, Agnes, whatever is the matter?" I asked her.

"Oh, my dearest friend, I am half agony, half delight! I hardly know how to behave. I so looked forward to tonight, and yet, now that it is here, all I can think of is that when it is over you will be leaving. How can I possibly enjoy myself with the knowledge of what will follow tomorrow?"

"Dear Agnes, you are such a sensitive lamb." I found my friend's inclination for seeing high drama in every circumstance both amusing and endearing. Indeed, I often thought it a great shame Agnes was so respectably situated, for she seemed to have been born for the stage.

"How I should love to have a season in Bath or London," she continued. "I only wish you could take me with you. It will be so dreadfully dull here when you, your brothers, and Arthur are all gone away. How shall I bear the solitude?"

"Perhaps you could come and visit us in Bath once Papa is on the mend," I suggested. "And in the meantime, I promise to write you about all my adventures."

"Yes, I simply *must* hear from you very often, yet it will be exquisitely painful all the same to discover what I am missing."

Despite her predictions of gloom, Agnes put her distress aside remarkably well in order to partake of the amusements the evening had to offer.

Meanwhile, I was far from neglected. The visiting Mr. Evans sought out an introduction and fawned over me so flagrantly that I felt sure someone had given him prior information of my monetary attractions, all twenty thousand of them. His overtures were so obvious as to be almost comical. The other present members of my band of suitors made every effort to please and charm me as well. No doubt they were keenly conscious that my imminent removal to Bath posed a considerable threat to their ambitions of securing my affection and fortune.

To break away from these unwelcome attentions, I sought out Mrs. Evensong. So close had been the fellowship between our two families that she was something like a second mother to me, and I a daughter to her. "My dear Mrs. Evensong, are you quite well?" I asked when I saw her. "You look a little pale."

"You mustn't always worry so much for me, my dear. I am very well today, very well indeed," she answered in her mild way. "What a lovely evening this is, which comes as no surprise, of course; your mama is such an accomplished hostess. I sometimes envy her energy and efficiency in such matters."

"There are few who can equal her, I grant you. How is little John? I'm afraid I have lately been remiss in my visits. Did he enjoy the tale of Mr. Pondwaddle?"

Mrs. Evensong broke into a lilting laugh at the reference to the story I had recently written as a present for her youngest son, a sweet but decidedly simple-minded boy of eleven. "He loves all your stories, Jo, but I think this one is his favorite. He insists I read it to him every night before bed and show him all the drawings as well."

"Oh dear. I am pleased he likes it so much, but I have created a lot of work for you, it seems."

"Nonsense. I think I enjoy it quite as much as John does. We shall both soon have it committed to memory at all events."

"Well, I have another story idea running round in my head – about a little pig and his brothers this time. I shall send it along from Bath as soon as it is finished."

Mrs. Bickford then pulled me to one side. "It is a shame about Miss Hunter, is it not?" she said conspiratorially.

"Why? What has happened? Is she ill?"

"No, my dear Miss Walker, it is something else entirely. She has broken off her engagement! Why, it is all over town. I thought sure you knew or I would never have presumed to mention it. I am no gossip, not like that horrid Mrs. Oddbody. In fact, she is the very person who told me about Miss Hunter. Personally, I tell no tales, so I will not say another word about it myself... except that it is a sad business when a girl from a good family behaves so irresponsibly."

"But, Mrs. Bickford, we cannot judge without all the facts. Perhaps Miss Hunter acted under severe provocation."

"Her reasons do not signify in the least, Miss Walker. Reputation is everything, and now Miss Hunter will always be known as a jilt. No respectable man will have anything to do with her. My own son had an interest in her at one time, but I will make very certain he steers well clear of her in future. He has political ambitions, as you may know, and can ill afford to be tainted by questionable associations."

Not wanting to listen to any more of Mrs. Bickford's slander, I immediately excused myself and went to find Agnes. By my design, she and I were seated together at supper with Arthur, Tom, and Frederick gathered close about us as a cozy, protective shelter. Perhaps it was selfish of me, but I wanted one last evening with all of us together.

Our conversation that night focused little on Bath and more on the destinations of the three young men. Frederick embarked upon a detailed description of Millwalk, to which he would soon lay claim. The extent of the property and the size of the house far exceeded anything he could hope to receive from his own father, so he rightly counted himself a fortunate young man. He brimmed with confidence bordering on conceit – not an uncommon fault in a man of six-and-twenty with independent means – about his grand plans for improvements and his sanguine expectations of success.

No one took offence at his brass. In fact, Agnes, whose interest was obviously piqued, encouraged him to continue by asking for more particulars about the size and style of the house, the number of servants employed there, and at what distance the place was from Wallerton.

"It would be my pleasure and my honor to show you Millwalk personally sometime, Miss Pittman," Fred continued. "I have it. Once I am settled, you must all come for a visit. The four of you can make an outing of it, for it is less than a day's journey from here. I shall welcome you like royalty and kill the fatted calf for your dinner when you come, by Jove."

"Oh, yes! It is the best plan in the world!" exclaimed Agnes, wild with delight.

"Capital idea, sir, but I hardly know when it might be arranged," said Arthur. "Tom and I may be home from Oxford at Christmas, but the party to Bath probably will not, from what I understand. In any case, December is an inauspicious time for travel."

"I suppose it must wait for spring, then," I concluded.

Agnes protested. "That is an absolute age from now."

"It cannot be helped," said Tom, decisively. "Brother, on behalf of my friends, I accept your invitation. You may expect us at Easter. I warn you, though, we shall come hungry, so begin fattening that calf at once." Frederick chuckled, and Tom continued. "Laying a feast fit for a king before us is the very least your conscience requires of you, Fred. I wager it troubles you severely when you consider your happy situation compared to mine and Arthur's."

"Must we reprise that same, sad tune, little brother? That tired complaint has lately grown quite thread bare. You really must resolve to give it up. Nonetheless, I shall overlook the offence this one last time. I stand by my offer and will expect to see you all at Easter," he said with his recently perfected air of *noblesse oblige.*

Tom and Arthur shared the mutual misfortune of having been born as second sons to their gentlemen fathers. Whilst the eldest could expect to inherit nearly everything by no more superior merit than having had the good sense to be born first and male, the younger might receive nothing from his father beyond a gentleman's education and the advice to look to the military or the church to make his living. The latter was the profession chosen by both these second sons.

Tom's situation was far from pitiful, his protestations of ill usage notwithstanding. Thanks to our uncle's posthumous gift, he held the distinct advantage over his friend of having already secured a good parish. Once his education was complete, he would take orders and assume the post that would in all likelihood provide him a very comfortable living for the rest of his days. Although, when pressed, Tom admitted having little true enthusiasm for the calling, he seemed reconciled to his fate.

A religious vocation was more to Arthur's taste but less immediately within his grasp, having no rich uncle, living or dead, to present him with such a fine rectory. Still, he was considered by all accounts to have a promising future. People who know about such things often remarked that Arthur's excellent record at Oxford was bound to attract the notice of an influential patron, who might not only have the means to give him his start but the power to advance his career in years to come. Toward that end, Mr. Pittman had already undertaken to solicit his many connections on his future son-in-law's behalf, a service the more necessary for the fact that Arthur's own father had died some months earlier.

As supper continued, Arthur and Tom proceeded to regale us with stories of their varied activities and acquaintances at Oxford.

"Did we ever tell you about our unfortunate friend Mr. Higgins?" Tom asked. "A most unpromising scholar! And he had the worst luck of any person I ever saw, especially when it came to curfew violations. I swear if he was out five minutes after nine o'clock, the proctor's bulldogs were sure to sniff it out."

"Those fellows show no mercy," Arthur added. "Poor Higgins. They finally sent him packing. I wonder what has become of him."

"He's not really a bad sort," Tom added, "and they never once found him in any serious mischief. He was just too distracted by other things to be bothered with keeping track of time. I put it down to the simple fact that the fellow did not own a reliable watch," he joked.

5

Taking Leave

Frederick left early next morning. He so keenly anticipated installing himself in his new home that he could hardly be prevailed upon to remain at Fairfield long enough to take some breakfast before setting forth to Millwalk. A carriage had been sent thence to collect the new master and his belongings. It awaited him whilst he hurriedly ate a few bites and bid us farewell.

Once he had gone, I seized the opportunity to broach a subject I had long contemplated. "Mama, Papa, I have a request to make of you," I began rather more seriously than I intended. "It is about our trip to Bath. I have decided it would be best if no one there knows about my inheritance. I want us to be as we were before. I shall be just plain Miss Walker again, instead of an heiress."

"I did not think being 'plain' was in fashion this year," Tom quipped.

"That is very droll, Tom, but hardly helpful," Mother scolded.

"Sorry."

Father took a more serious view of the subject. "Has this bequest from your uncle really become such a burden that you would forsake it entirely? I would not have thought you capable of such ingratitude, Josephine."

"No! Of course I am grateful. The inheritance itself is a good thing and Uncle was very kind to make me such a gift. The difficulty is that the knowledge of my inheritance has turned Wallerton into a camp full of fortune hunters. The motives of all single men are now suspect. And even the women treat me differently. I do not wish the same thing to happen in Bath. When I meet new people, Papa, I should like to know that any regard they show for me is sincere, not a symptom of avarice. I want to be valued for myself alone, not for my bank balance. Is that so difficult to understand?"

"It sounds reasonable enough, I grant you. However, I think you will find that reason has very little to do with the way society operates. It is all perceptions and appearances, money and manners, posturing and position. Although I should support any practical measure that might prevent you falling victim to a fortune hunter, Jo, you must be realistic. You must consider that concealing the information will limit your access to the good company that you can now command. You have the opportunity to raise yourself, to set your sights higher, to make a superior match. That is what I want for you... and what your uncle no doubt intended as well."

"So, no more Mr. Summeride, Papa?"

"Mr. Summeride? I should think not! No poor parsons of any description for you, my dear. Everything has changed. We may now entertain much more elevated expectations, I daresay. With your fortune, you will be considered eligible in the eyes of many of the best families. By disclaiming it, you lose your advantage entirely."

"I appreciate that fact, but it cannot be helped. My inheritance frees me from the constraint to marry, and I should much rather never marry at all than to find myself in an unhappy union."

"Josephine!" Mother cried. "You cannot mean that you intend to end an old maid."

"No, Mama. I make no such resolution, but there would be no disgrace in it either. A single woman of good fortune is always respectable. At present, I must say that I have very little intention of marrying. Yet, under the right circumstances, I suppose I might be persuaded. Agreeably married or not married at all, I am convinced I could be content either way. But I should be miserable bound for life to a man who does not care for me. *That* is what I am determined to avoid."

"You present a strong case, Daughter; I find your arguments quite compelling," Father admitted. "If you had been born a boy, I daresay you would have made a fine barrister."

"As for that, I might have made a fine barrister as a woman if it were allowed. At present, though, all I seek is your discretion. Shall I have it, sir?"

"I still believe it is a mistake. You should not hide your light under a bushel. However, I will agree to let you try it your way for now. You will always have your fortune to fall back on in the end."

I then reminded Tom of the similar promise I had exacted from him months before. "Oxford is not that far from Bath, and gossip travels quickly. If news of my inheritance becomes known at your college, it could spoil everything, Tom. You must stand by your pledge that you will not say a word about it."

"I shall keep my promise," said Tom with mock resignation, "though it costs me dearly. More than once already I have had to hold my peace as a friend told me how much he should like to meet an agreeable girl with fifteen or twenty thousand pounds. I daresay I could have pocketed a tidy profit by now, making introductions for a price."

Mother rebuked him for such a shocking speech. I just laughed, and then went on, "Pray, do be serious, Tom. You do not think Arthur has told anyone either, do you?"

"You needn't be uneasy on that head, Jo. Arthur is the last man whom you should suspect of discussing a lady's affairs out of turn."

The next morning, that same Mr. Evensong called at Fairfield to collect Tom for their return to Oxford. He sat with me a few minutes whilst Tom finished getting his things in order upstairs. After exchanging pleasantries, I ventured, "I daresay you are not sorry to be returning to your college, Arthur. With your education nearly complete, you must be impatient to get on with your career."

"I should be in more hurry to finish at Oxford had I the road ahead clearly in view."

"According to Agnes, you have your future mapped out for the next twenty years complete," I teased. "Come now, Arthur, there is no need for false modesty between friends. Admit it; you have your eye on a bishopric and a seat in the House of Lords."

He colored profusely and looked down at his folded hands mumbling, "You will say that I have a pretty high opinion of myself to even think of it."

"No, I will say you have a healthy ambition. Whether you can live up to that ambition remains to be seen, Mr. Evensong. Your friends may think very well of you indeed, but you will have to prove yourself to others in the end."

"I shall be grateful to anyone who will give me the opportunity to try. That is all I can say for it." Presently, he continued in a new line. "So, I perceive that you are very enthusiastic about this expedition to Bath, Jo."

"Why, I have traveled so little that every fresh place would be interesting to me."

"Then I trust you will not be disappointed. It is said to be quite a stylish town. Agnes certainly envies you your trip. She complains that everybody has somewhere to go excepting herself."

"You have already called on her to say your farewell, then?"

"Yes, on my way here. According to how she carried on, one would think she had not a single friend left in the world. You know her disposition."

"It is only natural that she should be excessively sorry to see you go."

"Thank you for the kind sentiment, but to own the truth, I believe she grieves more over your departure than mine. She is grown relatively accustomed to my absences whereas she has never had to do without you for so long before. I do sympathize with her."

Papa came downstairs at this juncture and abruptly interrupted our conversation. "Ah, Mr. Evensong. I thought I heard your voice. You must excuse my daughter now. Josephine, you are needed upstairs."

I found little to do upstairs other than to accompany Tom back down, as he was ready to set off. Mama made a valiant effort to keep her composure in the face of Tom's departure, but she could not quell the quiet tears that flowed just as they had the day before when Frederick took leave. Watching Arthur and my brother ride away down the long drive, I felt a few pangs at the separation myself. I tarried on the front porch and waved once more when Arthur looked back just before reaching the road and disappearing behind the hedgerow.

My melancholy reflections on the parting lingered only a very few minutes after the riders were lost from sight. Then a bolt of excitement raced through me as I comprehended that, with both my brothers now gone, the next event on the calendar was my own departure. We had talked about it for weeks, and all the plans were long since made. Yet it had never seemed real until that moment. "Two days from now, we will be on our way to Bath!" I said aloud before rushing back into the house to begin final preparations.

Mama and I spent the morning of our last day in Wallerton making calls, mostly of a charitable nature. We first visited the Miller sisters, a pair of spinsters who had come down sadly in the world in recent years. From there, we went on to a small cottage where a family of nine lived on next to nothing. Whilst Mama ministered to Mrs. Bateman, who had been ill, I read stories to the four youngest children. Both these households had long been under my father's protection. With his tacit endorsement, a week never went by without Cook discovering that there were too many eggs to use, more potatoes than could be conveniently stored, or a side of bacon that was in danger of going to waste. These and other staples of life invariably found their way to the Millers and Batemans, and would continue to do so even during the weeks we were away.

A brief stop to see Mrs. Evensong and little John completed our circuit. Then I had one last ride on Viola, my bay mare, after which I bathed, dined, and spent a restless night. Rising early, I dressed with more than my usual degree of alacrity, anxious to get underway as soon as possible. Unfortunately, my parents did not share my sense of urgency. In my excited state of mind, our normal, leisurely breakfast seemed an endless ordeal, and the loading of the carriage interminable. Mama could not be satisfied to leave without a lengthy consultation with the housekeeper to review every detail of her previously given instructions.

Agnes, who came to see us off, provided some distraction as I waited. "It still does not seem right somehow that you should be taking this consequential step without me," she lamented. "We have always done everything together before. And now, here you are, about to be launched into the good society in Bath, all on your own. There are sure to be balls and parties every night. How shall I endure the thought that you will attend them without me?"

"Dear Agnes, how you do exaggerate!" I could not help saying. "Remember, we shall be going out into the town very little until my father is better. After that, who knows? Perhaps you will be able to join us by then. I promise I shall speak to Papa about it just as soon as he is well enough." An inspiration for how to cheer her popped into my head. "And you ought not to begrudge me a little head start, dearest. After all, once the men catch sight of you, they will hardly give me another thought. You know that is what always happens."

"Nonsense, Jo," Agnes objected. Nevertheless, I noticed her gloomy aspect brightened considerably.

Encouraged by this success, I piled on more praise with a dramatic flare of my own, "No, 'tis all too true. I have seen it happen time and time again. It is your beautiful yellow hair that beguiles them. Men simply cannot help themselves; they are powerless before it."

28

"This time you have gone too far and I am sure you are joking," Agnes said, laughing. "No matter; you have made me feel better in spite of myself. I was determined to be miserable for at least a week. My plan is completely spoilt, Miss Walker, and I am quite put out."

Agnes made her final farewells at the carriage door. "Oh, I honestly do wish for you a very pleasant time in Bath, Jo."

"Do you also promise to write to me faithfully... and not to mope about feeling sorry for yourself?"

"Yes, I promise the first willingly, the second, if you insist."

"I insist."

"Very well then, I shall do my best. What about you? Do you still propose to keep to this silly ruse of concealing your inheritance from all the poor, unsuspecting men that you meet?"

"Certainly I do! I intend to conceal it from everybody – the rich and *especially* the poor. As for the unsuspecting men for whom you feel so sorry, they will come to no harm. This is not a husband-hunting expedition. I am only out for a bit of sport."

6

Arrival at Bath

Our journey was accomplished without incident if not without inconvenience, and at length we arrived at Bath. The unrelenting rain, for which the place is well known, did little to dampen my enthusiasm and nothing to stem my insatiable curiosity. I would happily have craned my head out the carriage window had I been allowed to do so. As it was, I had to be satisfied with the more restricted – but far more proper – view from within as we wound down out of the surrounding hills and into the town.

My first sight of Bath's fine and striking environs delighted me. The scene was a far cry from the country verdure to which I was accustomed. Still, the place had an undeniable beauty about it all the same – a beauty born of human rather than of natural composition. Everywhere I looked, there was some new sight to be admired: honey-colored stone townhouses strung together in long rows and curves; a variety of classically designed public buildings; and the occasional park or monument. The Abbey easily qualified as the most impressive edifice of all.

Approaching from the south, we crossed the River Avon twice – once as we came into town and again as we turned toward our lodgings in Great Pultney Street. Papa had taken a comfortable house for us there, and, when we were settled, I was irresistibly drawn to the windows overlooking that broadest of Bath avenues. A steady stream of people and commerce flowed in front of me, giving even this stationary viewpoint more animation than I would find at home. There, the only passersby I could reasonably expect were the occasional tenant farmer or stray goose.

When the rain left off that first evening, I received permission for a brief excursion to Sidney Gardens, the western boundary of which reached to within a dozen houses of our own. I passionately longed to further explore my new surroundings, but I contained my excitement out of respect for my father, lest he begin to suspect that his health was not of primary importance to me after all. Visits to the various assembly halls and even the famous Pump-room had to be put off for the time being. A call by Dr. Oliver, the physician to whom Mr. Trask had referred my father, was sought as the highest priority instead.

Despite a torrential downpour, the doctor came promptly the next day to examine his new patient, prescribing a series of treatments according to his findings. He gave a favorable prognosis, provided his instructions for taking the waters and moderating the diet were faithfully followed. Hence, the first of Papa's many visits to the Pump-room, to drink and bathe in the healing waters, was scheduled for the next morning.

Like a petulant child faced with the unhappy prospect of taking bitter medicine, the invalid once again voiced his dissatisfaction with a scheme so little to his taste.

In response, Mama informed him, "I will listen to no more of your grumbling, Mr. Walker. We have both promised Dr. Oliver that his orders shall be obeyed, and so they shall be. It is of no use to complain." She paused, but no further remonstration issued from her husband. "Good. Then it is settled."

Papa glowered at her and inquired peevishly, "And what shall you and Jo be doing whilst I am subjecting myself to the degradation of public bathing?"

"Suffer no anxiety for us, my dear. We shall entertain ourselves quite nicely."

"I harbor no fear as to that, Mrs. Walker. I assure you, it is simply a matter of idle curiosity."

"Well then, since you ask, Jo and I shall accompany you to the Pump-room and have a long promenade about that great hall. I daresay the exercise will do us both good, especially after being confined to a carriage for so many hours in recent days. I am very keen to consult the registry book there to see if anyone of our acquaintance is in town. What a fine thing it would be to discover old friends here. Do not you think so, Harold?"

"Most definitely. If we are to pass some weeks in this foreign place, it would indeed be a consolation to know that we shall have more than only each other for company. Conversation must eventually lag under such a strain, after all. But do you have any reason to expect someone we know?"

"No particular reason. It is only that Bath is very popular just now amongst our set. I do not think it at all unlikely that there will be at least one of my former schoolfellows, or perhaps one of your associates from business or Oxford, currently in residence. We must keep our eyes wide open. It would be pleasant for us and a material benefit for our girl if it were put within our power to introduce her to new people of quality."

I silently agreed that it would be a decided advantage. For the moment, though, the promise that we could go out into the town without further delay satisfied all my hopes.

~~*~~

Everyone in Bath, for health or holiday, inevitably finds their way to the Pump-room, the heart of the town and the reason for its existence. Crowds of fashionable people pass daily through its portals seeking the healing waters and the company of their peers. Reputedly, so many valuable acquaintances are renewed and favorable alliances formed within its hallowed walls that each visit holds as much promise for social as medicinal advantage. Thus, with high expectations, we joined the throng of pilgrims drawn to the Pump-room.

As Papa bathed in the warm, spring-fed pool below, Mama and I filled our time by parading up and down the main room in concert with all the others similarly left with no more-useful employment. The scale of the place gave even this ordinary exercise a feeling of grandeur. The vaulted ceiling, the massive columns supporting it, the sparkling chandelier, and the polished floor awash with the light spilling through soaring casements: it was quite a sight to behold. To one side in a windowed alcove was situated the ornate fountain, named The King's Spring, from which continually poured the healing water for all to drink.

Mama focused her energies on locating someone she knew within the multitude, whilst I contented myself with being in the presence of so many interesting strangers – ladies and gentlemen of every age and description. Without an introduction, I could speak to not a single one of them. Still, it was felicity enough on our first foray into Bath society.

After nearly an hour and a half, Papa rejoined us.

"How was your bath, my dear?" asked Mama. "Did the mineral water suit you?"

"Well enough, I suppose," he admitted begrudgingly. "I was neither drowned nor cured, but it was not an entirely disagreeable experience. If more of the same is the price for my recovery, I believe I shall be able to bear it after all."

"I am so glad, my dear. I was certain you would be a model patient when once you got started."

He muttered something unintelligible and then asked, "Did the two of you pass the interval pleasantly?"

"Oh, yes, Papa. Although I think the water does not so much agree with me. I have felt a bit unwell ever since I sampled it."

"Smells foul; tastes infinitely worse," was his appraisal of the same. "Count yourself as fortunate, Jo, that you are not the one obliged to drink it day after day."

Ignoring these grievances in favor of her own, Mama reported, "I have been disappointed in my hopes of discovering anyone of our acquaintance. I examined the registry book and every single face that entered this room without a single point of recognition. Still, it is only our first day out. I shall not so soon despair of success in the matter. In fact, I think I will get the Bath paper, and look over the arrivals. What do you say to that, Mr. Walker?"

"A very sensible attitude, my dear Doris. I would hate to see you cast down into despair when we are come to be merry in Bath," he said with a recurring edge of sarcasm. "We shall hope for better luck tomorrow."

"Yes, but now we must get you home so that you can rest. Then a little later, I thought I might take Jo out to visit the shops if you have no objection. She and I will need some new things for our stay here."

"I foresaw that this trip would take a heavy toll on my pocketbook. Do *try* to keep your purchases within reason, Mrs. Walker, I beg you."

"Of course, my dear. Moderation and economy shall be my watchwords."

So, after resettling my father and taking some refreshment, Mama and I set forth to explore the town. Although I daresay I am far less consumed with style and finery than most young ladies, I am not completely immune to their allure. Just as any other female, be she eighteen or eighty, I would rather be smartly dressed than not. And in Bath were shops enough to thrill and delight even the most devoted patrons of fashion, all suddenly within my reach.

The windows of each establishment we came upon enticed us with displays of the desirable wares within. We personally perused more hats, shawls, gowns, and gloves in that one afternoon than we would have ordinarily come across in a year's time in our own out-of-the-way corner of Hampshire. In the end, we came away with neither so much as the shopkeepers might have hoped, nor so little as Papa would have undoubtedly preferred.

"Your father will like to see how well you look in your new things," Mama advised me on our way home. "Be sure to show them off and thank him for his kindness. But there is no need to worry him at all about the cost. Believe me, he will be much happier not knowing."

In this, as in most other matters, I relied upon my mother's sound judgment. Far be it from me to plague my father with unimportant details.

7
New Friends

In a similar manner, we passed our first week in Bath. Except for Sunday, we attended the Pump-room for some portion of every day. Then, if the weather permitted, Mama would take me out to visit another shop or look at some new part of town. In the process, we also discovered the location of the lending library and bought a subscription to keep us supplied with books for the duration of our stay.

Day by day, there remained the continued expectation that, with enough patience and persistence, we should locate some acquaintance in residence. After more than a week of searching in vain, Mama's tenacity showed the first sign of bearing fruit. She found the name of a Mrs. Graham in the registry book at the Pump-room, and began to be convinced that it must be her former schoolfellow, a Miss Phoebe Banks, whom she knew to have married a man by that name many years earlier.

Although the two women had not seen each other in the intervening decades – and probably had not devoted a great deal of time to lamenting that fact – it now became a matter of utmost importance to the one that she confirm the presence of the other without a moment's delay. Therefore, Mama immediately dispatched a note to Mrs. Graham at her lodgings in Milsom Street to make inquiries. She invited the lady to call round at Pultney Street if she indeed turned out to be the former Miss Banks, of whom she remembered to have been excessively fond.

Accordingly, Mama stayed at home the next afternoon in anticipation of receiving her guest, sending Papa in my care to take his treatment at the Pump-room. Fortune smiled; my mother's conviction of Mrs. Graham's identity proved accurate. When we returned to the house, we found the two women in the midst of a joyful reunion.

"Mr. Walker, Jo, come and meet my old friend from my school days, Mrs. Graham," Mama said when we entered. "She and her family have only just arrived in town from Kent for a holiday."

Mrs. Graham, a short, plump woman, was dressed in flawless taste. Her manners seemed likewise impeccable. The only thing that created some discordance in her overall presentation was the surprising volume of her voice, which belied the size of the person at its source. It seemed somehow incongruous that such a substantial sound should emanate from one so small in stature.

"Now that we have met again, Doris, we should make the most of it. You and your daughter must come to call on me tomorrow," said Mrs. Graham in a commanding tone. Then addressing me, she continued with equal volume, "I have a girl about your age, Miss Walker, as well as two younger ones still at home. Susan will be delighted to make an acquaintance so soon after arriving in Bath."

"May we go, Mama?" I asked.

"Certainly we may. This is exactly what I have wished for, that you would find a suitable friend to keep you company."

So, on the morrow, Mama and I ventured to Milsom Street whereupon Mrs. Graham made it her first order of business to introduce us to her daughter, who resembled her in every important particular. She was diminutive and lady-like with a confident voice bigger than one would expect, at least without benefit of first knowing her mother.

I liked Miss Graham straight away, a surprising unity of interests and attitudes forming the foundation of our immediate friendship. Within half an hour, I found myself insisting that she call me by my Christian name, and she instantly returned the favor. I was pleased to discover that Susan had a rational mind and very sensible ideas on all manner of subjects, including romantic attachments.

"I have no objection to marrying," she declared. "Yet I am not so much at a loss that I will take the first man who comes along. One must have standards; one's principles simply cannot be surrendered."

"Very true."

Susan continued. "Were I to fall in love, indeed, it would be a different thing!"

"And, without love, I am sure I should be a fool to change such a situation as mine."

"Then we are in agreement. But, as for being a fool, I have often observed that it is exactly when people *do* fall in love that they become very stupid indeed, which does worry me."

"I will take care to guard you against it, my dear Susan. I should hate to see you nonsensical."

"And I shall watch out for you. Let us make a pact of it."

In order that our two families should spend the maximum time in each other's company, we ladies deemed it necessary for the men to form as warm a friendship between them as we ourselves had already so expeditiously established. Toward that end, Mama invited the Grahams to dine in Pultney Street the following day.

Mr. Graham turned out to be a man of acute contrast to his wife in both person and manner. Whereas she was petite and decidedly assertive, he was quite a tall man with a soft-spoken, unassuming way about him. They made an odd-looking, mis-matched sort of happy couple.

Father and Mr. Graham did not share the source of immediate camaraderie that their wives enjoyed – that of having attended the same school – for Papa had gone to Oxford and Mr. Graham was a Cambridge man. With a little exertion, however, that substantial obstacle was successfully surmounted. It seemed they were prepared to be friends, and, with their wives and daughters so determined that they should be, they really had little choice but to find by the end of the meal that they got on remarkably well indeed.

After dinner, the men furthered their friendship over a glass of port whilst we ladies withdrew to the sitting room for conversation.

"Have you been to the ballrooms yet?" Mrs. Graham inquired of my mother. "Susan has talked of nothing else since we arrived in town, and we have consented to take her at the first opportunity. I thought you might advise us."

"No, I can offer you no first-hand account as we have never been there. Mr. Walker's health has not allowed for it thus far. Still, I have managed to glean some information that might be of use. I understand that the Upper Rooms, the newer ballrooms farther up the hill, are very fine. However, I would still recommend the Lower Rooms, especially if you have no other acquaintance in town. The master of ceremonies there is reputed to be most accommodating. He will make introductions, so Miss Graham will have a dance partner. And I believe there is to be a ball there tomorrow night."

"An excellent suggestion. But what a shame it is for Miss Walker to have been in town so long without a ball. If you and your husband would permit it, Mr. Graham and I should be happy to convey her to the dance tomorrow. I can serve as her chaperone, and she will be a companion for Susan."

The men returned just in time for Mr. Graham to second the invitation and for Papa to give his consent. Being now absolved from any guilt for going by my father's own insistence that I should, I certainly made no objection. Susan and I soon had our heads together making plans for the ball and speculating at length about the gratification it was sure to bring. At parting, we agreed to continue the subject on the morrow, the topic being far too consequential to canvass adequately in only one afternoon.

The next day, when we reconvened at the Pump-room, Susan and I were excused from the monotony of walking up and down indoors in favor of the fresh occupation of walking up and down outdoors. So, with umbrellas in hand as a precaution against the real possibility of inclement weather, we ventured onto Stall Street and set off with no particular destination in mind.

"My dear, I could hardly sleep for thinking about tonight," said Susan. "It has been ever so long since I have had a dance. In our small village, there are rarely enough young people together in one place to support the idea of a ball. And you? Do you often go to balls and parties, Jo?"

"They are not so very rare in Wallerton. Still, what I long for, what I dare to hope this evening will supply, is a more agreeable choice of partners."

"Have you met any young men since you have been in Bath?"

"Not yet, but I have seen one or two that I should very much *like* to meet," I said, giving my new friend, by the inflection of my voice and the smallest inclination of my head, the hint to glance across the street. There she and I discretely observed a relatively tall, well-dressed gentleman of about five- or six-and-twenty advancing with a self-assured gait, apparently totally oblivious to our existence. We were equally careful not to betray any consciousness of him.

"He is fearful handsome. Perhaps he will be at the ball tonight." Susan said a little too loudly for my comfort.

At that very moment, a violent rain commenced causing us to exclaim in alarm, deploy our umbrellas in unison, and reverse our course to return to the Pump-room. This flurry of activity in-

38

advertently brought us at last to the notice of the gentleman across the street. And, when a sudden gust of wind tore my umbrella from my grasp, he was there in three strides to retrieve it. He placed it back into my hand without a word, leaving me flustered by being brought so unexpectedly face to face with such a fine-looking stranger.

"Thank you, sir," I managed to say despite my not inconsiderable degree of perturbation.

"I am honored to be of service, madam," he answered, fixing my gaze for a moment with his formidable dark eyes. Then he dropped me an elegant bow and departed as quickly as he had arrived.

The brief encounter left me surprisingly shaken. Never before had I found any man capable of so thoroughly discomposing me by his aspect and proximity. Miss Graham gave me a quizzical look, evidently expecting some kind of coherent remark but finding me dumbstruck instead.

"What an impressive gentleman – so fine a figure and so gallant," prompted Susan.

Still in a bit of a daze, I mused, "How extraordinary that he should have been brought to us just as we were… just as I was…"

"…wishing to meet him?" Susan volunteered. "Yes, what an amazing coincidence. One might be tempted to think you lost hold of your umbrella for precisely that purpose," she teased.

This roused me from my earnest reflections, and I laughed. "I will forgive your impertinence this time, Miss Graham. We are not yet well-enough acquainted for you to know that such a scheme would never occur to me. Since it did to you, however, I shall remember where to go for that sort of assistance in future."

"Yes, I possess an untapped wealth of scathingly brilliant ideas. I shall put them completely at your disposal. Yet you may not need a one of them, for I think you have already made your first conquest in Bath without my help."

"Do not be ridiculous! My dear Susan, you make far too much of this. The gentleman was merely being polite. I'm sure he would have done the same for my mother or any other woman."

"Perhaps, but I daresay he would not have been so eager nor enjoyed it half so much. I saw the way he looked at you, the way you looked at each other. I wonder who he is… and if he has a friend for me."

We laughed, and I continued to make light of the incident. Yet the memory of it held me tightly in its grip for the rest of the afternoon. I could not stop thinking about the stranger, nor could I resist hoping that he would not remain unknown to me much longer.

8
The Lower Rooms

Upon returning to the house, my parents and I found that the post had come in our absence bringing a letter from Agnes at Wallerton and another from Tom at Oxford. On a single sheet, Tom reported that he had already settled back into the hospitable embrace of his college, and he pledged – as indeed he did every term – to apply himself to his studies with renewed vigor and devotion. The brief, perfunctory note hardly seemed to merit the tender reverence with which Mama handled it. Apparently, she alone could discern the fonder sentiments and more noble aspirations concealed beneath and between the words so carelessly scrawled upon the page.

My letter from Agnes was not intended for general consumption and held no fascination for anyone but myself. Accordingly, I carried it off to my room for a private perusal. The thick folds of paper promised well for its being a more generous and edifying correspondence than the other. However, even though Agnes was very liberal with her words and far more candid ex-pressing her sensibilities, she ultimately related little information. That very lack of news figured prominently in the theme of her discourse.

"I declare that nothing interesting ever happens in Wallerton," she wrote, *"and I am convinced that I shall never enjoy so much as one ounce of excitement as long as I remain here. My dearest friend, I depend on your letters so. Let me hear from you very often, so that I may sample vicariously that which I hope will soon be mine to savor in person. The prospect of joining you in Bath is what sustains me."*

"Poor Agnes," I thought aloud, "I do pity you. Well, I shall write you a good, long letter tomorrow, I promise. By then I hope to have some news worth telling, some experience truly deserving of your envy."

After dinner, I began the delightful ritual of dressing for the ball. As I did so, I pictured the scene in my imagination and wondered who my dance partner would be. In answer, the face of the intriguing gentleman I had encountered earlier that day once again sprang unbidden to my mind. He had made quite an impression on me. One minute I fervently prayed that he would come to the ball and procure an introduction, and the next I reproached myself for allowing such an idle fancy to dominate my thoughts. I was not accustomed to this sort of emotional agitation.

Mama, coming in to check on me, discovered me fully ready to go and impatiently pacing the length of my room.

"My dear, how well you look," she said. "That gown is so becoming. I am glad you chose it for tonight. Green has always been your best color. But why so anxious? It is not like you to become overexcited by the prospect of a ball."

"This is no ordinary ball, Mama. At a dance in Wallerton, one knows exactly what to expect – who will be there, how they will behave, what dances we will have and in what order they will be played. Tonight, everything is different – new people, a new place. Anything could happen."

"And you are hoping that something does, I suppose."

"What?"

"I was once your age, you know, and it does not seem so long ago either. Believe it or not, I can still remember how nervous I felt before a ball. That was always the way with me, but I have never seen *you* like this before."

"I am sorry, Mama. I do not know what is wrong with me."

"No need to apologize; I rather like it. It makes me feel as if we have a little more in common. I never thought that I had much to teach you. Perhaps now, at this juncture, you may find that you need a mother's advice after all." Taking my hand, she continued, "I will never force a confidence from you, but I want you to know that you can come to me with your problems at any time. I have some knowledge and experience with affairs of the heart. I was quite admired in my day, and your father was not the first to notice me."

"Mama!"

"Why so shocked, my dear? Did you never consider the possibility that your mother might know what it is like to be pursued by a man, or even more than one?"

No, I had never given it an instant's thought in the whole course of my existence.

She went on. "I do not suppose that you have, any more than I did at your age. Well, nevertheless, it is true. So remember, you can talk to me about such things if and when you have the need."

I promised to bear it in mind.

At length, my party arrived and Mr. Graham came to the door to collect me. The afternoon rain had left behind a pattern of puddles of various sizes, scattered at random like so many mushrooms sprung up across the forest floor. Lest my carefully arranged dancing clothes be spoilt at the very outset of the evening, I held my skirt and carefully picked my way to the carriage. Mrs. Graham and Susan waited therein. One glance at my friend's face was sufficient to convince me that she felt the same exhilaration of spirits that I myself could hardly contain.

The brief ride to our destination had no very soothing effect upon either of us, and we arrived with nerves still on edge. As Susan and I entered the crowded ballroom, arm in arm for mutual support, Mr. Graham had a word with the master of ceremonies. An august personage with a fitting appellation, Mr. King reigned over the dance, directing decorum and introductions as he saw fit. In his hands rested the power to dash or delight the hopes of all the young ladies in the room, including my friend and myself.

We counted ourselves fortunate to find seats where we could view the large company engaged in the spectacle of the dance. Once settled, I cast my eyes over the throng, looking for the gentleman I had encountered that afternoon on the street. I saw instead Mr. King approaching with quite a different person at his side. The young man had a pleasing countenance but was rather shorter than average, giving me one more reason to hope that he was intended for my petite friend instead of for me. Unfortunately, that was not the case, as I soon discovered. Mr. King, with proper formality, introduced Mr. George Ramsey to me as my partner for the next dance. I smiled as graciously as possible, and allowed him to lead me out onto the floor for a quadrille.

Had I not already been entertaining thoughts of someone else, I would no doubt have found Mr. Ramsey's company completely acceptable, even agreeable. He was an excellent dancer, and he expressed himself well in conversation. After politely inquiring about my home and family, he in turn informed me that he lived in London, where he was a student of the law. If I could not have the partner I had envisioned – and he was nowhere to be seen – Mr.

Ramsey would do as well as any other and probably better than most, I decided.

By the commencement of the next dance, Susan had been provided a partner as well. His name was Mr. Cox, as I later learned. The pair of them stood up together in the same set with Mr. Ramsey and myself. Soon the lively music and the animated scene captured my spirit completely. I set aside my reservations and threw myself altogether into the fray, feeling the satisfaction of exhausting my excess energy by means of the vigorous exercise. Thus we continued until the break.

At tea, Susan and I introduced our partners to the others in our group. Whilst Mr. and Mrs. Graham engaged the young men in conversation, I had opportunity for a few moments' private discourse with my friend.

"What a lucky girl you are, my dear," whispered Susan. "You have made another splendid conquest. Mr. Ramsey appears very agreeable, and oh so handsome too."

"Do you really think so, Susan? He is pleasant enough, I agree, but hardly the man I had in mind, as you well know."

"In that case, would you consider switching partners? Mr. Ramsey may not be your first choice, but I believe he will do very well for me."

I had no very high hopes for finding Mr. Cox any more to my personal taste than my first partner. Still, seeing Susan's excitement at the chance to further her acquaintance with Mr. Ramsey, I willingly acceded to her plan. Advancing my friend's happiness seemed a worthwhile and more achievable goal for the evening than accomplishing my own. The gentlemen made no objection when changing partners was proposed, and Mrs. Graham firmly supported the idea.

"Yes, by all means, make the change. It would not do to start tongues wagging by keeping too long to one partner," she reminded us stridently. "I cannot speak to what may be acceptable in other places, but where we come from, it simply is not done."

So it was settled accordingly. When the orchestra struck up a fresh tune, we made our way back onto the floor, keeping side by side in the set for maximum companionship. Mr. Cox danced nearly as well as Mr. Ramsey, and his address was pleasing enough. Nevertheless, his society held no particular charm for me.

We had been about our business several minutes when Susan caught my attention with a small gesture toward the room's main entrance. There the gentleman so earnestly sought before could be seen surveying the company. The dance presently carried me in his direction, and I felt my embarrassment increase as the distance between us narrowed. I attempted to keep my eyes averted. Yet, when I passed so near to where he stood that we could almost have shaken hands, I looked up to find his gaze fastened upon me. He smiled and gave me a nod of recognition before my partner and I were swept away again.

I caught only a glimpse or two more of the handsome stranger during the course of my obligation to Mr. Cox. When I was free to look about myself thereafter, he was nowhere to be seen.

"You are a little flushed, my dear," said Mrs. Graham upon my return to our seats. "You must be fatigued from all this exertion. Do sit down and rest yourself. Mr. Graham has gone to the card room, so you shall keep me company for a little while, until you recover your strength."

"Thank you, Mrs. Graham. I believe I shall," I agreed, sitting down as instructed. "I am suddenly quite weary indeed."

"I cannot catch Susan's eye or I would direct her to do the same."

"No. I believe Mr. Ramsey claims her full attention."

"Well, he seems a nice young man, and I am glad Susan is enjoying herself."

I sat out the next two dances on the chance that the gentleman who had so thoroughly captured my interest might return with Mr. King to be introduced and claim my hand. He did not. In fact, I saw nothing more of him that night, rendering the evening sadly lackluster in my final estimation.

Mr. Graham returned from the card room to join us when the dance was almost over. "Well, Miss Walker," said he directly, "I hope you have had an agreeable ball."

"Very agreeable indeed," I replied, vainly endeavoring to hide a great yawn.

9

An Introduction

I stayed behind from the daily pilgrimage to the Pump-room next morning for the purpose of fulfilling my sworn obligation to Agnes, that of sending her a long, newsy letter. Having written before about the town, the shops, the Pump-room, and our acquaintance with the Graham family, the body of this missive could be devoted to the proceedings of the previous night. I flatter myself that I waxed quite lyrical about the scene at the Lower Rooms, describing in detail the look of the place, the finery of the ladies, the quality of the music, and the liveliness of the dancing – all subjects that I knew would be of special interest to my friend. I fancied what Agnes would ask if she could.

"What gown did you wear, Jo? Tell me about the size of the room and the look of the people there. Was it as grand as we have heard? Were there enough gentlemen to go round? The ladies were all dressed very elegantly, I suppose, in the latest fashions from London and Paris. How large and how many were the sets of dancers? Did you see anyone of your acquaintance? Tell me all about your partners!"

I answered each of these imagined inquiries as thoroughly as possible, the last question being the most difficult of which to give a satisfactory account, my partners having been so distinctly unremarkable from my own point of view. I omitted any mention of the man to whom I compared them, against whom they came up curiously wanting in my mind. Instead, I gave each one credit on his own merit, with Mr. Ramsey receiving the best review for pleasing Susan so well.

Despite the advantage of having more than enough information to relate, my letter progressed but slowly, the movement of my pen frequently pausing in suspense of further direction as I reflected upon the events at the dance. On the whole, it had been a success, I decided. I certainly had no just cause to be dissatisfied. After all, I had been allowed an evening out in Bath society far sooner than I had dared to hope, and spent it in altogether agreeable, if not particularly stimulating, company. My mistake had been in allowing my expectations to soar so high that there was no living up to them, in staking all my hopes on a man I knew nothing about.

"You are being quite ridiculous, Josephine," I told myself, "and it must stop now." I resolved to think of the man no more, finished my letter, and posted it at once.

Although somewhat improved, Papa still was not well enough to go much abroad. His limitations continued to govern his wife and daughter's activities as well. With the exception of our regular forays to the Pump-room, we three kept to the quiet of our house over the next few days. The Grahams were temporarily gone out of town, further securing our isolation. Much as I cared for my new friend, this brief separation suited me exceedingly well, assisting me to quiet my thoughts and emotions into the more composed state to which I was accustomed.

As a deliberate distraction, I set myself the task of writing out the story I had promised to send to Mrs. Evensong for little John. It had been gathering itself, bit by bit, in my brain until there was no more room to contain it; it needs must spill out onto paper at last. So the tale of Percival, a stout-hearted, seafaring pig, and his troublesome brothers, Peter and Pim, began to take shape. With my mind thus occupied, I was largely able to refrain from indulging the romantic reflections to which I had proved so susceptible of late.

~~*~~

Our comparative seclusion lasted about a week until the Grahams returned and gave a dinner party to mark the occasion. By then, we were all ready for an outing; we accepted the invitation to Milsom Street immediately. In addition to the felicity of seeing our friends again, the event promised the advantage of expanding our acquaintance in Bath. As it turned out, however, the party was small with only one person attending who was as yet unknown to me.

Susan met us at the door when we arrived, her countenance shining with excitement. From her animated expression and sparkling eyes, I knew at once that something out of the ordinary was afoot. As my parents proceeded upstairs, Susan drew alongside me, taking my arm.

"I am vastly glad that you are here, Jo. I have missed you excessively!" she said in hushed enthusiasm.

"I am very happy to see you as well, but what on earth has you so agitated, my dear? Has anything happened?"

"Not yet, but it is about to. Oh, what a surprise is in store for you! You will never guess who has come to dine with us."

Since, indeed, I had no idea at all, I waited to be enlightened. "Well?" I prompted impatiently as we neared the top of the stairs.

"Mr. Ramsey is here, and someone else whom you will be pleased to see, I daresay. No time to explain; just ready yourself for a shock, my dear."

As we entered the drawing room, the mystery guest stood not ten feet in front of us. His name I did not know, but his person was by no means unfamiliar to me. I suddenly found myself confronted with the very gentleman I had so diligently avoided thinking of for the last several days. It was all I could do not to gasp in surprise. Whilst he was first introduced to my parents, I had a moment to recover my composure before his attention – and those penetrating eyes I remembered so well – turned to me. His name was Richard Pierce.

"Miss Walker, I am delighted to make your acquaintance at last after very nearly meeting you twice before," he said in rich tones, following the formal introduction. "Do you remember?"

"Yes, sir, I believe I saw you briefly at the dance in the Lower Rooms a week ago, and when you were kind enough to retrieve my umbrella earlier the same day," I answered with measured control.

"I say, that was a job well done, young man," said Mr. Graham. "Mr. Pierce is the son of an old friend of mine from Cambridge," he informed us. "We discovered each other in the card room whilst the rest of you were dancing last week. I thought it would be pleasant to add some other young people to our party this evening, and these two gentlemen were good enough to oblige me."

"So you prefer cards to dancing, Mr. Pierce?" I pointedly inquired.

"I hope you will not accuse me of equivocation when I say that, in good company, I am equally content with either entertainment."

"Then, apparently, you liked the looks of the company in the card room better than the ballroom last week."

"Not at all, I assure you. I would in fact be mortified if you should believe I meant any such slight. However, if I do not mistake, you only toy with my words. For you, Miss Walker, I shall endeavor to choose them with more circumspection in future. I anticipate the challenge with the utmost pleasure."

"As do I, Mr. Pierce. And I shall be more than happy to accommodate you. In my experience, a gentleman only does his best work when tested."

"Then I am your ready pupil, Miss Walker," he said with a bow.

Despite a vague, pre-Bath notion of curbing my tongue in favor of a milder, more universally palatable brand of conversation, I had already thrown down the verbal gauntlet at Mr. Pierce's feet. What was more, Mr. Pierce had picked it up without hesitation. In the continuing contest of repartee that followed, he matched me point for point, only giving ground when hard pressed by claim of chivalry.

Dinner afforded me a fine opportunity to further observe Mr. Pierce's pleasing manners, to hear his correct opinions on a variety of topics, and to assess his many other amiable qualities. His comportment showed him to be a well-bred gentleman of style and taste. Toward me, he behaved very charmingly indeed. I was still more impressed by the civility and deference with which he treated his elders – my own parents and Mr. and Mrs. Graham. Everything I saw and heard contributed to my good opinion of him and my desire to know him better.

As soon as the ladies withdrew, Susan and I put our heads together on the subject of our dinner companions.

"Susan, I know you have all manner of brilliant schemes at your disposal, but how on earth did you manage it?"

"Is not Papa an angel for inviting such affable young men to dine with us?"

"He is a saint, without a doubt. But surely *you* must have a share of the credit for arranging this."

"It is true that I dropped a hint about his including Mr. Ramsey. Mr. Pierce was all his own idea, I swear! Not that I would have had the least scruple in suggesting it for your sake, but how could I when I did not even know Papa was acquainted with him? It was just a stroke of incredible luck, or perhaps we should call it fate. What do you think, Jo?"

"I hardly know."

"And are you pleased with him?"

"How could I be otherwise? I was already disposed to think well of him, so perhaps I am prejudiced. But, so far, I find much to admire and nothing to criticize. His sensible, lively mind is just what I value."

"The fact that he is tolerably pleasant to look at is of no importance to you, I suppose."

"You cannot fault me for approving his quick mind, Susan, although I admit he seems to have other highly estimable qualities as well." We both laughed. "Now, that is quite enough. We should not speak of Mr. Pierce in this way, as if there is room in our heads for nothing other than gossip. Remember our pact; we promised to guard each other against becoming stupid over men."

"Yes, of course. I shall try to think of a more serious subject… Mr. Ramsey, for example."

The card table was set out when the gentlemen reappeared, providing employment to the two older couples for the remainder of the evening. Left to our own devices, the rest of us took seats at the other end of the long drawing room and settled into conversation. What began as a foursome shortly divided into a pair of twosomes. Susan and Mr. Ramsey, who sat side by side, embarked on an earnest discussion of poetry – the relative merits of Scott versus Cowper – leaving Mr. Pierce and myself to entertain each other as well as we might. I viewed this circumstance as no hardship. Mr. Pierce seemed equally content with his lot. He moved away from the others and placed himself next to me.

"So, you are come to Bath for your father's health, I understand, Miss Walker."

"That is correct. What about you, Mr. Pierce? What brings you here?"

"My father has sent me on holiday, and to look out a good place for him to stay when he joins me later. You see, I lobbied him to be sent on the grand tour of the continent to round out my education before taking up my responsibilities at home. He would not hear of it. Far too extravagant, to his way of thinking. So this trip to Bath is intended as a substitute, I believe. Hardly an even exchange, I grant you, yet I mean to make the most of it."

"How are you enjoying your stay thus far, sir? Are the amusements, scenery, and society all to your taste?"

"Until very recently, I was undecided on the question."

"And now?"

"Now I have good reason to revise my opinion," he said with a meaningful look.

"In which direction? For the better or for the worse?"

"Oh, for the better. By all means, for the better."

I accepted this pleasantry as the gentleman clearly intended it, as a compliment to myself. I cannot deny the thrill of satisfaction it gave me. When my spirits recovered from this little flutter, I invited Mr. Pierce to tell me about his family and situation. He explained that he was the only son of his widowed father, his mother having died some five years earlier. His two sisters – one his senior and one his junior – were unmarried and still resided at home, that being an estate called Wildewood, in Surrey.

"Have you been to that part of the country, Miss Walker? It is known for its beauty. 'Surrey is the garden of England,' as the saying goes. Have you not heard it called such yourself?"

"Oh, yes, and I quite agree. I visited my uncle there many times. My brother Frederick has just inherited his estate, in fact. Perhaps you know of it; it is called Millwalk."

"No, I cannot recall that I ever heard of it. Still, Surrey is not that large. It may be that your brother and I are neighbors after all. So, now I know that you have at least one brother, and your honored father and mother I have met. Tell me the rest. Tell me about the place you come from and all your friends there."

In my limited experience, it was more usual for young men to rattle on and on about themselves and their own concerns, without thought for anyone else. Therefore, Mr. Pierce's interest both flattered me and spoke well of his character. By this time, I felt so at ease in his company that I did as he asked. I told him about Tom, Frederick, Arthur, Agnes, and our home in Wallerton. About myself, I had little to say. As I saw it, nothing much had yet happened to me (except for receiving my inheritance so unexpectedly, and that I was not willing to divulge). "I fear there is not much more to tell. I have lived a very quiet life," I concluded.

"Well, this trip to Bath will add another chapter to your book, and a few more friends to your list, I daresay. How long have you known the Grahams, Miss Walker?"

"Only a short time; just since they arrived here. My mother was acquainted with Mrs. Graham years ago when they were girls at school together. Apparently, Bath is the perfect place to find and renew old acquaintances. You and I both discovered a connection with the Grahams, which gives us something admirable in common, Mr. Pierce. They are excellent people – so friendly and obliging."

"Salt of the earth, I make no doubt. I must say that Mr. Graham seems a very worthy sort of man, although..." He chuckled, leaning forward and continuing in a much lower voice. "... my father is fond of saying that it is a great mercy that the man inherited his money for he is rather too simple to make his way in trade."

"Dear me. That is hardly fair, is it, Mr. Pierce?" I said, stifling a laugh.

"My father's words, not mine," he disclaimed. "And they were spoken with good-natured affection, I assure you. As for me, I make no such judgments. I find the whole family quite delightful."

"I am relieved to hear it."

"Observing people is prodigiously interesting. Would not you agree, Miss Walker? It has become rather of a hobby with me. I am always diverted since I am always meeting with something un-expected. Mr. and Mrs. Graham are the perfect example," he continued for my ears only. "Without a doubt, two of the finest individuals you will find anywhere. Yet together they certainly qualify as one of the oddest couples I have ever come across: a domineering little lady married to such a big mouse of a man. It really is quite comical, you must allow."

"Truly, Mr. Pierce, you mustn't say such things," I scolded mildly. "I know you only jest, but I am afraid you go too far."

"Do I? Then I am sincerely sorry," he said with comfortable grace. "I would not offend your sensibilities for the world. I suppose I shall have to find some other means of entertaining you, then, since you do not care for my style of humor. Perhaps we should keep to safer subjects. What shall it be, Miss Walker? Poetry? Politics? Social reform? What is your pleasure?"

My pleasure was listening to practically anything Mr. Pierce cared to say. He had such an engaging manner, such a charming way of expressing himself, that whatever he said sounded un-commonly clever. The fact that he demonstrated equal regard for my opinions only heightened his appeal.

Mr. Pierce set the tone for a refreshing openness between us by his relaxed attitudes. From the outset, no awkwardness hindered our conversational intercourse; ideas, wit, and humor flowed unre-servedly in both directions. I doubt Mama would have approved our uninhibited discourse, had she known of it, but I found a private satisfaction in setting aside the undue restraint of artificial niceties. Yes, I saw a new world of delicious freedom expanding before me, thanks to Mr. Pierce.

10
Courtship

After such a promising beginning to our acquaintance, there was nothing to hinder Mr. Pierce and myself from progressing on to what can only be described as the early stages of courtship. With my cavalier attitude toward men and marriage, I would have been hard pressed to admit it at the time, but so it was. He began with invented excuses to call on me, and I with contrivances to go out where we might happen to meet. When we encountered no opposition at home, these pretenses were swiftly discarded in favor of a more open acknowledgement of our mutual regard.

I saw him nearly every day. On an even footing and without reserve, we talked about every topic under the sun. The more Mr. Pierce made clear his preference for me above any other, the more sincerely I began to return his affection. After knowing him a fortnight, it first occurred to me that I might be in a fair way of falling in love. He showed unmistakable symptoms of the same, and all without the promise of fortune to tempt him. He had not asked for, and I had not volunteered, any specific information about my financial status. The general means of our family he could approximate from our style of living and from my talk about Fairfield. It appeared that was enough to satisfy him, just as I would have hoped.

Once it became clear that Mr. Pierce was developing serious intentions, my father made prudent inquiries into the gentleman's background and character through our solicitor. According to all available information, Mr. Pierce hailed from a very respectable family, and no one had ever heard any harm of him. He had recently earned his degree from Cambridge and, as an only son, looked forward to the happy prospect of inheriting the prosperous estate of Wildewood. In the meantime, his allowance kept him in stylish comfort. With all his questions answered satisfactorily, Papa declared that he would not object to such a creditable match for his daughter.

Mr. Pierce also won my mother's approbation with little difficulty, partly on the strength of seeing her daughter made so happy and, I suspect, partly due to the working of the same manifold attractions which had fixed my interest. Being a woman herself, I suppose she was not entirely immune to these influences, even at her different age and station in life. Still, her maternal instinct had not been so thoroughly overcome as to forget her responsibilities altogether.

"Jo, my dear, I thought you and I might have a little chat," she said one morning, coming into my room.

"If you wish, Mama."

She sat down upon the bed beside me. "Mr. Pierce is a delightful young man, and you like him very much." It was a statement, not a question. "As do I, to be sure. Yet I do feel it is incumbent upon me to recommend a bit of caution. I can well imagine what you must be feeling. A first romance is a very intoxicating thing. It is easy to find oneself... swept away... by a flood of unfamiliar emotions," she said with a far-off look in her eyes. "Still, you mustn't lose your head. Use the good sense God has given you, as you would in making any other important decision."

"Mama, really, I do not think this is necessary."

"I know, and you are probably right, my dear. Yet I could not bear to see you hurt when I might have prevented it with a word or two of warning. So humor me just this once, and then we shall say no more about it. All I am advocating is that you proceed slowly; take plenty of time to get to know the gentleman before you commit yourself in any way. It is for his protection as well as your own that you should. Nothing will give me more pleasure than seeing you well married someday. But you are still young and there is no reason to rush."

"You needn't worry, Mama. I have no intention of 'losing my head,' as you call it, for Mr. Pierce or anybody else. My wits have not as yet deserted me, I assure you."

"I am glad to hear it. See that they do not, and remember to come to me if you need advice. That is all I ask."

Mother seemed satisfied, having done her duty and being reassured that her daughter was in no immediate danger of making a fool of herself over the dashing Mr. Pierce. I was equally pleased to have soothed her unwarranted fears. And I meant what I said.

My growing regard for Mr. Pierce notwithstanding, I still felt in full control of my faculties.

~~*~~

The next two weeks passed most agreeably. Thanks to Mama's conscientious supervision, my father continued his treatments at the Pump-room with impressive regularity, and followed his dietary guidelines with similar faithfulness. As a result, he steadily improved and began to feel equal to a more ambitious social schedule. Concerts, the theatre, and even an occasional ball were now within our reach.

True to my word, I remembered to speak up on behalf of Agnes, who, by her own written account, continued to languish most grievously in Wallerton for lack of society and diversion. Now that Papa was feeling so much better, his spirits had improved as well. "The more, the merrier," he said to my surprise when I asked permission to invite Agnes to join us. I posted a letter to her forthwith.

Mr. Pierce's behavior during this interval could not have been more effectively designed to please. His devotion knew no bounds other than what decorum and basic civility to others demanded. Miss Graham and Mr. Ramsey's mutual fondness, though perhaps less ardent in nature, held fast as well. And since being introduced at the Grahams' dinner party, Ramsey and Pierce had established a comfortable rapport between them. Being forced to choose between the society of my new bosom friend and that of Mr. Pierce would have been a painful proposition. Fortunately, I seldom had to sacrifice the company of one for the other since we were all four content to go about together.

Although it was now November, exploring the streets and avenues of Bath remained our preferred choice for daytime activity. Winter clothing and exercise easily overcame all but the coldest temperatures. Precipitation could be more bothersome. Whenever the appearance of the sky was arguably in our favor, though, we would set forth on the gravel walk to the Royal Crescent or for a stroll along the Avon, umbrellas in hand. On those occasions when not even the most optimistic imagination could reasonably predict a dry outing, we were forced to be content with indoor entertainments, collecting at Susan's house, or at mine, or at the Pump-room.

On one such dreary, gray morning, Mr. Pierce called early at Pultney Street with an equally gloomy aspect. After leaving his dripping greatcoat at the door, he came up to deliver distressing news. Papa was at the Pump-room, so Mama and I received him, immediately noticing his uncharacteristically low spirits.

"Is anything the matter, Mr. Pierce?" she asked.

"I have unpleasant news, I am sorry to say, although it will doubtless hurt me far more than it does either of you. Alas, I must take temporary leave of Bath and of all my excellent friends here. My father has recalled me to Surrey; I have just received his summons. He needs me at Wildewood and then intends to send me on to London from there, to attend to some business on his behalf. Much as I am loath to quit this place where I have been so happy, I have no choice."

"This is unlucky," exclaimed Mama. "However, as you say, you are obliged to obey your father. I hope your absence will not be lengthy, Mr. Pierce."

"You are too kind, Mrs. Walker. Yet I cannot tell you how long I shall be detained. I really do not know myself. It may be as little as a week or as much as a month. My father does not say, and these things are difficult to predict. I will on no account stay away a single day longer than I must," he declared, looking intently at me for a long minute. Then, upon rousing himself, he lamented, "Of all horrid things, leave-taking is the worst."

I had been too disheartened by his news to speak before. Finally I asked, "Must you go immediately?"

"Tomorrow."

That dismal word heralded the end of my season of peculiar bliss, the heady days of early infatuation. At least Mr. Pierce and I were to have the benefit of one last evening together before we endured the trial of separation. Thus the ball at the Upper Rooms that night took on new significance, serving as the culmination to our first month's acquaintance and as Mr. Pierce's take-leave ceremony. The Grahams and Mr. Ramsey were expected to attend as well, so it would be a proper sendoff.

That night supplied all the magical delight that failed to develop at my first ball in Bath weeks before. On the earlier occasion, I had lamented the lack of a partner who could please me and be pleased by me. Now, I rejoiced in the fact that I had found one who did both. Instead of only glimpsing a handsome stranger across the room as I had done then, I gazed at him across the set, dance after dance, counting him as my very particular friend.

Mr. Pierce escorted me to the dance floor once again after the tea break, boasting glibly, "With you on my arm, Miss Walker, I daresay I am the envy of every man in this room."

"Mr. Pierce, really! You exaggerate most alarmingly. I am sensible enough to know that there are probably dozens of girls in the room much prettier. If you would but open your eyes and look about yourself, you would see that it is true."

"Well, perhaps I am prejudiced. Still, if the men are not envious, it is only because they do not know you as I do. Your beauty they can judge for themselves, but your other charms may not be so readily apparent. How can anyone who has never had the pleasure of speaking to you know the melodic tones of your voice, for instance? How can he be expected to appreciate your clever wit?"

"Yes, I believe you *are* prejudiced in my favor, Mr. Pierce, possibly to the point of blindness," I said, pleased nonetheless. "No one else has yet discovered me half so amiable. Unfortunately, now that you have spoilt me with this sort of high praise, I am bound to grow quite desolate when I am once again deprived of it."

As we reached our places on the floor, he pressed my hand and whispered in my ear, "Henceforth, you need never be without my praise and adoration, Miss Walker."

In that instant, Mr. Pierce had exchanged his light, flirtatious tone for one quite serious. When I faced him across the set, I found his look equally earnest. His statement was tantamount to a declaration of love; the words implied it and his manner confirmed it.

I could still feel his warm breath against my hair, hear his words echoing in my mind as the dance began. I barely noticed the music or saw the other couples, so fixed was my attention on Mr. Pierce, and his on me. We moved through the entire dance in a trance-like silence.

At its conclusion, Mr. Pierce continued resolutely. "Miss Walker... Jo... when I return to Bath, my father will be with me. I have written him about you, and he is most eager to make your acquaintance."

"I shall be very pleased to meet him, sir."

"Will you not call me Richard?"

"If you like... Richard."

"Yes, that is much better. In fact, I quite like the sound of it," he said with a satisfied smile.

11
Agnes Arrives

Mr. Pierce's absence cast a pall over his friends left behind in Bath. No doubt I felt the loss most acutely, but my pain was eased by the remembrance of all that had passed between us at the ball before his departure. He left me in little doubt of his intentions and wishes. My own feelings were more difficult to define. I could no longer deny being completely enamored with him. He charmed and fascinated me beyond anyone I had hitherto encountered, and my preoccupation with him defied my own reason. But was that love? Since mental confusion is said to be one of the most promising symptoms of the disease, I decided it was perhaps just as well that Richard had gone away, so that I could ponder the question in solitude.

My isolation lasted but two days before Miss Pittman made her entrance onto the scene. We were all three at home to receive Agnes and her unavoidable effusions of happiness. She declared Bath the most charming place she had ever seen, and her kind hosts the most obliging creatures in the world for enabling her to visit it, thereby securing her felicity and her eternal gratitude. My parents accepted this extravagant praise with grace and relative composure.

Agnes and I demonstrated less restraint. After such a pro-tracted separation, we required fully ten minutes to reaffirm our mutual affection before the flood could be stemmed and our sen-sations returned to tolerable good order. When this unbecoming display proved too tiresome for my father's nerves to bear, he gave us leave to continue the reunion in private.

"I am so grateful for your invitation, my dearest friend," Agnes resumed after we retreated to my own chamber. "I shall be forever in your debt for taking me away from dreary old Wallerton to such a fresh, exciting place. I can hardly wait to see the famous Pump-room and to meet all your friends! Your last letter was full of hints of some new development but very little solid information. What a tease you are! Now, do not keep me in suspense any longer; tell me your news. What has happened?"

For a moment, I held back, anticipating with pleasure what the effect would be of the intelligence I had to share with Agnes. Then, at her insistence, I confessed. "I do have news that will surely surprise you, Agnes, for indeed it has astonished me exceedingly. You see, I have a suitor – Mr. Richard Pierce, from Surrey. He has been courting me these four weeks."

Agnes squealed with delight, and then demanded a thorough description of the gentleman's person, situation, and manners, along with a detailed account of all events leading up to the present. I gladly obliged her with an exhaustive report on the amiable Mr. Pierce and his solicitous behavior toward me, including the current state of affairs between us.

"You imposter; I have found you out. 'Just a bit of sport,' you boasted before you went away, as if you were somehow immune to the attractions of the male sex. Now look at you – blushing at the very mention of Mr. Pierce's name. You are no different, after all. It only took the right man to teach you to know yourself."

"I daresay you are right, Agnes. I am quite embarrassed to remember what I said then. What arrogance to think I could play with fire and not be touched by it. Mr. Pierce has opened my eyes."

"Do you really think he means to make you an offer?"

"I can scarce believe it myself. Yet can there be any other interpretation of what he said to me at the ball? I think he is only waiting on his father's approval."

"And he knows nothing of your inheritance?"

"No. He must presume that I have a dowry appropriate to my station, although he has never asked and I have given him no reason to hope for more."

"So, it is just as you desired. But you have not said how you will answer Mr. Pierce. Do you wish to marry him?"

"My father considers it an eligible match," I hedged.

"I should think so! To be the mistress of a fine estate instead of a curate's wife; that is a vast improvement. You are to be congratulated, my dear."

"For my part, the decision has nothing to do with rank. Had I loved Mr. Summeride, I would have accepted him at once, regardless of his lowly state. But as you know, I have sworn never to marry anyone without benefit of love."

"Then the only question that remains is do you love Mr. Pierce?"

"'Tis a difficult thing to answer with certainty. I admit that I like him very much. He excites and interests me more than anyone with whom I have ever been in company. I think most probably I am in love with him. That is, I believe I must be. Oh, I cannot seem to think straight where Richard is concerned."

"My dear Jo, many people consider that the most positive proof of love."

"I hope not, Agnes. I should be sorry to discover that I must surrender my reason in proof of my affection. In any case, I do not have to decide the matter this minute, which is clearly just as well. Now, as we are speaking of affairs of the heart, it is only right that you should have your turn. What do you hear from Arthur?"

"Arthur?" she snorted. "You should know better than to class him with your Mr. Pierce. Arthur is no romantic hero."

"What? Surely there is no finer man in all the world."

"Do not mistake me. I quite agree with you, Jo. I am dotingly fond of the dear boy. And I do not require grand passion. It will be enough for me to marry a gentleman of some prestige with a handsome income, which Arthur shall be when he is well established in his career with a sizable living in hand, or better still, more than one. You know how he excels at all things academic and moral. Barring any serious scandal, he is sure to make bishop someday. The Right Reverend Arthur K. Evensong: how well that sounds! I should much rather he had a *real* title, of course, but I intend to be satisfied with being wife to a bishop. No, all Arthur's other merits aside, I only meant to say that he is not particularly romantic, not as you describe your Mr. Pierce – dashing to rescue your umbrella, contriving ways to meet you, wooing you so persistently, and saying exactly what a girl desires to hear."

"Naturally, I am in no position to judge; Arthur would hardly show his most tender side to me. I thought perhaps with you, however…"

"You suppose wrongly if you imagine him more demonstrative in private. It is simply not in his nature."

"A minor shortcoming, you must admit."

"Yes, and one that I am perfectly willing to accept considering his other advantages. I thoroughly intend that he will make me an excellent husband one day, just as my father and his arranged together years ago."

~~*~~

I wasted no time fulfilling Agnes's wish to become immediately familiar with the people and places of Bath. The very next morning, we began by attending the Pump-room, to there parade up and down with the rest of the company – a ritual by now common enough to me but irresistibly novel to my friend. The exercise served the additional purpose of introducing Agnes to nearly all our acquaintance currently in town. As luck would have it, the Grahams arrived shortly after we did, enabling Agnes to meet the family about whom she already knew a great deal from my information. Susan joined us, and ten minutes later Mr. Ramsey appeared, undoubtedly by design. He took up his usual place at Miss Graham's side and was introduced to the newcomer. After the customary civilities, he and Susan broke away to navigate their own course through the room.

As Agnes and I drifted about in the circulating sea of humanity, I soon became sensible of the effect my pretty friend was having on the members of the opposite sex. They had directly detected the presence of an attractive new prospect in their midst, and they apparently could not help but admire her beauty to the temporary exclusion of all other considerations. I was hardly surprised at this reaction; I had seen it a dozen times before. Heads always turned when Agnes entered a room.

Their resolute interest in Miss Pittman notwithstanding, the majority of the poor, simple fellows could do no more than look; it was not within their power to procure an introduction. There was one exception, however. Mr. Cox, on the strength of his prior acquaintance with me from the dance some weeks earlier, approached.

"Miss Walker, I am very pleased to see you again. How do you do?" Though he addressed me, his eyes were fixed steadfastly on Agnes.

"Very well, I assure you, Mr. Cox."

Undoubtedly expecting the coveted introduction to come next, he waited and continued gazing at Agnes.

I was suddenly struck by an irresistible impulse to toy with him a bit first, so I insisted on hearing his considered opinion of the current break in the rain, and on the prospect for the weather continuing fair. Then, when I had delayed as long as I decently could, I gave him what he wanted. "Oh, I do beg your pardon, sir. Where are my manners? You will think me very badly brought up, I fear. Allow me to present my good friend Miss Pittman. Agnes, this is Mr. Cox."

The lady curtsied and the gentleman complimented her with a deep bow. "I am honored to make your acquaintance, Miss Pittman. Have you been long in Bath?"

"No, sir, I arrived only yesterday."

"Ah, then you are yet to discover all the place has to offer. There is much to amuse a refined young lady such as yourself – so much to entertain."

Mr. Cox made it his business to act as our escort for the duration of our time at the Pump-room that day. On no account could he be persuaded to leave us unprotected and friendless in such a crowd. When he at last returned us to the safety of my father's care, he left Agnes with this parting thought:

"I hope you will allow me to be of some small service to you during your stay here, Miss Pittman. I should be only too happy to show you the sights – and Miss Walker as well, of course – at any time you wish. Perhaps I might be permitted to call on you in a day or two."

Given leave to do so, Mr. Cox reluctantly bid us farewell.

We left the Pump-room behind and turned toward home on High Street. Papa, who was in rare form, asked after Miss Pittman's first impressions of Bath, and received a very favorable report. He then proceeded to expound on his own opinions of the place after a considerably more lengthy exposure.

"I must tell you, Miss Pittman, that when my wife and daughter first proposed this trip, I was less than enthusiastic. I did not think such a place would suit me at all, but I have since been converted. I find that a change of scene and society is just the thing; it gives new strength to the body and revives the spirit most remarkably. I feel like a new man."

"Papa has been a model patient, and you see how much improved he is." As if to emphasize the point, my father added a little spring to his step.

"Yes. You seem quite recovered, Mr. Walker," agreed Agnes.

"Indeed, I am. Indeed, I am. Dr. Oliver says that two or three weeks more should do the trick. I shall be right as rain by then and ready to return home. Still, other considerations may detain us. We are in no great hurry to quit Bath, are we, Jo?"

"No, Papa. We certainly are not."

~~*~~

The next two weeks flew by in a whirlwind of activity. On the pretext of entertaining our house guest, Mama indulged her own inclination for a wide variety of social intercourse. She filled our days with shopping and calls, and our evenings with dinners and visits to the ballrooms, theatre, and concert hall. Her efforts were not thrown away. Agnes felt her luck at being the recipient of such uncommon benevolence, and we both took every opportunity of enjoying ourselves.

Mr. Cox did his part by way of contributing to Miss Pittman's entertainment. He kept his word, coming to call on us in Pultney Street and doing his best to shadow our public movements, with or without the invitation to do so. He seemed always to be turning up at the same assemblies and parties we attended, and encountering us on the street, invariably discovering that his way lay in exactly the same path as our own. I did nothing to promote these attentions. Agnes, however, seemed perfectly willing to accept them. If she did not precisely encourage Mr. Cox, she did precious little to discourage him either.

Finally, I felt compelled to express a word of concern. "Agnes, my dear, do not you think we have been seeing entirely too much of Mr. Cox? Perhaps we should give him a hint to direct his interest elsewhere."

"Good heavens! Why on earth should we do that? I find him so very diverting. I should dislike giving up the pleasure of his company above all things."

"I am afraid that the pleasantness of an employment does not always evince its propriety. Moreover, it seems unfair to accept his attentions when neither of us is really free."

"As far as I am aware, you are not engaged and neither am I. Until such time as we are, we break no rules of propriety by keeping company with Mr. Cox."

"Strictly speaking, you are correct, I admit. Still, I believe it would be most impolitic to encourage him. Consider how it would appear to Arthur. Consider Mr. Cox's eventual disappointment. No good can come of it, surely. Your own conscience must tell you it is so."

"My dear friend, I would not vex you for the world, and for your sake I would be prepared to sacrifice a great deal. But I truly believe you are over scrupulous in this case. You needn't fear for Mr. Cox. He is a grown man; he knows what he is about. As for Arthur, his sensibilities are in no danger. He would not be alarmed by this trivial business, even if he were to learn of it. It is a harmless flirtation that has nothing whatever to do with him."

Further remonstration proved pointless. I had no choice but to let the subject drop for the moment, hoping that my word of caution would serve to reign in my friend's enthusiasm for Mr. Cox. Although my solicitude for Arthur knew no bounds, Mr. Cox would have to look out for himself, as Agnes suggested. I was unwilling to jeopardize my friendship with her by officious interference on his behalf.

12
Richard Returns

The additional diversions generated by Agnes's presence went a long way toward consoling me for the absence of Mr. Pierce. Yet at certain times, I could not help but miss his particular attentions. A dance held less pleasure because he was not my partner. No one solicited my company half as earnestly as I had become accustomed to Richard doing. And when I was alone, my thoughts inevitably wandered back to dwell on him – the way I felt when he looked at me, his ability to make me laugh at the oddest things, my thrill of pride in knowing that he preferred me above any other. Only the fact that the separation was temporary made the deprivation tolerable. All these reflections added strength to my growing conviction that, indeed, I was in love with him.

I weathered the first fortnight of Mr. Pierce's absence without too much consternation, but my courage wore more ragged with each succeeding day. I began to watch for him round town, to stare out the windows in the hope of catching the earliest possible glimpse of his return, and to examine the incoming post for word of when he could be expected. He would not take the liberty of writing to me directly, yet I reasoned he might send word to me through my father. At last, his letter came. My patience was tested to its limit as I waited for Papa to read it through.

"Good news, my child," he said when he had finally finished. "Your Mr. Pierce has nearly concluded his business and will soon be free to return to us."

"How soon? Does he say when we may look for him?"

"I apprehend that it cannot be soon enough to suit you, eh?"

"Do not tease me, Papa. When is he coming?"

"In two or three days, if I understand him correctly. He begs to introduce his father to me at the first opportunity."

"What else? Is there more?"

"He gives some narrative about his travels, the nature of his business, and so forth. Oh, and he makes a particular point of sending his regards to my family, saying he will not be satisfied until he is back amongst us. Perhaps you would like to read the letter yourself, my dear. I make no doubt that it was written more for your benefit than mine."

After I had spent fifteen minutes alone in my room with Richard's letter, Agnes knocked and let herself in. "Well?" she asked.

"Oh, Agnes, Richard will be here Thursday – Friday at the latest – and you shall meet him. Then you shall see for yourself why I love him."

"So you *do* love him, then? And do you have your answer ready for him as well?"

I took a deep breath, in and out. "Yes, I am ready."

~~*~~

I endured the torture of the next two days, which seemed to crawl by at a snail's pace, in a state of heightened suspense. Had I been forced to confine myself to the house, the tension would have been unbearable. Fortunately, a break in the weather allowed me to relieve my restlessness by stalking the length and breadth of Bath with Agnes struggling along at my side.

"Pray, do slacken your pace, Josephine!" pleaded Agnes as we made our way up Bond Street. "I cannot keep up with you. Hurrying your gait will not bring him back any sooner, you know."

"What? Oh, I am sorry. I did not realize."

"Distraction, irritability, thoughtlessness – yes, these are all very promising signs. Now, if you should go so far as to forget your own name, the case for love will be settled beyond a doubt."

"Agnes, really, you mustn't mock me so! Surely you can understand how I feel, how eager I am for Mr. Pierce's return. Have you not felt the same yourself in anticipation of seeing Arthur again after a separation?"

"Oh, Arthur and I have been acquainted so long that his comings and goings no longer inspire such severe agitation. Look," she said, and I followed her direction. "Are not those your friends, Miss Graham and Mr. Ramsey, coming out of that shop at the turning of the road? Perhaps they will be good enough to engage you in conversation so that I may recover my breath."

The chance meeting was very agreeable to me as well. Since Agnes's arrival, I had seen little of Susan and Mr. Ramsey. I missed the easy camaraderie Richard and I had shared with them during the past month. After greeting the couple, I communicated the good news of our mutual friend's impending return.

"Capital!" said Mr. Ramsey. "We shall have to celebrate. What do you say to a little party, Miss Walker, the first night he is back?"

"I would be delighted, Mr. Ramsey, but it does not depend upon me. Mr. Pierce's father is coming with him; his plans must take precedence."

"What sort of a man is he, Jo?" asked Susan. "My father has known him for years, but I have never set eyes on him myself. What has Mr. Pierce told you about him?"

"Well, Richard says he is a good man at heart, but that his reserved nature tends to put people off at first. Still, I think there may be more to it than that. I gather that Mr. Pierce has very definite opinions about everything of consequence, and he will brook no opposition to his authority. I know Richard never dares to cross him, so he is clearly not a man to be trifled with."

"Good lord!" cried Susan. "No wonder you look a bundle of nerves. With such a description in mind, I shall be more than a little intimidated to meet the man myself, though it does not signify in the least what he thinks of me. How much worse for you!"

"So much depends upon his approval that I cannot help trembling a little at the possibility of being examined and found wanting."

"Take courage, Miss Walker. I am sure Pierce is right; you will win the old man over the moment he meets you," said Mr. Ramsey, confidently. "My dear Susan faces a far more daunting trial. She must convince my contentious mother that she is worthy of keeping company with her darling son. Since my father died, my mother's rule has been absolute. There is no one more fastidious where her children are concerned, no one more vigilant in guarding the nest against the undeserving. Even without meeting old Mr. Pierce, I can assure you that you have the better bargain."

"They sound like two of a kind, your mother and the senior Mr. Pierce," said I. "I wonder what would happen if two such strong-minded people ever met. They would either get on famously or, more probably, end at each other's throats, I should think. What is your opinion, Mr. Ramsey?"

"I think you may be right, and we should perhaps take care not to attempt such a volatile experiment."

~~*~~

By Thursday afternoon – the earliest moment that Mr. Pierce could be expected – my impatient wanderings necessarily came to a close. I refused to stir from the house again for fear of missing his visit. At about two o'clock, he came, his father with him. But in those first few moments, I had regard for Richard alone. I drank in the sight of him, anxious to reassure myself that he was the same man I had fallen in love with, and that he was truly mine. Our eyes met, my heart leapt, and all was confirmed.

It was far from the reunion of joyful abandon for which I might have hoped, however. The senior Mr. Pierce's presence ensured that the meeting was marked by an awkward tension rather than the rekindling of more tender emotions. Unlike me, my mother and father had been given no reason to suppose Mr. Randolph Pierce unpleasant or to fear their own inadequacy. Consequently, they received him with more equanimity than I could boast on the occasion.

Mr. Pierce did not have the look of a man expecting to be pleased. Nevertheless, upon being introduced to me, he said, "I am delighted to make your acquaintance, Miss Walker. My son told me so many good things about you and your family that I made up my mind to come to Bath without further delay, in order to meet you for myself. Richard is not inclined to exaggeration, so I fully anticipate finding that his praise is well deserved." His stern voice and grim countenance unfortunately detracted from this generous sentiment. Hence, the compliment was little felt.

"I am honored to meet you, sir," I answered with tolerable composure. "I hope your son has not built us up too high. I would hate to disappoint your expectations, Mr. Pierce. We are a very ordinary set of people."

"Your modesty does you credit, I am sure, Miss Walker." He flattered me with a stiff bow and the faint intention of a smile before turning back to my father.

Conversation continued in the drawing room, the older generation supplying the lion's share with periodic contributions from Richard and even less frequent offerings by Agnes and myself. The senior Mr. Pierce clearly lacked the easy, inviting manners of his son, but I noticed he took great pains to be courteous and civil at all times. I suppose such an exertion could not long be sustained; after only half an hour, the gentlemen took their leave, agreeing to return the following day for a longer visit to include dinner.

Before they departed, Richard managed to take me aside for a few moments. "He likes you already, my dear," he whispered. "And your parents made a good first impression as well. I told you there was nothing to fear."

"I am vastly relieved to hear it, although how you can be convinced of his approbation so soon, I cannot imagine. To me, he seemed aloof, almost cold."

"That is just his way. He cannot help his reserved nature. He was trying to please, though, which is a good sign."

"Then I yield to your better judgment in the matter. Will I see you later, Richard? Mr. Ramsey thought we might celebrate your return."

"No, though I would like nothing better, believe me. I must spend the evening with my father. He would not take kindly to being abandoned on his first night in a strange place. We have made a good beginning here today, Jo. I daren't risk turning the old man against us now."

"Of course. It is only that you were away so long. I had hoped…"

"I know. It was deuced difficult to leave you in the first place, and nearly as hard to be back now without yet being free to… But we must be patient a little longer. It will be worth it in the end." With that, he quickly pressed my hand to his lips and was gone.

Richard's confident words notwithstanding, I was far from sanguine after this brief, first meeting. I soon turned to my friend for reassurance. "What is your opinion, Agnes? Do you like Richard? What did you think of his father? Do you really believe he approved of me?"

"I daresay the old man likes you as well as he does anybody. He's a bit of a cold fish, though, is he not? As for your Mr. Pierce, he is just what a young man ought to be – handsome, charming, clearly devoted to you, and conveniently rich into the bargain. You are a lucky girl, my dear. I am sure you will be very happy."

13
An Offer

The gentlemen arrived punctually in Pultney Street next day. Although there was still an air of formality in our discourse, the senior Mr. Pierce seemed less constrained on this second visit, and consequently, so did we all. The topic of our mutual friends, the Grahams, went a long way toward easing the lingering awkwardness and facilitating conversation. On that agreeable subject, everyone present could contribute a good opinion. Mr. Randolph Pierce had called on them earlier in the day, to pay his respects and renew the longstanding acquaintance. So he was in position to confer their warm regards, and to relate the latest news of their activities to the rest of the company.

Dinner passed uneventfully, after which we three women withdrew, leaving the men to their tobacco and port. Before long, Richard joined us in the drawing room. "I have been dismissed as well," he told us in good humor. "I must have said something amiss, or perhaps my elders have subjects too substantial to discuss in my presence. No matter. My instructions were to join you and make myself as charming as possible. I will certainly do my best to entertain but, as I told my father, it is you ladies who have the upper hand when it comes to captivation."

By so disclaiming his own talents for the social graces, Richard once again showed himself master of the art.

When Papa and Mr. Pierce finally emerged from their conference in the dining room, they were both in excellent spirits. Mr. Pierce gave a meaningful nod to his son and bestowed upon me a more convincing smile than I had seen heretofore. I took it to mean that he was now prepared to give his blessing to an alliance between his son and myself. Richard and I exchanged a look of satisfaction, each of us apprehending that the only potential obstacle to our union had just been cleared away.

After our guests had gone, my father invited me into the study and closed the heavy doors. "My dear," he began, "I believe you will soon be hearing something serious from your young man. I trust that such an offer will not be unwelcome."

"No, Papa."

"I thought not. It is a good match for you. I shall be proud to see you married to a gentleman of consequence, and installed as the mistress of a fine estate such as Wildewood." Before continuing, he gestured for me to take a seat next to him. "Well then, as you may have guessed, my private discussion with Mr. Pierce concerned that very topic. He told me of his son's intentions, and recommended that we come to an understanding without delay. Apparently, nothing can go forward without his approbation."

"That I can well believe. I imagine he wished to be assured that I would do the family credit; he wanted to know how much wealth I would bring to the union by my dowry, no doubt."

"Exactly so. But there is nothing unconventional in that. Mr. Pierce is well within his rights to make such an inquiry. No need for false delicacy about it."

"What did you tell him? You did not divulge my inheritance, did you?"

"Well ... yes, I'm afraid that I did, my dear."

"No!" I protested, coming out of my chair. "Little wonder, then, that Mr. Pierce left so cheerful! Papa, how could you?"

"Now, Josephine, you mustn't blame me too severely. I only acted in the interest of your happiness, I assure you. Sit down again, my dear, and let me explain," he said, patting the chair beside him.

I reluctantly complied.

"Now then, I could see that Mr. Pierce was none too impressed with what I disclosed to him at first: the amount of your dowry and what you will receive from your mother. He hemmed and hawed, making sour faces of a most unpromising nature, and muttering something about it being far less than what his son had the right to expect. In short, I am convinced he would have denied his consent altogether if I had not offered him something more to go on. And after all, the young man had already made up his mind to marry you without knowing about your fortune. What possible harm could it do to reveal it now? It would have come out soon enough anyway, when the engagement became official."

"I suppose that is true enough. It galls me that Mr. Pierce could not be satisfied without the money, but so long as I can be sure Richard has not been influenced by it, I shall be content."

~~*~~

Richard came next morning to state his case in form. No one was surprised at his arrival or shocked at his request for a private audience. Elated and suddenly embarrassed, I led the way into the study and slid the doors closed with trembling fingers. Richard lost no time on preliminaries; he proceeded to the business at hand as soon as I seated myself. With his characteristic flare, he dropped to one knee before me.

"My dear Miss Walker," he began, taking my hand in his. "Josephine. You can hardly doubt the purport of my discourse. I'm sure my attentions have been too marked to be mistaken. You know that I love you, and you have given me to believe that you are not completely indifferent to me. So, let us delay no longer. Tell me now. Will you do me the great honor of consenting to be my wife?"

It was the moment I had pictured in my mind a hundred times over the course of the last few weeks, still somehow, never quite like this. Instead of the dream-like quality of my imaginings, this had the unmistakable stamp of cold reality upon it. I had prepared my answer, and yet, now that the time was at hand, I wavered, feeling the weightiness of the question before me. From this day forward, my life would be changed forever; it both thrilled and terrified me to consider it. But when I looked into Richard's dear face, as he waited in calm anticipation of my answer, all reason and hesitation melted away.

"Darling boy," I said. "Yes, of course I will."

With that, Richard rose from his genuflection to demand what was due him in his new position as my betrothed; he enfolded me in his arms and claimed his first kiss – his first kiss from *me*, that is. He performed the maneuver so proficiently and to such dazzling effect that I suspected he had some prior experience in the field... or a very natural talent. At that moment, I did not much care which.

A party of three waited to offer the first round of con- gratulations when we issued forth from our brief tête-à-tête. I embraced my father and mother in turn, and then received the most enthusiastic reception from Agnes. Richard and Papa retreated briefly to the study to execute the ritual of begging the father's permission. In this case, it was a mere formality comprehending no suspense or trepidation on either side.

Mama took the opportunity afforded by the absence of the men for a few personal words. "I am so happy for you, my dearest girl! What a fine young man he is – so handsome and obliging. And you are quite certain that this is what you want?"

"As certain as may be, Mama."

"Then, I am satisfied. Oh, but how shall I do without you when you are married and settled so far away? I have come to rely on you so."

"We shall see each other often. It cannot be more than forty or fifty miles from Fairfield to Wildewood, and what is that in this day of improved roads? Yes, I call it a very easy distance."

After the initial excitement, Agnes had grown quiet. Now, with a touch of melancholy, she said, "You must visit Wallerton regularly, Jo. Your friends shall miss you as sorely as your family will."

"Do not despair, Agnes. I shall be there very frequently; depend on it. And you must come to Surrey. Now that county will hold two points of interest for you: Wildewood and Millwalk. Remember, we all agreed to visit Frederick at Easter. There is no reason to abandon the outing. We shall simply invite Richard to join the party."

When Richard reappeared, I suddenly wanted nothing more than to be alone with him, to revel in our mutual joy and make plans for our future. Accordingly, the two of us embarked upon a protracted walk, taking a circuitous route to his lodgings in order to announce our news to his father. The bite of winter freshened the air, but I felt no chill wrapped in my woolen cloak and snug on Richard's arm. In my euphoria, my feet barely touched the pavement as I made my first public promenade as an engaged woman. My heart brimmed with emotion, and my mind overflowed with ideas to discuss with my beloved. Yet, now that we were alone, neither one of us seemed in a hurry to break the companionable silence.

Finally, Richard commenced, saying mildly, "You might have told me, Jo."

"Told you what?"

"About your inheritance. There was no need to hide it from me, surely."

"Pray, do not take offence, Richard. I did not conceal it from you in particular. Long before I came to Bath, I made the decision to tell no one about it."

"It would have made no difference to me."

"Unfortunately, that is not the case with most people. I am glad you proved yourself the exception, however." I continued in a lighter vein. "And I trust you were not too displeased to learn of it."

"Not at all. I only hope that everything I henceforth discover about you is equally pleasant, my dear. Do you have any other wonders in store for me?"

"One or two perhaps, but no more fortunes hidden away if that is what you mean. And lest you think me in the habit of keeping secrets from you, I should tell you one other bit of news. I shall soon have the honor of introducing you to my brother Tom and our dear friend Arthur, of whom I have told you. We have just had a letter to say that they are both coming from Oxford to celebrate my birthday. Now it shall be a celebration of our engagement as well."

14

Getting Down to Business

During our courtship, romance had its glorious day in the sun. After the engagement, the business of getting married began in earnest, for serious business it certainly was, as I quickly learnt. No sooner had Richard and I issued the formal announcement of our joy than a series of meetings between the interested parties commenced for the purpose of negotiating settlements and drawing up agreements, all relating more to the transfer of funds than to the exchange of lovers' vows.

I discovered, to my amazement, that Richard and I had very little share in the proceedings; the fathers and the solicitors handled nearly the whole of it without us. My duty, it seemed, as a direct consequence of accepting the match, was to take the financial bargain that came with it. What had belonged to me would henceforth belong entirely to my husband. That is the way of things. There was nothing whatever that I could do about it, so I chose not to grumble. Instead I counted myself fortunate to have been allowed my choice as to marriage partner, and to have a prudent father now representing my interests in the disposal of my future happiness.

There were other compensations as well. Since our help was not wanted for framing contracts, Richard and I were free to devote most of our time to each other. A variety of social events competed for the remaining hours. Something in the special circumstances seemed to demand a more frenetic pace of activity from us all. With the three families – the Walkers, Pierces, and Grahams – sharing the honors, barely a night was allowed to pass without a party, dinner, or outing planned amongst us.

On one of the few evenings that my parents and I were to be found at home and alone (except for Richard and Agnes), Tom and Arthur arrived, fresh from completing their term at Oxford. A welcoming celebration immediately ensued as parents were re-united with son, sister with brother, and dear friends with dear friends all round. Arthur and Agnes greeted one another with a shy awkwardness as befits lovers kept apart by circumstances for a long while. When my brother and Mr. Evensong were introduced to Mr. Pierce and informed of his important new standing in the family, they were both taken quite by surprise, having received no word of our engagement beforehand.

Tom recovered from the shock quickly enough, embracing me and wringing his future brother-in-law's hand enthusiastically. "What outstanding news! Congratulations, Mr. Pierce. I hope you appreciate what a fortunate man you are."

Richard responded in his easy, urbane manner. "Thank you. I am very sensible of that fact, sir. I'm sure I have done little to merit the favor your sister has shown me or the kindness of your excellent parents."

"Perhaps in time, however, you may prove yourself worthy, Mr. Pierce," said Arthur, leveling something of a measured glare at him. "I would certainly advise that you endeavor to do so,"

"Easy, Arthur," Tom interceded. "There's a good chap. You needn't pretend to be so menacing. If anybody should be jealous for Jo's honor, it should be me. She is *my* sister, after all. Mr. Pierce will see her right, or he will have me to deal with."

Before the skirmish could escalate, I cut in. "That will suffice! Mr. Pierce will have a very pretty first impression of the pair of you. After the way I have built you both up too, I daresay he will never credit me with good judgment again. Pay them no mind, Richard."

"It is quite all right. I take it as a compliment to you, my dear, that you have such... loyal... protectors. I hope your friends will soon be convinced that I am chief amongst them."

The little tempest passed, but I noticed Arthur remained subdued. He sat a bit apart from the group throughout the evening, unable or unwilling to fully enter into the otherwise festive mood of the gathering. It disturbed me to see him looking so low, so I finally took myself from Richard's side long enough to speak to him.

Arthur began before I could. "Jo, you must allow me to apologize. I beg you would forgive my rudeness earlier, for how ungraciously I received your good news. May I wish you all possible happiness in your marriage, as I should have done before?"

"Thank you, Arthur."

"My surprise at your announcement is a poor excuse for bad manners, but it is my only defense. I know I have no earthly right to object to your choice."

"You have no *reason* to object, more like. You do not even know Richard, and when you do, I hope you will be great friends."

"He must be a fine man. He could hardly have won your respect and affection otherwise. Still, I very much doubt that Mr. Pierce and I will ever be good friends," he concluded darkly. "There, I have done it again. Forgive me, Jo. Perhaps I should not have come; I shall only spoil your celebration with my disconsolate attitude."

"Nonsense. You are always welcome in our home, Arthur, regardless of your state of mind. Yet something must be troubling you. Truly, you do not seem at all yourself tonight. Are you unwell? Or is it your mother?"

"No, I am in exceptionally good health, and my mother is tolerably well also. I had a letter from her just before I quit Oxford. Please do not concern yourself; there is nothing whatever the matter with me."

"I know you far too well to believe that, old friend. Come now. Let us have no secrets between us. Tell me what is responsible for this gloomy aspect of yours."

"I suppose I am a little preoccupied," he suggested after some further hesitation. "I have a lot on my mind at present. You see, I came to Bath not just to visit friends but on an errand of business, a matter of no small importance to my future. I am invited to call on a certain gentleman visiting here who has a fine parish in Surrey at his disposal. At the generous recommendation of a mutual acquaintance, he has agreed to consider me for the post. This is a man of uncommon influence, I understand, so his endorsement could be the making of me, Jo."

"Why, Arthur, this is wonderful news! It is precisely what you have been hoping for, what you have worked so hard to secure, is it not? You needn't be uneasy; the man could never find a better candidate."

"Thank you. Unfortunately, I cannot share your optimism. I very much suspect there is something in the situation that will not suit me at all. From what I hear, he – the fellow who holds the living – is a very formidable person, not to be easily won over."

"No doubt you have excellent references at the ready. But if you need someone else to put in a good word, I daresay my father would be happy to oblige. Of course, we are nobody to him, whoever he is."

"By a strange coincidence, I think you may know him after all. I believe it can be none other than your future father-in-law of whom I speak. The man's name is Pierce, Mr. Randolph Pierce."

"Really? Indeed, that is the man. How extraordinary! Well then, you do have a daunting challenge before you; Mr. Pierce is a formidable man, to be sure. Only think, should he appoint you rector, I would see you – and, if I may be so bold, Agnes – constantly in years to come. How cozy we should all be in Surrey together: you, me, Richard, Agnes, Tom, and Frederick. Yes, you must try your best for the appointment, Arthur. Why not start tonight by learning to get on with Richard?"

"Must I? I am not sure I feel up to it just now."

"My word! You *are* in an odd humor tonight, Arthur. I have only asked you to become acquainted with my very particular friend, for your own sake as well as mine. You act as if I had proposed you have a tooth drawn."

Against his will, I pulled Arthur back to the conversation circle as I seated myself next to Richard again. Arthur made a half-hearted effort to join in; he nodded and smiled unconvincingly, spoke when spoken to, and treated Richard with tolerable civility if not cordiality.

After he and Tom left that night for their own lodgings at the White Heart, Richard rose to go as well. I followed him to the door, saying, "You will put in a good word with your father for Arthur, won't you? I should be ever so grateful if you would."

"Of course, my pet, if you wish it. Although I cannot say that I find his manners especially engaging. Still, I know you think very highly of him, and that is recommendation enough to satisfy me of his good character."

"Thank you, Richard. I really cannot account for Arthur's behavior tonight; he was not at all himself. I do so want the two of you to be friends, but you have got off on the wrong foot, I fear."

"Yes, Mr. Evensong seems to have taken an instant dislike to me for some reason. I daresay he will get over it in time."

~~*~~

Tom rejoined our family party shortly after breakfast the next morning, but Arthur did not arrive until mid-afternoon because of his appointment with Mr. Pierce. Everybody waited in suspense for the outcome of the interview, with Agnes suffering the most perturbation due to her vested interest in the case. We gathered round when Arthur came in, expecting a full report.

"Well, Mr. Evensong, what can you tell us? How goes your business with Mr. Pierce?" my father inquired on behalf of us all.

Arthur begrudgingly informed us that, after a long discussion, the two of them had concluded their business without coming to any satisfactory understanding. "There is very little chance that I will ever be rector of Wildewood parish. I can tell you that much."

"Why are you so pessimistic about your chances? Has Mr. Pierce definitely decided to give the preferment to another man?" I asked.

"Not exactly, no."

"Then what exactly did he say?" pressed Tom.

After a thoughtful pause and a heavy sigh, Arthur explained. "He said that although he would reserve his final decision until my ordination, the job was as good as mine. *However*," he hastened to add as the group reacted to this news, "I told him I was not interested."

"You did what?" exclaimed Agnes.

"Oh, Arthur! Surely you are only joking," said I. "You would not really refuse such an advantageous situation, would you?"

"I would and I have."

"But, why?" Mama chimed in.

"Because I was fully convinced that the outcome of accepting would have been insupportable. For various personal and professional reasons, which it can serve no purpose to enumerate here, I am quite certain that such an arrangement would have suited neither myself nor Mr. Pierce in the end. I will not be put into such an untenable position. I am sorry to disappoint you all, but I assure you that it cannot be helped."

As the protests rose again from more than one quarter, Papa came to Arthur's aid. "Now, now, there's an end to it. Let us say no more about the matter. We must trust Mr. Evensong's judgment. I am sure he knows what he is about."

~~*~~

Arthur's unpopular decision put a stop to all the blissful speculation between Agnes and myself over the delightful prospect of living always as neighbors together in Surrey. Immediately upon discovering that such a possibility existed, our imaginations lost no time in fixing it as a certainty of fate and adding to the picture such embellishments as our lively minds naturally supplied. Now the dream with all its trimmings lay dashed to pieces at our feet.

"How could he do it?" demanded Agnes that night in my room. "He knows we cannot marry or even be engaged until he has secured a living. What was he thinking of, to throw away such an ideal situation where we could all have been so happy?"

"He must have had his reasons," I offered weakly. "You know that Arthur has exceptionally high principles and standards."

"Do not defend him! 'Principles and standards,' you say. Pig-headedness more like." She stomped about the room, eventually dissipating some of her exasperation. "Perhaps you could speak to him, Jo. He listens to you. If you could only persuade him to reconsider, it might not be too late. He could apologize to Mr. Pierce – say that he has changed his mind and wants the appointment after all."

"I think there is little chance of that. You give too much credit to my influence with Arthur, and I highly doubt Mr. Pierce would be prepared to overlook such an insult in any case."

"Oh, very well, then. I suppose we shall have to resign ourselves to it, but it is all extremely vexing! If we must suffer such a setback, he could at least have had the courtesy to offer some kind of credible explanation."

"As disappointed as I am at the outcome, I believe Arthur may be right. Indeed, when I consider it, I cannot image that he and Mr. Pierce would at all suit one another. Between them there is too great a disparity of mind. Added to their philosophical differences, perhaps Arthur disapproves of Mr. Pierce's character."

"That may well be. Mr. Pierce would not be my first choice for a neighbor either. But if you can tolerate having the man as your father-in-law, Jo, I would have thought Arthur could put up with him as his patron. No, he had better have a more compelling reason than that or I'll not soon forgive him."

15

On the Town

In contrast to Agnes's lingering distress over the failed negotiations between Arthur and the senior Mr. Pierce, everybody else
diplomatically forgot the incident entirely, or at least had the manners to pretend as if they did. Richard appeared at our door next
morning at the appointed hour, followed directly by Arthur and
Tom, none of whom alluded to it in any way.

We had already determined that the day should be spent
showing the newcomers the sights of Bath. Their stay would not be
long, so there was no time to lose. Accordingly, we set forth
shortly after breakfast – Agnes, Tom, Arthur, Richard and I. I had,
by then, been in Bath over three months, and Richard nearly as
long. So, the two of us served as guides for the tour of the now
familiar streets, landmarks, shops, and views. The weather, though
cold, remained agreeably dry for our long outing, which began
with a visit to the magnificent Abbey followed by a stop at the
Pump-room. Almost as soon as we arrived at the latter, Mr. Cox
appeared to pay his compliments to the ladies and be introduced to
the two unfamiliar gentlemen. He attached himself to our party
whilst we remained there but did not attempt to follow us beyond.

Milsom Street being directly along our way, we paid a brief
call on the Grahams before moving on. Afterward, Richard remarked, "Jo, I meant to tell you that I saw Mr. Ramsey and his
mother yesterday. Being in Milsom Street again has reminded me.
My father and I had errands here and we chanced to meet them
coming out of Molland's. I must say that Mrs. Ramsey is quite an
imposing woman – a force to be reckoned with, I'll be bound."

"Ah! I have not met her myself, but that agrees with Mr.
Ramsey's description. I venture to guess that it must have been an
interesting encounter. How did your father and Mrs. Ramsey get
on?"

"Hmm, yes. Well, they began awkwardly enough, to be sure –
each one sizing up the other, I believe; neither willing to give

ground. For a long moment, I thought sure there would be fireworks. Yet incredibly, before the conversation broke up, they seemed to have struck an accord of some sort between them."

"Perhaps we can put it down to the regard one feels for a kindred spirit," I suggested with a mischievous glance at Agnes.

Our route took us through the Circus and on to view the magnificent houses of the Royal Crescent, then back toward town via the gravel walk, and south past Queen's Square and beyond. As we five strolled by Westgate Buildings in the course of our travels, a well-looking young woman walking on the other side of the street attracted our attention. I had never seen her before, but I thought I caught a look of recognition pass across Richard's face. He tipped his hat to the lady who nodded in return, confirming it. Though I resisted the powerful urge to quiz Richard about it, Tom did the honors for me.

"Who was that fine young woman, Mr. Pierce?"

"Oh, just an old acquaintance from Surrey; nobody of any significance."

"Not to you, perhaps, but I think I'd quite like to meet her," rejoined Tom.

"I should be only too happy to introduce you, sir, if the occasion arises."

Richard and I had saved the walk up to Beechen Cliff for the culmination of the tour. Poetically, and in actual fact, it could be nothing less than the high point of the day. The stately hill encrusted in a glorious tangle of greenery was a sight in itself, surpassed only by the prospect from the top, which overlooked the entire town and surrounding area. Upon gaining the summit, the whole party took some minutes to admire what could be seen from the elevated vantage point, and some minutes more to rest from the exertion of the assent.

Tom would not waste the view by sitting down, however. "What a very fine thing it is for Bath to have a high hill located so commodiously, as if it had been erected here expressly for the purpose of providing visitors the means to properly appreciate the grandeur of the place. Look how the Avon winds round the town, hemming it in on two sides. There is the Abbey, Queen's Square and, afar off to the left, the Royal Crescent where we walked earlier. The facade fairly glows where the sun strikes it. Remarkable. Indeed, the whole town quite exceeds my expectations. A triumph in classic architectural design flawlessly executed, in my humble opinion. Mr. John Wood and his son have left a great legacy behind them here."

"Good gracious, Tom!" I said with amusement. "Your enthusiasm astounds me. I have never known you to speak so lyrically on any topic before, let alone the value of fine architecture and a picturesque view. It must be your expensive education finally showing some effect; our father and mother will be so pleased."

"I cannot make out if that is a compliment or an insult. With you, dear sister, it is often difficult to tell. I think you give far too much credit to Oxford regardless. Perhaps my education allows me to speak with more understanding on such subjects, but I trust no one need teach me to appreciate a thing of beauty, be it a Gothic cathedral, a view from a hilltop, or the face of a pretty woman," he said, gesturing to the named articles in turn and finishing with a nod to Agnes's remarkable countenance as a case in point.

Agnes glowed with pleasure.

"If it were admissible to contradict a lady, I would have to side with your brother against you on this occasion, Miss Walker," said Richard. "Any man with an ounce of sense will recognize *true* beauty when he sees it," he added looking at me, not my more-handsome friend, and bringing my hand to his lips.

Arthur, who looked uncomfortable at the direction the conversation had taken, declined to join the other two gentlemen in their *ode to woman*. He turned instead to more practical matters. "Well then, if the ladies are sufficiently rested, we should start back. We only just have time to get them home by dinner as it is. Come now, Agnes, take my arm. The path is very rough."

~~*~~

That evening, when we – the same group of five – attended a ball in one of the assembly rooms, we saw the lady from Westgate Buildings again. She spied us also and made her way directly toward Richard.

"It seems as if you will get your wish to meet the 'fine young woman' after all, Mr. Walker," he said. "Miss Fennimore, how do you do? Allow me to present my friends: Miss Walker, Miss Pittman, Mr. Evensong and Mr. Walker. Everybody, this is Miss Fennimore, an old friend of mine from Surrey."

"A pleasure to make your acquaintance, I'm sure," she simpered. "But, Richard, why so formal? 'Miss Fennimore' indeed. La! You know you have called me Margaret forever."

"Yes, of course. How good of you to remind me, Margaret."

"Now, that's better. I hope you and these charming friends of yours," nodding to the men, "will each spare a dance for me, for I have as yet no other acquaintance in Bath, and I am vastly fond of a ball."

Tom very willingly petitioned for the honor of the first two dances with Miss Fennimore. Arthur took his turn without complaint. And later, Richard did his duty by her as well. Whilst Richard was thus occupied and Agnes continued distracted by the ever-present Mr. Cox, Arthur asked me to dance.

"Now tell the truth, old friend," I responded. "Do you feel obliged to stand up with me in Richard's absence, or do you honestly wish to dance? I seem to remember that you dislike the amusement."

"Dancing in general, perhaps, but not this opportunity in particular. Nothing should give me more pleasure than to stand up with you, dear girl. I have not had the privilege these many months and may not again... for a long while."

"Very well, then." I allowed him to lead me out onto the floor. "But I should more easily believe it a pleasure if you had the face of a happy man instead of the melancholy bearing of one who has just lost his best friend. Are you still brooding over your disagreeable interview with Mr. Pierce?"

"Perhaps I am."

I could think of nothing helpful to contribute on that topic, so I held my peace several minutes as we danced. It was good to be with Arthur again, to look across at his steady gaze, to feel the warmth of his firm hand through my glove. I realized that, even with all the excitement of the last few months, I had sorely missed his company. Now, who could say where he and Agnes would finally settle, or how seldom I might see them in future?

Arthur broke in upon my thoughts. "Now *you* are the one who looks as if you had lost your best friend."

"Do I? I am too transparent, it seems. I'm sorry, Arthur. I have no doubt that you made the correct decision about Mr. Pierce's offer. But I cannot help thinking how heavenly it would have been to have you and Agnes always living nearby... and how much I shall miss you both after I am married. So it is like losing my best friends after all, you must concede."

"Yes, I too regret the way things have turned out... more than I can say."

When our dance concluded, Arthur begged me for a second. "Agnes will not miss me. As you see, she is going to dance with Mr. Cox again. She prefers his company to mine tonight," he said evenly. "Tell me, is he a man of good fortune?"

"Yes, I believe so. You mustn't mind him, though; he means nothing to Agnes. I am sure of it. She is only flattered by his preference... and I fear she has not quite forgiven you yet for turning down Mr. Pierce. I daresay she will rally in another day or two."

"No doubt. I shall follow your example of forbearance in the meantime. I notice that it bothers you not in the least to see your Mr. Pierce lavishing similar attentions on Miss Fennimore."

Richard's whereabouts and behavior had quite escaped my notice whilst I danced with Arthur. Now, however, I saw that he seemed to be talking with Miss Fennimore in an unnecessarily familiar manner, his eyes holding hers with that same intensity that I had come to know so well myself. As I watched, they laughed together conspiratorially, as if they shared some secret joke. Was it my imagination, or did their hands hold longer and their bodies pass nearer each other than the movements of the dance strictly required?

"Never mind, Jo. She is nothing compared to you," Arthur was saying. "Even a fool should be able to see that," he added dryly.

16
Happy Birthday

My father and mother hosted a dinner party the following evening in honor of my twenty-first birthday, to which all our friends in Bath were invited. The wedding plans were well in hand, and the arduous work of the complicated marriage settlement had been completed only that morning, lending the occasion additional cause for joy. With good company and reasons to celebrate, it should have been the best of times. Instead, most everybody seemed out of sorts to one degree or another.

The party collected in the drawing room until the last of those expected should arrive. Mr. and Mrs. Graham appeared as jovial as ever. They plunged straight into conversation with my parents, with whom they were by now on the most intimate terms. But Susan, try as she might, could not hide her low spirits, even for my sake. And that which afflicted her necessarily affected Mr. Ramsey as well. I learned the cause of the trouble presently.

"Mrs. Ramsey called at Milsom Street this morning," Susan explained when I joined them in the alcove by the windows. "At first, I hoped it was a compliment to me, a sign that she accepted my attachment to her son. It soon became apparent that it was quite the reverse. She said she considered it her duty to apprise me of certain facts: first, that her son is totally dependent on her good graces for his financial future; second, that she would not scruple to use her influence, up to and including the threat of disinheritance, to ensure that he makes a suitable choice of wife; and finally, that she does not have me down on her list of eligible candidates for the office."

"Oh, Susan, she didn't!" I groaned.

"She did."

"Yes, I am ashamed to own that my mother is quite capable of such a speech," Mr. Ramsey confirmed, "of making such a threat and probably of carrying it out as well. Although I have always believed myself her favorite, she will be at no great pains to secure an alternate should I invoke her displeasure. I have three younger brothers, Miss Walker, any of whom would be ready to take my place and happy to receive my inheritance. My father, God rest his soul, would have been more sympathetic to my situation, I daresay. A person's wealth and status were of little consequence to him; he was a friend to one and all. I can only fault him for one thing, and that is leaving Mama in control of the purse strings." He sighed.

"So, you see the desperation of our circumstances. We are entirely at her mercy."

"Perhaps you will be able to win her over in time," I suggested.

"God grant it, but I doubt it," said Mr. Ramsey.

"Time is no remedy for what she finds objectionable in me. It cannot sufficiently aggrandize my family connections or double my small fortune," Susan concluded sadly.

My birthday party was off to an inauspicious beginning.

Dinner awaited the arrival of Richard and Mr. Pierce. Whereas the rest of the company idled away the intervening minutes in artless conversation, Agnes applied them to a more specific purpose. She had not yet exhausted her displeasure with Arthur, and she lacked the self-command which might have made the prudent concealment of her feelings possible. Consequently, she once again turned to Mr. Cox as the most convenient means for demonstrating her resentment to Mr. Evensong. By conspicuous attention to one and complete neglect of the other, she effectively drove home her point. Although I had long been in the habit of excusing my friend's whims of behavior as harmless folly, even part of her charm, in this case my sympathies were entirely on Arthur's side.

When the Messrs. Pierce, father and son, arrived nearly half an hour late, Arthur's fortunes suffered another blow. Although reasonably civil to everybody else, Mr. Pierce addressed *him* with a distaste bordering on contempt. Even Richard, who could generally be trusted to provide a joke or a droll story to support the morale of his companions, was of no assistance. As soon as he entered the room, I apprehended that his customary conviviality had slipped a notch. Irritable he arrived, and irritable he remained.

"Is everything all right, Richard?" I asked at my earliest opportunity.

"Yes, quite all right," he said with more annoyance than conviction in his tone. "But, I detest being late! It renders it quite impossible for one to start the evening off well. Do not you agree? Unfortunately, I am at my father's disposal, and he would… Well, never mind. I just hope we have not spoilt your birthday, Jo."

"If your being late was the only threat to the success of the evening, I should think we could withstand it well enough. But I have observed a worrying trend."

Although the party carried on, supported by the good spirits and determination of the livelier members of the group, the quality of the celebration suffered from these detractions. The event was meant for my gratification, but I could not be happy with my friends in such distress. Richard's uncharacteristic peevishness disturbed me more than anything else for reasons that I could not well define.

Dinner afforded a temporary reprieve from one source of aggravation. I had foreseen the problem of including Mr. Cox in this little gathering. However, he had by his frequent visits so insinuated himself into our society by this time that Mama considered it a serious breach of etiquette to exclude him. I could give her no just cause for doing so without casting aspersions on my friend as well. So invited he was, but placed as far from Miss Pittman at table as possible, thanks to my interference. This put it completely out of Agnes's power to talk to, make eyes at, or court Mr. Cox's attentions in any way during the whole course of the meal.

Mama had ordered a very good dinner with my preferences in mind. We began with a delicate soup and finished with cherry-water ice, with everything in between being equally agreeable to the palate. To accompany these dishes, hearty servings of discourse on a variety of topics were brought forward.

Mrs. Graham shared the contents of a letter she had lately received from Kent, in which the governess apprised her of the excellent progress toward proficiency in music, drawing, and French that her younger daughters had made during their parents' absence.

She boomed out proudly in conclusion, "There are few young ladies in all the county who can equal our girls for grace and accomplishment, though I do say it myself. Did you know, Mr. Ramsey, that Susan has a very fine singing voice? Madeline's performance at the piano-forte grows more exquisite every day. And our little Laura is quite talented as well, I am sure. She is only just sixteen but already shows remarkable ability. Why, she painted the sweetest little table for us last spring, all covered with flowers – dog roses and honeysuckle, I think she said they were. I couldn't quite make it out myself; I have no eye for art. But her drawing master raved about it excessively, and everybody who sees it remarks its beauty."

Mrs. Graham then called upon her husband to verify all her assertions about their daughters – which he did with some diffidence – leaving the rest of the company little alternative. No evidence to the contrary, we had to allow that the Miss Grahams were the finest girls in the world. Mr. Ramsey had no cause to doubt it; Susan, with her spirits so depressed, had not the strength to oppose; and my mother diplomatically suppressed any impulse she may have felt to put her own daughter forward as being entitled to a share of the honors. Mama talked about her sons instead, an altogether safer choice. Mrs. Graham could not possibly take offence at this since she had no sons of her own to suffer by the comparison.

"Tom is doing very well at Oxford this year. Are you not, my dear? In fact, I shouldn't be a bit surprised if you take a 'first' in your exams."

Tom laughed heartily. "Well, I shall be excessively surprised if such an improbable thing should occur."

"I am sure you are too modest," said Mr. Graham.

"Not at all, on my honor. Now, if you want a true scholar, my friend Arthur, here, is your man."

I instinctively glanced at Mr. Pierce to see how he bore hearing Mr. Evensong praised. With knife and fork firmly gripped, he directed his concentrated attention – and any feelings of hostility – against the defenseless roasted guinea fowl on his plate.

Mama gave Arthur his due, then turned the conversation to her other son. "Our oldest boy, Frederick, has already finished at Oxford, you understand. He is now at Millwalk, his estate in Surrey, and getting on splendidly. Why, we never hear from him but what he tells us of some clever plan he has for improvements. I am sure he will make a great success of the place. Mr. Pierce, how near is Millwalk to your estate? Wildewood is it called?"

"Yes, madam. I think it might be as much as twenty miles from one to the other."

"Oh, what a shame," Mama continued. "How comfortable it would have been for Josephine to have her brothers close by. Tom will be at Millwalk too, you know, at the rectory."

The rest of the dinner came and went without incident, after which we all repaired to the drawing room, the men following not long behind the ladies. Claiming fatigue and an early business appointment next day, Mr. Randolph Pierce departed as soon as the rules of civility would allow him to do so. Before he went, however, he did take the trouble of thanking his host and hostess quite handsomely, favoring me with a fine parting sentiment in recognition of my birthday, and dismissively giving his son leave to continue in my company.

Much to Susan's dismay, Mr. Ramsey left shortly thereafter under curfew orders from his mother. Half an hour later, Tom began to make noises as if restless to go as well, citing the long ride he and his friend had before them on the morrow. Mama, of course, opposed any further diminishment our party, and Arthur showed no sign of taking himself away so precipitously. He seemed instead determined to prolong his torment at the hands of Agnes and Mr. Cox, whose flirtations had recommenced forthwith.

I did not wish Arthur away, yet I wondered at his will to linger in a situation that must only bring him pain. As the evening wore on, he repeatedly glanced from the pair of them to the clock and back again. Mr. Cox showed no inclination for an early relinquishment of his claim. At length, Arthur crossed the room and spoke to Agnes despite the presence of the third party. "I leave Bath at first light, Miss Pittman. May I have a few words with you now, before I go?"

"Certainly, Mr. Evensong," replied Agnes, formally.

"Thank you. Mr. Cox, if you would be so kind…"

Mr. Cox began to rise.

"No, I beg you would stay where you are, sir," Agnes told him. "Mr. Evensong can have nothing to say to me that anybody need not hear."

"Agnes, please," Arthur said with impressive self-control. "I wish to speak to you in private. Surely you owe me that much."

"Owe you? I hardly think you have the right to demand anything from me, sir."

"Perhaps that was an unfortunate choice of words, but I thought, after so long an acquaintance, a few minutes of your time was not an unreasonable request to make."

Arthur waited. Agnes held her ground and kept Mr. Cox obediently by her side. As the exchange had grown more heated, it had fixed the attention of everybody else in the room. Accordingly, all eyes were turned in their direction to see the outcome. The awkward silence was unendurable. Arthur finally broke it.

"Very well, then. I will bid you good-night, Miss Pittman." He turned and made his farewells to the rest of the company with more composure than could reasonably be expected under the circumstances. Tom recognized his cue and began his leave-taking as well. Arthur saved his parting words for me as I walked him down to the door. "I am sorry for the unpleasantness, Jo. I never meant to create a scene. This is a fine thing for your birthday."

"Think nothing of it, Arthur. If an apology is due, I believe it should come from a different quarter. Now then, when shall we see you again?"

"I cannot say. I make for Wallerton tomorrow, to visit my mother and brothers, and thence to Oxford."

"But you will come to Millwalk at Easter as planned, and then home again in May for my wedding."

Arthur hesitated, a pained look in his eyes. "I doubt it will be possible. I think it unlikely that my commitments at Oxford will allow me so much time away. A short excursion at Easter may be manageable, but as for your wedding…"

"Do try, Arthur. It would mean so much to me – to all of us – to have you there."

"I shall make no promises. If I can see my way clear, I will come. Failing that, permit me to give you my best wishes now: all imaginable happiness, Jo. Goodbye and God bless you." He pressed my hand and was gone, Tom following behind him.

17
From Bad to Worse

With the loss of Arthur and Tom's company, little pleasure remained in the offing. The evening could not be over soon enough to suit me. I was tired from the strain of all that had passed, and yet I could not expect to rest until I claimed a few minutes tête-à-tête with Richard, in hopes of easing his trouble and making my own mind comfortable again.

Agnes dismissed Mr. Cox shortly after Arthur left, and the Grahams were not far behind him in taking leave. With Mr. Ramsey gone, Susan could no longer support any guise of cheerfulness. In kindness, her parents took her home where she could be miserable with more convenience. Agnes soon made her apologies and went to bed, after which my parents discretely disappeared as well.

At last alone with Richard, I collapsed into an armchair and relaxed my countenance, abandoning any further attempt to conceal the true state of my feelings. "That was a bit of a grueling exercise, was it not?" said I. "I hardly know when I have seen a more unhappy set of people so unsuccessfully trying to look as if they were enjoying themselves."

"Well said, my dear." He took a seat beside me. "The trouble between Miss Pittman and Mr. Evensong was plain for all to see, but what the devil was wrong with Ramsey and Miss Graham? I did not like to ask in front of the others."

"It amounts to this. Mr. Ramsey has nothing to live on without his mother's pleasure, and she intends to deny her consent for his ever marrying Susan. I pray they may yet come to some understanding, but at the moment there seems little chance of it. So, you can appreciate their distress."

"Yes, of course. How glad I am that we do not face that obstacle. Fortunately, my trouble with my father is far less serious. He and I got into a whale of a row just as we should have been leaving the house today. That is what detained us, and that accounts for our contribution to tonight's *festive* atmosphere," he finished with heavy sarcasm.

"Did you settle the matter between you at last?"

"After a fashion. He shall never admit that he was wrong, of course, but I think he is now resigned to do his duty. It is a question of basic propriety, of common courtesy really. When a call is due, it must be made without delay. I fail to understand why he insists upon making such a to-do about paying his respects to an old acquaintance."

"An old acquaintance? Do you mean Miss Fennimore?"

"Quite."

"You have called on her yourself, I suppose."

"Yes, earlier today. However, it seems that she is now beneath my father's notice, although he was friendly enough with the family not that long ago, until Mr. Fennimore's affairs collapsed. Now he does not scruple to snub them, one and all. Yet I maintain that Miss Fennimore deserves our consideration, despite her father's reduced circumstances!"

This little discussion, which I had anticipated being equally therapeutic for us both, had tended instead toward providing far more relief for Richard than for myself. Whilst his burden presumably lightened as he gave expression to his frustrations, that very venting served only to add to my trouble. After having observed Richard's familiar manner with the lady at the ball the other night, his mere mention of Miss Fennimore might have been enough to disturb my peace of mind. Now I could not help noticing the feeling with which he defended her claim on his attention, the passion he suddenly demonstrated for the observation of proper civility to this "old acquaintance."

Despite my effort to conceal it, a hint of my consternation crept into my reply. "Miss Fennimore is fortunate indeed to have such a champion looking out for her honor. I hope she appreciates your loyalty and enthusiasm on her behalf."

"Now, Jo, you cannot seriously be jealous. I told you, she is nothing to me personally – just an old friend of the family. And as an old friend, I should hate to see Miss Fennimore ill-used by anybody, especially by one of my own relations."

My battle for self-command waged on. "Do not say it," I silently counseled myself. "If you are wise, you will hold your tongue for once." However, as is so often the fate of good advice, this example also went unheeded. Instead, against every fiber of my better judgment, I escalated the confrontation. I could not seem to help myself; I opened my mouth and pure poison poured out.

"Oh, *do* call her Margaret, Richard," I said, mimicking Miss Fennimore's affected coyness credibly. "Remember, she insisted that you should. After all, you have known her 'ever so long.' And, as anyone at the dance could plainly see, you are on very familiar terms with her!"

Richard's reaction to this pretty speech was immediate and severe; it struck me like a physical blow. He froze, gripped me with a cold stare, and then delivered an equally icy reproof. "Do not take that mocking tone with *me*, Josephine. I will soon be your husband – your lord and master, if you please. I believe I have the right to insist you to treat me with more respect. There is a fine line between pert opinions and impertinence; you have just crossed it." He stood, adjusted his cravat, and fiercely tugged his waistcoat into smart order. "I know this has been a trying evening for you, so I am prepared to overlook your remarks. Perhaps tomorrow, by the clear light of day, you will recover your sense. For now, I must go before I lose my temper altogether. I bid you good night, madam."

Before I could say a word to stop him, Richard turned on his heel and was gone. No kiss; no embrace; no tender parting word. I was left alone and utterly wretched. It was a misery of my own making, of course; that glaring fact did nothing to ease my pain. Richard would never have gone away angry had I not been so horrid to him. His annoyance with me was completely justified.

For half an hour, I stared out the drawing room window, down at the darkened street, praying that Richard would return so that I might humbly beg his pardon. When he failed to appear, I resigned myself; I had no alternative but to wait until the morrow to make amends. I went to my bed that night with a heavy heart, my confidence in the power of our mutual affection to overcome this difficulty my only comfort.

~~*~~

During the course of my uneasy night, I resolved to linger in suspense of Richard's forgiveness no longer than necessary. The trouble had been my doing – solely mine. Hence I intended to be the one to seek out the remedy as well. Yet before anything could be done toward that end, another event intervened. While we were all at breakfast, the morning post arrived with a letter for Miss

Pittman. Stating that it was from her father, Agnes opened it, silently read the contents, blanched alarmingly as she did so, and hastily excused herself from the room.

The remaining three of us looked at each other in puzzled amazement.

"Perhaps I should go to her," I proposed. "Shall I?"

"Best allow her time to recover her composure first, my dear," Mama advised. "She will not thank you later for witnessing her current suffering, whatever the cause. I wonder what Mr. Pittman could have communicated to unsettle her so completely. I do hope none of her family has been taken seriously ill."

In deference to my mother's recommendation, I tarried longer than my own sensibilities would have advocated before going to my friend. I found her in a state of considerable agitation, crying fitfully and filling her trunk.

"Agnes, dear, what on earth has happened? Why are you packing your things?"

"Here. See for yourself," she said, thrusting her letter toward me. It read as follows:

My Dear Child,

I do hope that you have enjoyed your stay in Bath. Unfortunately, I must now insist that you return home at once. This will no doubt come as quite a blow to you – both cutting short your holiday and the reason for it – but it cannot be helped. You see, my dear, I have suffered a severe financial setback, the complexities of which I will not attempt to describe here. Suffice to say that we must retrench immediately. My attorney has drawn up plans for economy which I hope will save us from total disgrace, but it will require great sacrifice on the part of us all. Do thank our dear friends, the Walkers, for their hospitality, and beg their continued fellowship through the difficult time ahead. Pray, get yourself home as soon as possible, Agnes. Your presence is wanted at every moment, most particularly by your mother, who has been very cast down by this grave disappointment.

Your Loving Papa

"Oh, Agnes, I am so sorry."

"Our family is ruined, Jo. Ruined! I shall never be able to show my face in society again. What will become of us? Are we to be cast out to starve in the hedgerows?"

"Do try to calm yourself, dearest. Surely the situation cannot be as desperate as that."

But Agnes would not be comforted. The depth of her distress was beyond the reach of my ministrations. Indeed, there was little of use that I could do, except to assist with the practical preparations for her departure and to solicit my father's help in arranging her transportation. Within the space of three hours following the arrival of the ill-fated news, Papa had supplied Miss Pittman with the necessary funds for her journey, and safely deposited her and her luggage on the next outbound post chaise for Hampshire.

"What a sad business this is, Jo," he lamented as the coach pulled away, wheels rattling on the uneven cobbles. "I feel the loss of our young guest and the misfortune of her family exceedingly. At the very least, I wish Miss Pittman might have remained until we could deliver her to Wallerton ourselves in another week or two. I hate to see her traveling post. Still, I can understand her father's impatience to get her home. A family must close ranks at such a time."

I saw Agnes's forlorn face once more as the coach turned the corner before passing out of sight.

"Well, well, there's nothing more to be done for them at present, I suppose," Papa continued. "And since this mission has brought us out into the town, I believe it shall be as well for me to take myself to the Pump-room now as later. Will you accompany me, my dear, or do you have errands of your own?"

The sorry business with Richard flooded back into my mind. "Now you mention it, I do have something to do on Bond Street, if that's all right."

"Perfectly, perfectly. I daresay your time will be better spent there than waiting on me. Go about your business and I will see you at home later. But keep your wrap close about you; it is very chilly this morning."

I fully intended to go to Bond Street as I had told my father I would. But I had to see Richard first, to make my apologies without further delay. I should have gone even earlier, with Agnes in tow for propriety's sake, had not fate taken a hand. Now my determination to be restored to Richard's good opinion gave me the boldness to march up to the door alone. The servant who answered recognized me and reported that the gentlemen were not at home. Since he expected them shortly, he invited me to await their return upstairs in the drawing room.

Not many minutes passed before I heard noise below – the sound of the front door closing sharply followed by the raised voices of Richard and his father quarreling.

"But, Father, why must I come away so abruptly? Give me another week."

"Absolutely not! This was never intended as a holiday, as you well know. Now, with our business successfully concluded, any more expenditure would be a pointless extravagance. You have thrown away enough of my money, sir. It is time you came home and earned your keep."

They were moving in my direction. As I considered my awkward position and if I should make my presence known, the opportunity to do so was lost. I remained where I was, immobilized by Richard's words, which I could not help overhearing.

"I have done everything you demanded of me, sacrificing my plans and the woman I preferred in order to secure you a rich daughter-in-law. Have I not earned a little gratitude for a job well done?"

"Gratitude? No, I'll not thank you for your trouble nor pity your sacrifice either. Need I remind you that securing Miss Walker's fortune would have been entirely unnecessary had you not gambled away so much of your own? You have no one to blame but yourself for your current situation."

With that, the two men opened the drawing room doors wide and discovered me within. They stared at me and I at them, all three of us momentarily stunned silent. Then, with an involuntary cry of anguish, I fled the room, the house, and Richard.

18
The Painful Truth

Richard attempted to detain me, babbling some sort of explanation, I suppose. I could hear nothing above the menacing roar building in my head. Once out into the street, I broke free of him. I simply had to get away, to extricate myself from the nightmare, to leave the horror behind. I cared nothing for the curious faces that swam before my eyes or for whither I ran. I hurried on as if pursued by a fearful apparition, striving to outdistance the specter of Richard's hideous betrayal.

How long and how far I fled, I know not. What little conscious control I retained was entirely employed in the office of self-preservation, which took the form of denying what I had just heard with my own ears. Whenever Richard's incriminating words rose up before me, I thrust them back down again. I refused to believe it could be true. It must be some sort of ugly joke, I told myself. Or perhaps I had misconstrued some critical portion of the conversation. Mr. Pierce might be to blame, but not my Richard. I could rather believe every creature of my acquaintance leagued together to ruin his reputation than believe his nature capable of such cruelty. He loved me; he must be innocent! I willed it to be so, for to suppose otherwise would be insupportable. With all the strength at my command, I endeavored to shut tight my mind against any dissenting voice, to resolutely deny the unthinkable a foothold in my consciousness.

On I ran. I did not surrender without a fierce struggle. Yet gradually, as I tired and the pace of my flight slackened, the real state of affairs began to overtake me. Importunate questions plagued me, demanding answers. Were he truly innocent, why had Richard's look been so guilty upon seeing me? What possible explanation could there be for what I had heard other than the obvious? And who was the woman Richard had forfeited by his father's mandate? No, it would not do. Despite my fervent attempt, I could deceive myself no longer. It was impossible that any contrivance could represent the matter in such a way as to exonerate Richard from the crimes of treachery and fortune hunting. Thus sank all my hopes of domestic bliss, and with them, my last ounce of strength.

Through a haze, I heard a woman say, "Are you ill, Miss? May I help you?" Not waiting for my answer, she wrapped a supporting arm about my waist. "Henry, call a chair for the young lady. She cannot continue on foot. The poor thing is quite done in." My weak protests were disregarded, and a sedan chair summoned to carry me to Pultney Street. I made no further objection as the kind couple helped me into it.

Although I rested my weary body on the way home, my mind could not be quieted. It had work to do, the most urgent priority being to reestablish some semblance of control over my unruly emotions before I reached my door. I prayed for the strength to keep new tears at bay until I could closet myself in my bedchamber, to be spared the need for any immediate explanation to my parents. I saw no sign of my father when I arrived and, thankfully, my mother was much occupied. I made my apologies to her as I hurried through on my way upstairs, saying only that I had a headache and intended to take a long nap before dinner.

When at last I gained the sanctuary of my own room, the dam broke wide open. Flood waters surged over me in successive waves of pain. The first carried home all the agony of my unrequited love. On top of that washed other suffocating layers: self-pity at having been ill used; grief for the death of tender dreams; anger at the cruelty of fate; and shame for my own stupidity at believing what had clearly been a lie. One after another, they crashed against me, each one eroding away a little more of my world's foundation, like so much sand from beneath my feet, until I was left with no solid ground to stand upon. Completely overpowered, I collapsed on my bed, sobbing into my pillow until at length I fell into a heavy slumber.

~~*~~

I woke hours later, and the awful truth burst in upon me again, now in a colder light. Richard was a fortune hunter. He did not love me. In fact, he preferred another woman. On some level, I knew these were the unalterable essentials, but I could not face them squarely. Not yet. Each time I tried, my mind reeled wildly and my heart lurched with a fresh shock. It seemed impossible that I might come through the calamity alive; I could barely imagine surviving the balance of the day.

The clock struck four, suddenly filling me with alarm. Dear Lord! I would be expected downstairs for dinner shortly. Much as I wished to hide myself away forever, wallowing in my private misery, I knew I could not. I must be prepared to go down or be forced into making explanations. And it was far too soon, the gaping wound too new, to contemplate discussing my trouble with anyone – my parents, Susan, or even Agnes, had she been available. I could not have formed the words. How could I explain to someone else what I was as yet unable to comprehend?

Reluctantly dragging myself from bed, I inspected the damage done by the morning's misadventures. It was not a pretty picture that I saw in the mirror. My gown was wrinkled and muddied, my hair in disarray, and my face... oh, my face! Bloated and blotchy from my fit of tears, the ill effects of which seemed only to have been compounded by my leaden sleep. Still, I had to try.

I methodically dressed myself in a fresh gown, arranged my hair into some order, bathed my face with cool water, and made an attempt at a cheerful countenance. A second look in the glass to examine the result gave little satisfaction. Yet I hoped my parents would not notice anything drastically amiss.

My pretense of normalcy was neither effective nor necessary as it happened. No doubt my complete lack of appetite and conversation would have given me away in any case. However, Mama had good reason to suspect the general nature of my malady, even without reading my symptoms.

"You needn't pretend for our sakes," she said after several minutes of watching me struggle. "We know why you are upset. Richard was here this afternoon whilst you were resting."

"Oh?" I said warily.

"Yes, my dear. He said that the two of you had some sort of misunderstanding this morning. He gave no particulars, and I daresay he would never have mentioned it at all except that I guessed something was wrong. He looked so miserable, poor soul."

"Waste none of your compassion on him, Mama!"

"I see you are quite vexed with him, and no doubt justifiably so. He claimed the trouble was entirely his fault."

"An accurate assertion," I muttered.

"Yes, well… in any event, he asked to be kindly remembered to you, and said he would call again tomorrow."

"No! I will not see him."

"There, there. You may feel very differently by then. I trust you will not be too hard on the young man, Jo. I am certain he will have a very good explanation to give for himself. And, you know, lovers' quarrels mend quickly where there is true affection, so there is no need to lose hope. Now, my dear, we shall say no more about it if you like."

I was vastly relieved by my parents' disinclination for interference. Even so, I could not stand to remain long at table. I soon excused myself to return to the solitude of my own room, where I could be alone with my thoughts.

Where there is true affection, my mother had said. But was there ever any true affection in this case? That was the key question. There certainly had been – still was – on my side; my whole being ached to think how much. What about Richard, though? Could he really have been playing a part to me all along? No! In my heart of hearts, I still could not believe it of him. Or perhaps that was only the answer my vanity wished to hear.

Oh, what was to be done about this disaster? I tried to consider the question rationally, yet how could I when the very idea of seeing Richard again sent me into a panic? How could I bear to look at him, to see now the face of a traitor instead of the man I loved, to hear again the voice that had led me astray with such silken tones? I could never hope to retain any self-command in that charged situation when even under ordinary circumstances his presence had such a powerful influence over me. That very quality – his ability to intoxicate me so completely – had been my downfall. Notwithstanding my confident promise to my mother weeks before, I had indeed lost my head over Mr. Pierce. I could not see it then, but it was plain enough in hindsight.

Still, face Richard I must… if not tomorrow, then soon. I could not expect to make the difficult decision before me without knowing the whole story, without hearing his explanation for what he had done, without assessing – this time with eyes wide open – his true sentiments toward me. The exercise, though painful, must shed some light on my predicament, although it was hard to imagine that anything I might learn could make much difference. Nothing could change the fact that I would soon be forced to choose between two equally unacceptable alternatives. Should I consign myself to a loveless marriage, or endure the pain and disgrace of a broken engagement?

19

Cards on the Table

At my insistence, Richard was turned away when he presented himself in Pultney Street the next morning and again the following day. Still, I had no peace. The more I anguished over my limited options, the more convinced I became that no course of action could be settled upon until I had seen him. By the third day, I felt strong enough that I thought I might endure his coming. At all events, there seemed little advantage in further forestalling the inevitable, as if by refusing to see him I could perpetually deny whatever of his father's evil intent or his own culpability the interview might forever confirm. I judged it best, therefore, to get on with it, unpleasant as the ordeal must be.

Convinced that a business-like detachment was my best hope for managing the awkward situation and my own precarious emotions, I hardened myself and composed a careful plan. I would receive him, but keep a safe distance between us at all times. I would make it clear from the start that I was in full control, and that he must dance to my tune. I formed what questions I would put to Richard and in what order. And I imagined how he might respond to them, trying to anticipate the worst and ready myself for it.

Papa made no difficulty when I informed him that I should like to be allowed to see Mr. Pierce alone. Mama optimistically declared that a private meeting was the very thing needed to ensure our reconciliation. So, when at eleven o'clock he came again, he was directed to the study, where I had seated myself behind the large mahogany table.

The first sight of him, looking just as appealing as ever, struck such a sympathetic cord in my heart that I questioned at once whether I could maintain my composure, much less my resolve. His air of contrition, his countenance of concern, those dusky brown eyes that I knew so well.... A torrent of tender feelings rushed over me, momentarily obscuring his misconduct and my injury from view.

"Josephine, my darling, I fear there has been a terrible misunderstanding," he began. "Things are not as they may seem. You must allow me to explain."

"Wait," I interrupted, holding up a hand and briefly closing my eyes to refocus my thoughts. When I felt I was once more my own master, I continued. "You will have your chance to explain yourself, Mr. Pierce. However, I have something to say to you first."

"Just as you wish, my sweet."

"I know what I heard the other day." I checked his immediate objection. "No! Please do not insult me by denying it. I think I can bear anything better than more deceit. If there is still any chance for us, Richard, there can be no more lies. You must understand that, and do me the honor of answering my questions as honestly as possible. Will you?"

"Yes, of course, my love."

"And for heaven's sake, do refrain from using such endearments. At the moment, you have no right, and I find it most annoying." He made no protest. So far, so good, I thought. Richard stood before me, submissive and penitent, and I was in command – of myself and of the interview. "Now, I have gathered this much. You have run up debts through gambling; the estate needs a fresh infusion of capital; and, consequently, you set out on purpose to capture a fortune by marriage." I paused to see how Richard would respond to this test.

He fidgeted uncomfortably, turning his hat in his hands, and looking from me to the floor and back again. At length, he said, "You put it very severely, but... yes, I suppose that is essentially the case."

I felt a little something die within me. In spite of harboring no real hope that it could be otherwise, it still hurt to have the brutal truth confirmed beyond a doubt.

Richard hastily added, "And I *am* sorry for it, my d... Miss Walker."

After taking a moment to recover from this first blow, I invited the next by asking, "How did you settle on me as your object? How did you learn of my fortune? The truth, please," I reminded him.

Another uncomfortable pause ensued – no doubt another struggle between conscience and saving face – before he answered.

"I had already made plans to come to Bath, my father considering it the most promising place for me to meet a... suitable lady. I then happened to mention my upcoming trip to an acquaintance of mine, a Mr. Evans, who had lately returned from visiting some relations in Hampshire. He informed me that, while there, he met a fine young woman of good fortune who was likewise bound for Bath. Although his own run at you had been unsuccessful, he suggested that perhaps I might have better luck. Do you remember Mr. Evans?"

I nodded with chagrin. "He came with the Bickfords to our take-leave party, but I had not given him another thought from that day until this."

"Well, be that as it may, his report of your attractions quite intrigued me. From his description, I thought we might suit nicely."

"Yes, I was rich, and I am sure that suited very well indeed."

"No, it was more than that. With Mr. Evans's account in mind, I thought, 'This Miss Walker sounds most agreeable. If I must marry for money, I could probably do much worse. Perhaps we might even be happy together.' So, I determined to look out for you when I arrived in Bath."

"Then you found me, procured an introduction with the assistance of the unsuspecting Mr. Graham – poor 'simple' fellow – and have been leading me a merry dance ever since. And I, so obligingly naïve, offered not the slightest resistance to your charms. How you must have laughed and congratulated yourself for the ease of your conquest!"

He winced at the charge. "It was not like that, really!" His voice wavered as he continued, leaning forward across the table and looking intently into my eyes, "You *were* obliging, yes... and lovely, and bright, and utterly delightful. I could not believe my luck when you agreed to marry me. I may have started with wrong motives, but I ended with such an honest regard for you that my proposal was quite sincere. You must believe me, Jo."

I wanted to... desperately. His story sounded entirely plausible, compellingly heartfelt, and even romantic, which made it all the more seductive. The division between us was miserable. He had suffered for it as well; I could see the pain in his countenance. In that moment, I very nearly gave way. Indeed, had there not been a ponderously heavy piece of furniture between us, I might have fallen into his arms directly, apologizing for ever having doubted his affection.

Then I remembered Miss Fennimore.

The thought woke me from my poignant reverie as effectively as cold water thrown in my face might have done. "What about Miss Fennimore?" I challenged him. "I presume she is the person to whom you alluded, the woman you preferred." Much depended on his answer. I watched his reaction with a pounding heart. He seemed genuinely taken aback. Perhaps he had not anticipated such a pointed reference to his 'old friend.' "Come now, Richard. It is useless to deny it; your guilty look has already confirmed it."

"I... I was not going to deny it. I only want to explain. Whilst it is true that at one time I might have preferred the company of Miss Fennimore to any other woman of my acquaintance, that was before I came to Bath, before I met you, Jo."

A smooth parry. "But if it is all in the past, then why your comment to your father only two days ago?"

"It was an argument! People say all sorts of things they do not mean in the heat of the moment. By throwing Miss Fennimore back in his face, I merely hoped to win my point, reminding him what I had supposedly given up to meet his demands. I never could have *married* Miss Fennimore. She is not at all suitable to be mistress of Wildewood, as you could certainly judge for yourself. So, in truth, it was no sacrifice."

"I see. Very neatly explained."

"Then you *do* understand... and you will forgive me."

"Understanding is not quite the same thing as forgiving, is it? Do you have anything else to say before you go, Richard?"

"Go? Surely you would not send me away, not now you have heard my side of the story."

"I shall indeed. I have an important question before me, and you must go so that I can think properly. I must determine what is best to be done. I shall not see you again until I have decided... and possibly not even then."

"Good God! You are not seriously thinking of breaking off our engagement, are you?"

I did not deny it.

"How could you even contemplate such an odious thing?" He stalked up and down the room, running an unconscious hand through his thick hair. "Consider the consequences. I know you are angry, and I daresay you have every right to be. But this misunderstanding will pass and in time be quite forgot. We can still be happy together. I am sure of it."

I shot to my feet. "How can I marry a man who does not love me?" I cried out, cutting to the core of the matter.

"But I do!" he declared, stopping to face me again.

I sighed and sank back into my chair, rubbing my temples. I was suddenly very weary. "Perhaps you do, Richard, in your own small way, but not as I thought... and not as you ought. I cannot help wondering if I could be content with such feeble affection. I hesitate to risk my whole future on that kind of speculation. *You* are the gambler, not I."

Richard continued to profess his contrition for his misdeeds, his mortification at having failed to fully redeem his honor in my eyes, his concern for his father's reaction to the possibility of a broken engagement, and his undying devotion to me until the front door shut between us. From his manner, I was persuaded that, until the last moments of our conversation, Richard had never doubted the outcome. He had never questioned his ability to bring me round to his way of thinking. My strength had surprised him. Whatever the eventual conclusion of our little drama, I could at least take satisfaction in that.

20

Taking Advice

Although I had narrowly retained my composure in Richard's presence, it had been a desperate battle, the continuance of which I could not long sustain after he quit the house. As soon as he was safely away, I surrendered to the misery that pressed upon me from all sides. I sobbed aloud, my tears flowing feely and without end. I made no further attempt to hold them back or to conceal my grief any longer. The whole world was tumbling down about my ears. What possible difference could it make if everybody knew it?

The interview with Richard had provided no means of consolation, only more pain. It had effectively stripped away the last vestiges of my hope for his innocence, and it had served to confirm the difficulty of my circumstances without showing me a clear way ahead. It seemed I was no nearer a solution than I had been before.

My parents, witnessing all this, no doubt began to grasp that there was more gone awry than they had previously supposed. Mama gathered me into her comforting arms and patiently rode out the storm with me.

I knew it was time for a family conference. My parents had a right to know the situation, and I needed their advice. So, when at length I was sufficiently recovered, I told them what had transpired the other day at Richard's house and the gist of his explanation just given. I finished with my quandary over what, if anything, should be done about it. Mama looked too shaken to speak, so I turned to my father.

"What do you think, Papa?"

"I hardly know what to make of it, my dear. A very disagreeable development. Mr. Pierce a gamester and a fortune hunter after all? Well, well. This is a hard blow, principally because of how it concerns you, of course."

He paused in thought before continuing. "The assertion that his father was behind the whole scheme, I can easily believe. That does not excuse his conduct entirely, however. Still, I would not condemn him out of hand. Seeking to improve one's financial circumstances by marriage – although particularly offensive to *your* sensibilities, Jo – is a commonly accepted practice. It might be forgiven him. And the gambling is likely at an end now he is away from his college. Removed from that environment, productively employed at Wildewood under his father's watchful eye, and with a prudent wife to settle him, I think it most likely Richard will yet turn out a fine gentleman. I must admit I have a partiality for him despite all this. Let us not forget, he has much to offer you in the way of a highly eligible situation.

"In short, if you are prepared to overlook this inauspicious beginning and be happy with him, I have no objection to your marrying Mr. Pierce as planned. You may have some rough patches ahead – all young couples do – but the alternative could be fraught with even more difficulty. Society can be very cruel in such cases. Should you break off your engagement, there may be major repercussions to your reputation... even legal ramifications. I daresay Mr. Randolph Pierce will have to be reckoned with; he is not a man to be gainsaid."

As if to emphasize this last point, a message addressed to my father arrived from the senior Mr. Pierce later that day.

Dear Sir,

In recent weeks, I have reflected on the upcoming alliance between our two families with great satisfaction. Imagine my distress, then, when I learnt from my son that your daughter has implied an inclination to end the arrangement over some trifling disagreement. Perhaps, as I hope, Richard has misunderstood her intentions entirely. Surely Miss Walker is too principled to break her word on this minor provocation. If, however, she is indeed showing signs of inconstancy, let me urge you, as her father, to use your influence to prevent her making such a grave error. A breach of her promise would result in serious consequences. Much as I esteem your family, I will not on any account see my son and our respected name insulted with impunity. As a sensible man, you understand me and would act the same in my place, I am sure. With best wishes for the proper outcome,

Randolph Pierce

111

"So you see, Jo," Papa explained, "herein lies a thinly veiled threat of legal action against you, should you renege on your commitment to marry Mr. Pierce. He will be disappointed in his reasonable expectation of taking control of your fortune. As the injured party, he would be well within his rights to attempt to recover some of his losses."

"Richard, not I, the injured party here?"

"In the eyes of the law, yes; I fear it may be so."

"Outrageous! But surely he would not go so far as to file an action against me. His questionable behavior notwithstanding, I cannot believe Richard would stoop to such vindictiveness."

"Nor can I think so ill of him. However, as you yourself have acknowledged, he is held hostage to his father's will. I would not put it past Mr. Randolph Pierce to carry out such a plan. I believe we must regard it as a genuine danger. Weigh carefully your course of action, therefore, my dear. I will help you where I can but, since you are of age now, the final decision must be yours."

"So, after having been tricked into an engagement by one man, I am now to be blackmailed into going through with the marriage by another. Is that what you are telling me? It is too much to be borne!" I was far more angry than hurt by the thought. Still, I could feel tears stinging at the back of my eyes.

"Things are not quite as bleak as that," Papa continued. "Although we must take the threat of legal action seriously, we are not entirely without recourse if it comes down to it."

With this latest complication, my spirits sank still further. The prospect of my private affairs being dragged into court heaped one more layer of wretchedness upon me. How was it possible to make a dispassionate decision under such duress? Parting with my first love would have been painful enough. Now it appeared that the choice to leave Richard could cost me my good name and a sub-stantial part of my fortune as well. Although I cared nothing for the money itself, it did afford me the precious luxury of independence. Without it, I would be back where I started – obliged to marry in order to support myself, only with fewer prospects than before. Even Mr. Summeride might not take me once I was known as a jilt. That would be a new low indeed.

These and similar gloomy contemplations fully occupied me until dinner. Over the meal, my parents had the consideration to talk of trivialities, to which I was neither obliged to contribute nor attend. None of us made any reference to the question uppermost in our thoughts. My father, having already spoken his mind, seemed content to let the issue rest. My mother, I suspected, was far less easy about it. Although she kept her conversation cheerful, I noticed the deepened furrows of her brow whenever she looked in my direction.

Real maternal solicitude had been awakened, and I was not left long in suspense of Mama's sentiments. When I excused myself to return to my room, she soon followed.

"Would you like to talk, my dear?" she asked upon entering.

Her invitation served as sufficient encouragement, calling forth from me a new flood of emotion. "Oh, Mama," I cried, "this whole affair with Richard... It's like a nightmare; the very thing I was so determined to avoid has overtaken me nonetheless."

She sat down beside me and pulled me close. "Not quite. You are not yet irrevocably bound to a man who does not care for you, if indeed that is what Richard be. You still have a choice. Perhaps these events may even prove a blessing in disguise. In fact..." She trailed off.

I looked at her expectantly. There was an absent expression on her face, as if her gaze reached beyond the walls of my room and her thoughts to another time or place. "Mama?"

"Oh, I'm sorry, my pet. I was just thinking..."

"About what?"

"Well... I was remembering, really... a girl I knew a long time ago." Another pause. "She found herself in... a somewhat similar predicament. Perhaps hearing about her would be of use to you, in coming to terms with your own situation, I mean."

"Does the tale have a happy ending?" I asked dubiously. "I do not think I can bear a tragedy just now."

"Oh, yes. She ended very happy indeed. Let me see. Where shall I begin? Well, there was this young lady, a close friend of mine..."

"What is her name?"

"Oh, uh... Maria. We shall just call her Maria."

I rested against my mother, ready for her to soothe my pain with a story, as if I were a child again.

"Now, Maria was a fine girl of nineteen from a good family. Not so very accomplished, perhaps, but quite admired all the same. Several of the local young men took an interest in her. One night at a dance, though, Maria was introduced to a certain gentleman, several years her senior, who was visiting from another part of the county. His name was Mr. Goring, the son of a prosperous London attorney. Well, she fell for him at once. He was handsome, charming, articulate and lively: everything pleasing that her mind could conceive and her heart desire. From that moment on, no other man had a chance with her. Mr. Goring could do no wrong, and no one else could hold a candle to his perfections.

"The couple soon fancied themselves in love but, for various reasons, Maria's father flatly refused his consent to their marrying. No amount of pleading could make him reconsider. His decision was final and for her own good, he said. My friend was beside herself with vexation of mind and spirit. So, believing it the only way they could be together, Maria consented to Mr. Goring's daring plan of eloping to Scotland."

"Oh, my! To leave everything and run off like that? There is an element of romance in it, to be sure. Still…"

"Yes, looking back, I can scarce believe it myself… that a well-brought-up girl like Maria could have done such a thing. But she was determined to have the man, and despaired of any other means to accomplish it. I suppose she thought that once the deed was done, her family would have no choice but to accept the match."

"So, what happened? Did they make it to Scotland and marry?"

"Nowhere near. When Mr. Goring came for Maria in the middle of the night, one of the servants heard the noise and alerted his master. The couple had not got more than five miles off before her father overtook them. He sent the young man packing, and carried his daughter safely home again. You can imagine Maria's mortification. She declared her heart was broken forever; she swore she could never love another man; and she refused to speak to her father for weeks. The affair was hushed up as well as possible, but rumors got round nonetheless. There is no preventing the spread of gossip in a small town," Mama lamented.

"But you said the story ended well," I reminded her.

"Yes. I was just coming to that," she continued more brightly. "Time and reflection ultimately did their work; Maria became reconciled to her disappointment. And resignation is never so perfect as when the blessing denied begins to lose somewhat of its value in our estimation. In hindsight, she perceived the serious defects of Mr. Goring's character and the impropriety of his actions, to which she had been blind before. She even came to wonder if Mr. Goring had meant to marry her at all, after spiriting her away."

"Dear me. So her father had been right about the man after all. I am sure your friend was better off for her narrow escape, but that hardly qualifies as ending 'very happy.'"

"I'm not finished yet. Because of her fortunate escape, Maria had a second chance, the opportunity to make a superior choice for herself. Although Maria's society was far less eagerly sought than before, one gentleman was not put off by the business. Mr... March – yes, that was his name – a man of a more noble character, showed himself the truest friend in standing by Maria through her troubles. By and by, she grew to love Mr. March with a tenderness – and a passion, I would venture to say – far deeper and more sincere than she had ever felt for Mr. Goring. The two ultimately married and are still happily so to this day... so I understand."

"Ah, now I am satisfied," said I. Then my own troubles rushed back. "But how can this story possibly help me? The situations are not alike."

"Not precisely, no. The obstacles are undeniably different, and I would not presume to say that your Richard is another Mr. Goring. You must be the judge of that. I only suggest that, as you deliberate on what to do about your current dilemma, you keep in mind the lessons learnt by my friend Maria.

"Your eyes have been opened now, Jo. Painful as it has been, you can turn it to your advantage. Use the opportunity to assess Mr. Pierce's character honestly. Compare his virtues and faults to those of the noblest and best men you know. If you can respect Richard as well, then marry him, by all means. If not, do not attempt it. Nothing will destroy your love more quickly than discovering that you cannot truly esteem your husband. I would have you choose deep disappointment and temporary disgrace rather than forfeit all hope of finding a truly worthy partner to share your future."

21

Deliberations

Toward deciding what to do about my endangered engagement, I had now achieved my first objective, that being to gather all potentially useful information and advice. Richard had given his explanations at my request, and his father his views without invitation. My parents had both had their say. One opinion only remained to be heard, and that was mine, which lingered undisclosed of necessity as I did not yet know it myself. Thus began my earnest deliberations.

I set out to review every fact concerning Richard with a ruthlessly rational eye. No simple task; the heart does not easily relinquish its claims. At every turn, I recalled a treasured moment or a tender word that threatened to divert my objectivity toward a caving-in to emotion. Yet I carried on. Through it all, my unspoken wish was that Richard would somehow emerge exonerated, thereby sparing me any necessity of parting with him. However, as the evidence weighed in, my hopes for that cherished result waned.

At the outset of our acquaintance, his appearance and prodigious social powers had granted him every advantage and lulled to sleep any cause for misgiving. How different did all Richard's words and deeds look when viewed in the light of recent revelations. His flirtatious manner and flattering style – which before seemed so innocuous, even endearing – now bespoke deliberate design rather than a playful nature. I had been aware of these excesses at the time, but had been happy to attribute his exuberance to his unbridled love for me. What absurd conceit that now seemed!

It had all been an act, at least in the beginning, with securing my fortune his goal. He had as good as admitted that much, and laid the blame for it at his father's feet. Still, had Richard strongly objected to the role, I question if he could have been so convincing in it. Even the best actor requires proper motivation, and it was hard to imagine him playing his part with more spirit than he had done. It followed that he was either a willing participant or highly proficient in the art of deception. No comfort could be found in either explanation.

If, however, as Richard claimed, he had come to love me in spite of his disingenuous intentions, I might have successfully conquered my scruples over his early treatment of me. The duplicity of his behavior toward others I found more difficult to overcome. He claimed Miss Fennimore was nothing to him, yet their familiarity belied it. One day he vehemently defended her honor, and the next he freely disparaged her worth. I could not help but wonder if he would treat his wife with the same inconstancy.

Still, the most damning of all was the recollection of Richard's conduct toward Mr. and Mrs. Graham – all respectful civility in their presence and yet laughing at them behind their backs, ridiculing them whilst at the same time enjoying their kind hospitality. I could not imagine my father, Arthur, or even Tom, with his irreverent sense of humor, doing such a thing. Not only had Richard slighted these good people, he had encouraged me – a total stranger at the time – to join him in doing so. I was ashamed to remember how mildly I had reacted to such obvious impropriety – more proof of Mr. Pierce's unhealthy influence over me.

With this solid character indictment before me, my choice should have been clear. How could I even contemplate trusting my future to a man who had shown himself so inclined to falsehood? Yet, when I considered never again knowing the bliss of Richard's arms about me, the delicious thrill of his kiss, his resonant voice in my ear, his look that seemed to penetrate to my very soul...

"Stop it, Josephine!" I commanded myself under my breath. "It can never be. It never was! That man does not truly exist; he is a product of disguise and imagination. You only prolong your pain by continuing to indulge the fantasy. Enough!" Before I could waver in my resolve, I quit the cloister of my room to inform my parents that I had decided to put an end to my engagement.

~~*~~

Mama accepted my verdict with grace and sympathy. My father was less sanguine. Nevertheless, he made it his first order of business to seek, on my behalf, the advice of Mr. Benson, the man who had represented us in drawing up the marriage agreement.

Under the circumstances, I certainly had no wish to see Richard again, much less his father. Another face-to-face meeting was more than I could countenance in my precarious state. Yet Richard had to be told something before we left Bath. A judiciously worded note; I hoped that would serve. Fortunately, the solicitor agreed that my taking that approach would be for the best.

"He said to make it brief and non-committal," Papa reported when he returned from the consultation. "Say not that you are breaking the engagement, only that you need to get away and think."

"Why? Does he suppose I will change my mind? I have made my choice and I want to have done with it as soon as possible."

"As it was explained to me, it is primarily to give us the advantage of time. There is no reason to tip our hand before it is necessary. In the interim, to prepare for the possibility of legal action, Mr. Benson advises that we take counsel with a colleague of his in London. He also said you must be careful to set nothing down on paper which you would be embarrassed to have read out in court someday, should it come to that."

With that sobering thought in mind, I wrote and rewrote the note several times until I was satisfied.

To Mr. Richard Pierce
Dear Sir,

Although I was entirely sincere when I consented to be your wife three weeks ago, circumstances are somewhat altered now. The deception you and your father perpetrated upon me from the outset of our acquaintance has seriously compromised the chance of a successful union between us. Therefore, I shall withdraw to give the question the prudent consideration such a weighty matter demands. Please honor my desire for privacy during this time, and refrain from attempting to contact me in any way. I will advise you of my intentions in due course.

Respectfully,
Josephine Walker

"That should do the job very neatly, I think," said my father upon reading it. "Although, before we send it on its way, I want Mr. Benson's approval as well." And he went out again.

Since the crisis began, I had quite deliberately thrown all my emotional and intellectual energy into solving my dilemma. By giving me a useful purpose, the undertaking had provided some protection against the desperation that I sensed every moment crouching at my door. With my decision made, and that safeguard thus removed, I believe nothing but my mother's intervention kept me from taking to my bed for a protracted wallow in grief and self-pity. She wisely headed off such a relapse by supplying me with a fresh occupation, enlisting my help in packing up the house toward the goal of starting for home early the next day.

"With a little luck, we may be back in Wallerton in time for Christmas services," she suggested. "Would that not be pleasant, dear?"

"I suppose so," I answered without enthusiasm. As we continued our work, I could feel her watching me. "You mustn't worry about me, Mama. I will survive this."

"Yes, I know you will, and you will be stronger for it in the end, I trust. Still, it does grieve me to see you in such distress, even though I am certain you have made the correct choice. Come what may, you can take consolation in that. And I truly believe things will turn out right for you in the end, as they did for my friend Maria."

"Yes, but she had Mr. March to rely on after her disappointment."

When my father returned, he reported that my letter had been approved by the attorney and sent off to its destination. Whilst he was out, he had also ordered horses for our departure and settled with the landlord, so all that remained was to call on the Grahams. Considering it a propitious hour of the day to find our friends at home, we set off for Milsom Street at once.

"When we arrive, leave everything to me," said Papa. "I will make a simple statement about the change in your plans, and then we will have a little visit before we say our goodbyes. I shall be excessively sorry to part from such good friends, but there is no help for it, I suppose. Mrs. Walker, what do you say to inviting them to stop in Wallerton for a few days when they leave Bath? It may not be in their direct road to Kent, but not very much out of it either, I should think. Perhaps Miss Graham would consent to staying on with us for a while, as a companion to you, Jo."

The Grahams were indeed at home when we arrived. They received us with great cordiality... and great curiosity, after our unexplained four-day sequestration. My father related to them the nature of our trouble as briefly and with as little fuss as possible. He concluded with our intention to decamp at once in favor of Hampshire, and with the open invitation to Fairfield Manor. When our parents moved on to other topics, Susan drew me aside for a more candid discussion of my situation. I held nothing back from her.

"I do not know when I have been more shocked!" said she, after hearing me out. "When I was turned away at your door, I hardly knew what to think. The servant would only say that your family was in seclusion. My poor Jo! You have been very ill used by that man. To think, Papa must have the blame for first introducing him to you."

"Please do not say that, especially to your kind father. He is not in the least responsible. How could he have known to what that event would lead? No, we were *all* taken in by Richard's pleasing manners. And, despite everything that has happened, I cannot bring myself to judge him the black-hearted villain you may suppose. If I could, I might have fewer regrets. He has been weak, and he has acted wrongly. Still, I believe that at least some part of the value we saw in him – and some measure of the regard he showed for us – must have been genuine."

"You are more generous than I should be in your place. Yet I hope you are right. If he has a conscience, and if he truly cares for you, then he will suffer as he ought for what he has done. Yes, leave him in suspense of your answer for as long as you like, but let it not be an invitation to waver in your resolve, Jo. I trust you are too wise to fall for his tricks a second time."

Despite my own troubles, I had not forgotten Susan's distress of circumstances. Before leaving, I inquired if there had been any progress made toward gaining Mrs. Ramsey's approbation.

"No, I fear not. Mrs. Ramsey has made her position abundantly clear, and everything gives way to her," said Susan, with a heavy sigh. "Now we shall all soon be leaving Bath. You go tomorrow, the Ramseys return to London next week, and we are for Kent. So I do not know when, if ever, I shall see my dear George again. It really is too cruel! Only a few weeks ago we were such a merry party, the four of us, and now we are to be flung apart forever."

"Do not despair, I beg you, Susan. Although it is true that one of that party must be permanently lost to us, surely there is hope for the other three. You and I shall not always be divided, and I daresay Mr. Ramsey will move heaven and earth if necessary to make his way back to your side."

22

Return to Wallerton

We had come to Bath full of optimism, but prepared to retrace our route now, three months later, with heavy hearts. We could not be away soon enough to suit me. And, but for the treasures there gained – my new friend Susan and my father's improved health – I could have wished we had never entered the town's fine environs at all.

Indeed, we were within half an hour of our departure when an agitated Mr. Richard Pierce arrived in Pultney Street. My father, who supervised the loading of the carriage at the curb, would no doubt have turned him away. That would have been the end of it, had I not at the same moment emerged unawares from the front door.

The unexpected sight of Richard sent a jolt of alarm right through me. Could I have retreated unobserved, I would have done so. But it was too late for that; he had seen me.

"Jo, I must speak to you. Please!"

Father moved to interpose himself. "I thought my daughter made her position perfectly clear in her letter, sir. She does not wish to see you," he said firmly.

"Never mind, Papa," I said, recovered from my initial shock. "I can deal with this myself. It will not take long. Mr. Pierce, shall we walk?"

"My dear Jo, surely someplace more private..." Richard broke off mid-sentence upon observing my warning look. "But of course; as you wish."

I set off down the street at a brisk pace. "Well? Speak your peace, sir. I have very little time to spare. As you see, we quit Bath almost immediately,"

He followed, struggling to keep up and put his words together at the same time. "This is too sudden. Your letter came as quite a blow, and now I find you rushing away like this... What am I to think?"

"You are to think that I am a rational creature who must weigh all the facts before rendering a decision about my future. I see no great mystery in that."

"The mystery is how you can speak so calmly about the possibility of throwing over everything that has passed between us. Josephine, do stop for a moment and listen to me."

I complied, crossing my arms and turning a look on him that I hoped would communicate a blend of boredom and disdain. "Yes?"

"Do you really care so little for me that you can treat me with such contempt? I would not have thought you capable of such calculated cruelty."

"I learnt it from you, sir," I said evenly.

"Fair enough; no doubt I deserve that... and perhaps more. At any rate, I did not come here to defend myself."

"I am glad to hear it. But then, why have you come?"

"I came to ask you to give me a chance to win back your regard. Tell me how I can prove myself. Allow me to convince you of the sincerity of my affection."

I tore my eyes from the handsome architecture of his face to study an altogether safer subject – the line of neat houses on the far side of the street. "This is pointless, Mr. Pierce. I have already had a three-month demonstration of your character. What more can there be to know of you? As for your sincere affection, you can only begin to prove that by doing as I ask. Allow me time away to consider what is best to be done." I turned round and started back.

"You are determined to give me up, then," he said, walking at my side again.

"I have said no such thing. I am only resolved to act in that manner, which will, in my own opinion, constitute my happiness."

"What of my happiness? Is that no longer of any interest to you?"

"Your current discontent, Richard, is of your own making. As for your future state of mind, I have yet to settle if that will be any of my business. I can tell you this much, however. Nothing will drive a wedge between us more surely than threats of legal action."

"I'm sorry about that, Jo, but you cannot reasonably hold me accountable for what my father does. I have no control over him."

I stopped and faced him once more. "That is unfortunate, for I doubt that my remaining regard for you is stout-hearted enough to survive the punishment meted out by the courts." He made no rejoinder. Instead, his eyes articulated his plea more eloquently than words. They asked for sympathy and forgiveness. They begged to be adored as before. I took one long, last look into their depths before breaking the spell. "It seems we have nothing left to say to one another, Mr. Pierce."

I walked away from him, and he let me go.

When I regained the safety of the house, I closed the door behind me and rested against it. I hardly knew whether to laugh or cry. It had cost me dearly to turn my back on Richard there in the street. But alongside the sharp pang of loss, there lay an undeniable thrill of satisfaction. It was good that I had been forced to confront him again. My emotions had been running the gamut and my reason vacillating for days. Even after my choice was made, I had been in continual danger of slipping back into doubt and disarray. Seeing Mr. Pierce again had reinforced my decision and made me feel my own strength. In taking command of the situation, I no longer felt myself the victim.

~~*~~

With tolerable equanimity, I bid farewell to Bath and faced the journey home. So much had transpired that it seemed like years rather than months since we had come away. How good it would be to fall back into the comforts of my settled home and the simple routine of daily life at Fairfield. I had dared to taste incandescence. Now I craved only retirement, peace, and the consolation of my closest friends. I wished to see Mrs. Evensong again, and to learn how little John liked the story I sent him from Bath. I would also call on the Batemans, the Miss Millers, and poor Agnes as soon as possible.

As we drew near Wallerton, Father suggested, "I believe we should visit the Pittmans tomorrow, to inform them of our return and to make it clear that they can count on our support in their current crisis."

"Yes, Papa. I was this very moment thinking how I long to see Agnes again. It has been barely a week since she left us, yet how much has happened?"

"A great deal indeed," he agreed.

"I suppose I should post a letter to Frederick," said my mother, "and one to Tom as well, unless we find him still at Fairfield. I hope you do not mind, Jo, but they must be informed of our early return and the reason for it."

"Of course. My trouble cannot be kept secret from my own family... and not long from everybody else in Wallerton, I imagine. Word of my engagement will have got round by now, and I daresay the report of its cancellation will spread even more rapidly when it comes out. People take such a disgusting joy in gossiping about the misfortunes of others."

"Yes, my dear," agreed Mama. "Folks are bound to talk. But you have done nothing to be ashamed of. You may hold your head up and look your neighbors in the eye same as before."

"Perhaps, if I am very lucky, something even more sensational will come along to divert their attention from me."

Mama was saved the trouble of writing to either of her sons in consequence of finding them both at Fairfield Manor when we arrived. She had reason to hope Tom would still be in Wallerton, but Frederick's presence was an unexpected prize.

After the initial greetings, Tom inquired, "What brings you home so soon? You were not expected until the new year."

"My convalescence was complete, and we all grew a little weary of Bath," said Papa. He continued more tentatively, looking at me, "And your sister has had a change of heart about Mr. Pierce."

"Yes, I am giving up my engagement. I have not yet informed Mr. Pierce or the rest of the world of my decision, but my brothers may as well know it." I then gave them a brief recital of what had transpired in Bath.

"Wretched scoundrel!" Frederick pronounced the offender afterward. "I never met the man, but he clearly did not deserve you, sister."

"I see you take my view of things," agreed Tom with like indignation. "If only this had come to light whilst I was still in Bath! I would have taken real pleasure in giving Mr. Pierce good reason to regret insulting you, Jo."

"Thank you for the sentiment, but I really have no desire to see Richard knocked about. I wish only never to see him again under any circumstances, if possible. Now, Frederick, we have explained ourselves, so it is your turn. What brings you to Wallerton? It is clearly not on our account, since we were not expected. Have you tired of Millwalk so soon?"

"On the contrary; I am quite content, except I must own that I miss my old friends. So I have come for a visit. I had been considering it anyway, and then I heard about the Pittmans' troubles. That decided the matter."

"I had no idea you took such an interest in local affairs, Frederick," said Papa.

"Not as I ought to have done in the past, perhaps. However, my new position in life gives me a keener appreciation for the cares and responsibilities of a gentleman such as Mr. Pittman. With you away, Father, I thought it my duty to pay my respects on behalf of the family."

"You have seen them, then? Are their circumstances so very bad?" asked Mama. "We know only the barest facts from the letter that summoned Miss Pittman home from Bath."

"Yes, I fear they are. I did not wish to trouble Mr. Pittman with pointed questions when Tom and I called on him. He seemed uncommonly low as it was. But I gather from what he volunteered, and from the talk I have heard about town, that he invested largely in an unsuccessful speculation – some sort of stock exchange swindle, as it turned out. The family's hard hit. They have already had to dismiss most of the servants; the spare carriage and horses are to be sold at auction; Henry has been recalled from Cambridge; and most of the money for the girls' dowries is gone as well, from what I understand."

I gasped. "Oh, poor Agnes!"

Part Two

23
Taking Sides

I take extravagant pleasure in the peace of the country night when I retire to my bedchamber and pick up my diary. As I peruse its pages, the crackling of the crisp paper stands out in sharp relief against the silence of the house, everyone else at Fairfield having likewise taken to their beds. The only sounds I hear from beyond my own room are the steady tick of the hall clock and the occasional bark of a dog somewhere afar off. After having been so long in the constant clatter of town, I welcome the quiet. I allow it to envelop me completely.

Despite weariness brought on by travel, the restorative of sleep long eludes me. I lie awake into the early morning hours, reading and involuntarily reliving events in Bath. Before going, I could never have predicted the way things would turn out. And now that I am away from there, I can almost imagine the whole misadventure with Richard never occurred, that it is nothing more than a bad dream to be put out of my mind so that I might return to the old life. I would gladly make it so if I could, for nothing less can blot out my torment for long. When I least expect it, a word or a memento of the past calls Richard back to my mind, and once again I am struck down by the same aching emptiness inside.

Snow falls during the night. When I arise at dawn, it rests an inch thick on the lawns and shrubbery surrounding the house – singularly appropriate, for the day is Christmas Eve. The fairy-land quality of the scene adds to my delight at finding the grounds of Fairfield, not Pultney Street, outside my windows. Although I suspect my troubles are far from over, this feels like the safest possible harbor in which to weather the storm.

As we gather for breakfast, I consider how agreeable it is to have things back as they were before. My father has resumed his proper place at head of table with his sons on either side – Fred to his right and Tom on his left, as always. Mama sits at the other end, with me beside her. The tacit agreement amongst us forbids spoiling the meal by speaking of any subject weighty or disagreeable. Therefore, our discourse canvasses all the little varied topics of polite conversation that are sure to promote good digestion by placing only trifling demands on the intellect and emotions. Thus, the pleasant picture is preserved for the moment.

Afterward, however, Papa restates his determination to call on the Pittmans, to see of what effectual aid and comfort we might be to our unfortunate friends. Tom excuses himself from the errand, but the rest of us willingly agree. The carriage is ordered and off we go, mentally preparing ourselves along the way for what we may find at our destination.

We arrive upon a gloomy scene indeed. The Pittman household displays the same air of desperation and grief as one in mourning is sure to exhibit. The servants – what remains of their numbers – hurry about their business with fretful expressions. The family looks infinitely worse. Mrs. Pittman makes the best show of rising to the occasion. Her well-entrenched habit of good manners enables her to receive us properly despite the trying situation. Mama naturally gravitates to her side with the sympathy of feeling afforded by their long acquaintance and common station in life. Mr. Pittman nods and mumbles his greeting, looking more embarrassed than gratified by the presence of visitors. He and my father soon withdraw to the study for a private consultation. I take Agnes aside, leaving Frederick to keep her brother and younger sister company.

Considering Agnes's temperament, I had expected to find her in the throes of some violent emotion. That rendering of my friend would be less alarming than the pale, subdued creature before me now. I hardly recognize her. I have never seen her so dull and spiritless before, her normal sensibilities and high animation nowhere in view.

"My dear Agnes, are you quite well?" I ask with real concern. "Frederick explained to us what has happened, so of course you are upset. But, seeing you, I fear for your health as well as your circumstances. What can I do for you? May I not send for a doctor? Truly, you look very ill."

"No. You needn't be alarmed," Agnes says languidly. "Mr. Trask has already been here. He has given me something for my nerves and pronounced me in no danger." She sighs and continues. "Oh, Jo… when I got Papa's letter in Bath… little did I imagine how bad things really were: the servants let go, our things sold at auction... and my dowry all but gone. The degradation and humiliation of it... No one will solicit our company now. We are ruined, ruined forever. Papa puts a brave face on the future and Mama tries to make out that she believes, but... it is useless. As for me, I have no more tears; they are all cried out," she finishes flatly.

I place my arm about her shoulders, and she slumps against me.

My heart aches for my friend, and my anger rages against those whose crimes have driven her to such a state. But I must be calm for Agnes. "I know the situation appears very bleak at present, but it is bound to brighten by and by," I offer, feeling all the feebleness of such platitudes. I long to be able to say something more to the purpose. After an interval of silence, I try again. "You must not lose hope, Agnes. Your family's fortunes will rise again. In the meantime, your friends will see you through. We shall none of us desert you in your hour of need."

At this, Agnes gives a cynical little laugh. "I am sorry, Jo. I do not mean to sneer at you; your sincerity I trust completely. But you give others far more credit than they deserve. Rats abandon a sinking ship, or had not you heard? We are already shunned by our neighbors, and even Arthur lost no time in forsaking me."

"Arthur? Impossible!"

"Nevertheless, it is true. He called the other day... to condole with us – ever the dutiful young man," she says with sarcasm. "He sat with us a full hour, working up his courage for the real purpose of his visit, I daresay. Finally, he asked to speak to me alone and it all came out. He said that before returning to Oxford he wished to... to 'clarify' our relationship... for *my* sake. 'In light of recent events,' as he so delicately put it, he wanted to be certain that I understood myself to be free from any perceived obligation to him. Was that not considerate? He would never admit it, of course, but he could hardly wait to be rid of me."

"Surely, in your distressed state, you simply misunderstood his intentions, dearest. I cannot believe Arthur would be inconstant or deliberately cruel. It is not in his nature."

"You take his part against me, then," she accuses, pulling away with a wounded expression. "Really, Josephine, I did not expect it of you."

"No! You have my complete loyalty, Agnes, always. I only wish to spare you the unnecessary pain that must arise from a misunderstanding between you and Arthur. I suppose, I would spare myself as well. I should feel the break up of our little group exceedingly. Are you absolutely certain he meant to cast you off by what he said?"

"Oh, yes. He used my flirtation with Mr. Cox as his excuse, but I am sure it has more to do with my reduced circumstances. It seems he will not take me without a proper dowry."

"Abominable! Oh, Agnes, I would not have thought him capable of such a thing. Yet who am I to judge? I can no longer trust my own opinion as regards any man's character, not after my blindness in Richard's case. Are all men born with such avarice, or are they trained up in the art?" I go on to apprise my friend of events in Bath, those which followed her departure and hastened my own. "So you see, my dear, we have both suffered a reversal of fortune at the hands of unscrupulous men, and we are both left the worse for it. You can at least take comfort in this. When the news of my broken engagement gets out, as the fresher scandal it will take attention away from your troubles."

We each solemnly swear to keep the confidence of the other. Agnes wishes to avoid the further humiliation of Arthur's desertion becoming known, and I hope to stave off rumors about myself as long as possible. For my sake, Agnes vows to loathe Mr. Pierce for all eternity, and I – although I cannot commit to the same extreme measure – pledge to henceforth spurn Arthur's company for his offences against her. When our conference of commiseration finally concludes, I leave satisfied that the session has noticeably cheered my friend, which was, after all, my primary goal. My own spirits, however, sag far lower than before under the added weight of what I have learnt of Arthur's defection, which increases my burden on my own account as well as Agnes's.

On the ride home, Papa remarks, "I have encouraged Mr. Pittman to engage a solicitor to attempt the recovery of his money. He says he was cheated by some dishonest businessmen who gained thousands at his expense. Perhaps if these men can be brought to justice, at least some of his investment might be salvaged. Mr. Pittman holds out little hope, but I think it worth a try."

We again lapse into a meditative silence. I am in no humor for light banter in any case. My thoughts dwell on the suffering heart I have just left. I am ashamed to think that I had recently begun to question Agnes's attachment to Arthur. If she did not care for him, she would hardly be so devastated now. Still, whether Agnes truly loved Arthur or not was immaterial. She had trusted to him for her future. Of that much I am certain. His ill-timed abandonment dealt Agnes the final blow by knocking out from under her the last remaining pillar of her formerly secure world. For that, Arthur is fully culpable.

This whole episode troubles me exceedingly, even beyond my solicitude for my friend. It shakes my confidence in the human race – and in my own judgment – to the core. When unscrupulous men behave dishonestly, it surprises no one. But when an honorable man acts against his known principles, it threatens to turn to quicksand the ground on which we all stand.

Unconsciously, I believe I have long held Arthur on a sort of pedestal in my mind, as the model of what a man ought to be. I have always admired him, valued his judgment and companionship, and rejoiced in his good character for Agnes's sake as well as his own. Even if the pair had never married, I should have liked to retain his friendship and my good opinion of him. That is impossible now. By his fall from grace, Arthur is forever lost to me. How can I bear such another disappointment so soon after parting with Richard?

When we arrive at home, we are told that Tom has a guest within – the man himself: Arthur Evensong. It seems the first test of my pledged loyalty to Agnes is already upon me. After what I have lately learnt of him, I half expect that he will look different somehow, that his outer form will now reflect the change in his conduct. If he appears the villain that Agnes represents him to be, my job may be more easily done. Yet, as I enter the drawing room, he looks precisely the same as before – the same solid frame, the same honest face, the same clear eyes. He rises when we come in, nodding to me and then paying his respects to my parents. If anything, he seems more artlessly open than ever.

When Arthur turns back to me, I unaccountably begin to tremble.

"I did not expect to see you again so soon, Jo. You are well, I hope," he asks gently, searching my face.

I have to look away. It is impossible to say what I must whilst meeting his gaze. "Not entirely, sir. I have just come from Agnes. Seeing her so unwell and hearing the cause of her misery has distressed me more than I can say. In fact, it has left me completely unequal to idle conversation. I beg you would excuse me, Mr. Evensong," I finish brusquely, stealing a glance at him.

133

A cloud passes across his countenance. "Of course," he says uncertainly.

As I leave the room, I hear my father make excuses for me. "You must forgive my daughter's bad manners, Mr. Evensong. I am afraid she has taken this unhappy business with the Pittmans very much to heart. And on top of her own disappointment too…"

I hastily retreat to the privacy of my own apartment, shaking and truly unwell after the encounter with Arthur. I did what I had to do, what my allegiance to Agnes required of me. Even so, I feel wretched, in my body and in my soul, for having treated an old friend so coldly.

24

Christmas

Christmas Day breaks clear and crisp over Wallerton, with only remnants of the previous day's snowfall preserved in shaded corners and hollows. Most of it has already dissolved with the sun. No similar warmth has come to chase away yesterday's trauma over Arthur and Agnes, however. The chill of that memory remains fully intact. It comprised the substance of my thoughts and prayers until I fell asleep last night, and my first consideration upon waking. Still, it is Christmas, and I am determined to set the distressing subject aside as much as possible in favor of more cheerful reflections.

After morning services, the rest of the day will be spent in the friendly confines of my own family. It occurs to me that this might well be the last Christmas that the five of us will share together on our own. Although I think it unlikely Tom will marry anytime soon, Frederick is four years older and well established at Millwalk. There can be no obstacle whatever to his taking a wife as soon as he wishes. With a pang, I remember that this would have been my last Christmas at home as well had my plans with Richard not run aground – another sore subject on which not to dwell today.

So much has changed lately that I appreciate the constant and the familiar more than ever before. Other than my family, and a dwindling list of true friends, I can think of nothing else so constant in my life as the church. The scriptures, liturgy, and hymns I have known since childhood never fail to bring me comfort when my own small troubles threaten to overwhelm me. As we walk into the village, I hope for that same consolation again.

The whole community will be in church; the pews are always full on Christmas Day. How glad I am that news of my failed engagement has not yet got out. At least the day will not be spoilt by the fear that every look and whisper makes me its object of derision. I am safe from that fate for now. Even so, I will likely have to endure some uncomfortable comments and questions. The possibility of another confrontation with Arthur worries me more.

We arrive just before the start of the service, and file into our pew without incident. The Pittmans, not surprisingly, are missing. One fleeting look confirms that Arthur is present, however, sitting with his mother and brothers straight across from me in the Evensongs' customary place. He catches my eye; I immediately withdraw it to focus on the words before me in my Prayer Book.

I lose myself temporarily in the music and message of the service. Afterward, Mrs. Oddbody makes her way with purposeful haste to my side. She is a talkative old lady with a nose for gossip, the very sort I should wish to avoid just now. Yet there is no evading her today.

"My dear Miss Walker, how glad I am to see you are come back. And looking so very well too!"

"You are too kind, Mrs. Oddbody."

"It is no wonder, after such a refreshing holiday in Bath – refreshing *and* fruitful, from what I hear. A little bird told me that you are to be congratulated, my dear," she says in a knowing way. "You understand that I am very fond of news – any kind of news but especially romance – so you can well imagine that I was uncommonly pleased when I heard of your engagement. Since I have had the great good fortune to get my own daughters so respectably married and settled these many years, I have made it my concern to see to it that all the other young ladies of the parish are similarly well disposed of. So I am simply bursting with questions. Tell me about your young man, my child. Is he a gentleman of good fortune? And how did you find Bath? Was it as delightful as the reports we hear? I have never been, you know, and I suppose I am not likely to at my age. You must pity me that and give me benefit of your experience. You have such a way with words, Miss Walker. Paint me a picture with your colorful descriptions."

As I cast about for some means of escape, I catch sight of Arthur hovering nearby, apparently waiting his turn to speak to me. Another awkward conversation with Mr. Evensong seems more to be dreaded than the one to which I am currently captive. Therefore, pretending not to notice him, I return my attention to Mrs. Oddbody with a plan in view.

"Oh, Bath!" I exclaim. "I could go on and on about the beauty and style of the place, Mrs. Oddbody. And the fast-paced society. I daresay, some of the stories I could tell you about what goes on in that town would stand your hair on end. We are both going in the same direction, are we not? Let us walk together…"

With a running narrative on Bath, embellished enough to hold the old lady's interest, I keep other subjects, and Arthur, at bay. His own home being in the opposite direction, he can hardly persist in trailing after us like a stray dog; he has little choice but to give up the attempt altogether.

"…And here you are at home again, Mrs. Oddbody. Goodbye," I say, beginning to move off.

"But you have not yet told me about your young man, Miss Walker. Come in and take tea with me, my dear, so we may continue our little chat."

"I thank you kindly, Madam, but I must get home to my family. It is Christmas, after all. Another time perhaps." I hurry along before she can raise any further objection. With a peek behind to reassure me that no one else follows, I rejoin my parents and brothers for the remainder of our way.

"That was very charitable of you, Jo, to humor Mrs. Oddbody for so long," says Mama. "I daresay she is as good-hearted a creature as ever lived, but she does try one's patience with her constant chatter. And I have never known her equal for poking her nose into other people's business. I hope she has not wheedled any secrets out of you, my dear."

"No. Doubtless she shall have her earful of news before too long, but she'll not have it from me for a Christmas present."

~~*~~

Our family party passes the afternoon quietly at home with no interruption from outside. Dinner is kept simple, most of it having been prepared in advance to lighten the servants' duties in honor of the holy day. Mama and I – neither of us a great talent – take turns at the pianoforte to add to the festivities. Still, the gathering is not spirited enough for her taste.

"At times like this, I do so wish we had a larger family, my dear," she laments to my father. "Now your brother is gone, it is only we five together on such occasions. We are become too quiet and sedate. What we need are children about us to provide a little noise and disorder, to make us sit up and take notice. That would be the very thing. I often think that I should have liked to have had one or two more to keep us company in our later years."

"'Tis too late now, I suppose," Papa says dryly.

"I should think so, Mr. Walker! I am afraid there is nothing to do but to wait for grandchildren."

Tom, just returning from the next room, hears the last. "Grandchildren? Is that not a bit premature? You will be a very long time waiting indeed if you have any such ideas with regard to me. Fred, here, is your man, but you must first find him a wife, Mama."

"I am quite capable of finding a wife for myself, I assure you," says Frederick.

"Really? You have shown very little aptitude thus far, I must say," Tom rejoins. "Have you a promising candidate for the office secreted away in Surrey? Ah, it is the curate's spinster sister, no doubt. Miss Claudia Summeride – once considered a great local beauty, I believe. How long has she been such a favorite? And pray, when am I to wish you joy?"

"Miss Summeride is not the woman. I will tell you that much. The rest is none of your affair," Frederick says, unperturbed.

"As you say, dear brother. Nevertheless, I shall have my eye upon you."

My mother intervenes. "That will do, Tom. Leave poor Fred alone. And I do not see why he should necessarily be the first to marry. You will be very well set up yourself soon – ordained and installed as the rector of Millwalk parish in a few months. Any young woman will be proud to have you then."

"Thank you for that fine endorsement, Mama. I will not deny that it is a very good living. Nevertheless, I cannot countenance the idea of settling down to be a country parson. Not yet. There is still so much I want to do first."

"What grand plans might you have, little brother?" inquires Frederick.

"If you must know, I wish to travel and to learn more about the world; to see the pyramids of Egypt; to explore the Roman Coliseum, the canals of Venice, the Parthenon and the Acropolis – all the great monuments of human civilization."

"You see, Tom has a private passion for architecture," I explain. "I heard him speak quite eloquently on the subject in Bath."

"Is that what you would do with your life if you could have your own way?" Papa asks him. "Would you choose to build houses and plan cities rather than serve God?"

"Surely not," says Mama.

"I would do both together if I could. An architect can serve God just as well as a clergyman, I believe. But have no fear. I shall never have the option to choose. I must take the living that has fallen to me and be grateful for it. To pursue any other course would require capital that I have not got. I only wish to experience a little more of what the world has to teach me before I take up my post. That is all."

From here, the conversation moves on to other things. Later, however, Frederick reopens the topic. "I say, Tom, perhaps you can do both after all," he remarks thoughtfully.

"What do you mean, sir? I have not the pleasure of understanding you. Of what are you talking?"

"I speak of your wish to practice architecture as well as serve God. Perhaps there is a way for you to do both at Millwalk. I have a mind to make some improvements to the estate. What would you say if I were to put you in charge of them?"

For a moment, Tom is quite speechless, but I take up the plan at once. "What an inspired idea, Fred! Tom, you could do it. I am sure you could."

"Well, I would certainly like to try. I never thought to have such a chance come my way. I must say, it is very decent of you, old fellow."

"I'm not promising, mind. You get some plans together and we shall see. If all turns out well, I might be in the position to send a little more work of that kind your way now and again."

Tom and Frederick continue with their heads together on the subject for the better part of the evening – the young squire describing the improvements he has in mind, the would-be architect asking questions and taking copious notes. With his intimate knowledge of the estate and a vivid imagination to assist him, Tom obviously has no trouble picturing each of the projects before and after the proposed modifications. He begins spouting ideas at once for how to go about the work and what the finished product will look like. In his enthusiasm, he proposes to begin his research immediately upon returning to Oxford, and to bring drawings of his plans to Millwalk at Easter.

"Take care, Tom. You cannot afford to jeopardize your ordination by neglecting your other studies," my father cautions. "This idea of Frederick's is all very well, but you must still look to the church to earn your daily bread."

25

Goodbyes and Correspondence

Our whole family makes a repeat visit to the Pittmans a few days later. They fare much the same as they did before: Mrs. Pittman wears a worried, vacant expression; her husband seems ill-at-ease in his own skin; Agnes continues as listless as before, with her siblings in somewhat better condition. Although Frederick goes out of his way to be agreeable, and Tom, who is always quick with a joke, does his best to lighten the general mood of the gathering, it is to no avail.

As we make ready to go after an extended stay, Tom informs the Pittmans, "Unfortunately, I will be unable to call on you again for some time, as Arthur and I return to Oxford tomorrow. But doubtless he has informed you of that himself."

"No, indeed," says Mrs. Pittman. "We have not seen the dear boy since before Christmas. I wonder that he stays away so long, but I suppose he has been much occupied at home with his mother's health being so delicate. I expect we shall see him before he goes, however. He would not leave without saying goodbye to you, Agnes."

Agnes lets the remark pass without comment. Her parents still know nothing of the falling-out between her and Arthur. Her low spirits raise no suspicion, since they can reasonably be attributed to the same business that oppresses the rest of the family.

I give my friend a sympathetic look and an embrace. "I shall come again in a day or two," I promise her.

Witnessing Agnes's overpowering woe helps me regard my own troubles as trifling by comparison. Not a day passes without many minutes spent anguishing over Richard, yet in truth, I feel much sorrier for my friend, with her limited inner resources, than for myself. I am the strong one. It is accepted between us without apology or reproach on either side. Hence, years ago I fell into something akin to a maternally protective role with Agnes. I like taking care of her; I consider it a privilege granted by virtue of my greater natural fortitude. Although it was out of my power to prevent the damage in this case, I am determined to supply whatever consolation my loyal service can afford her.

The next morning, Arthur calls at Fairfield to collect Tom for their return to Oxford, just as he did before Michaelmas term. How different are my sentiments on this occasion. Then, I welcomed the chance to spend a few minutes with him, and regretted his departure. Now, Arthur cannot be gone soon enough to suit me. I would avoid him altogether if I could. However, for me to refuse to see him would alert everyone that something is amiss, which Agnes still wishes to avoid doing for the time being. So I join the others in the drawing room with the resolution to be civil to him, but no more than civil. I do not speak unless spoken to, and my every glance in Arthur's direction I carefully transmute into an icy glare.

Although I have had several days to become accustomed to the alteration, I still find this forced coldness painful. Deeply embedded bonds of friendship are not rent asunder without a bitter sting, I find; each one tears away a little part of me as it crumbles. I know Arthur is not insensible to the change in my demeanor, which he astutely attributes to the proper cause, as I soon discover.

When he and Tom have made their good-byes and are ready to go, he takes me by surprise, saying, "Jo, it is a fine day. Will you not accompany your brother and me outside, to see us off as you have done so many times before?"

I stammer, vainly searching for a reasonable excuse to decline.

"Come along, Jo," Tom cajoles. "Give in gracefully. Do not make us beg. After all, it has become something of an honored tradition, you taking up your post on the porch to see us ride away. You cannot deny us this small favor when we shall be deprived of home and of your company for months to come."

I have no alternative but to comply, so I take my wrap and follow them. Once outside, though, Tom makes an excuse to return to the house for some supposedly forgotten detail, leaving me alone on the porch with Arthur. The awkward situation now made infinitely worse, I turn from him, pondering a strategic retreat.

"Pray, do not run away, Jo," Arthur hastens to say. "In consideration of our longstanding friendship, I beg you would listen to me for one minute. Let me speak my peace, and then you shall be rid of me."

I remain, but I steel my heart against whatever he may say, lest I be completely taken in again.

With my implied consent, he continues. "I know what you must think of me. I believe I can guess what Miss Pittman has told you, and no doubt you have accepted her interpretation without question. Your loyalty and devotion to your friend do you credit. Indeed, I would have expected nothing less of you. I am glad for her sake that Agnes has such a champion beside her now. Despite what you probably believe, I do wish her well and happy.

"Jo," he says with infuriating tenderness. "I value your friendship more than I can say. To have lost your good opinion, even temporarily, pains me deeply. Nevertheless, I will not force upon you an explanation that I fear would only distress you further. I am patient; I choose to forbear. God willing, in time both you and Agnes may see things differently. I shall trust to that eventuality for my vindication. In the meantime, I pray you will not judge me too harshly. Well…"

While he stands, as if meaning to go, but not going, I sense he is waiting for some sign of encouragement. I stubbornly refuse to give it, denying him the comfort that a single word or look might supply.

"Well…" he says again as Tom reappears. "I must be off. Goodbye, Jo, and God bless you."

Tom kisses my cheek, and then he and Arthur mount up and ride away. As in the other instances, I stay rooted on the spot until they are out of sight. I should properly be sorry to see my brother go, but I feel only relief that Arthur's unsettling presence is not likely to trouble me again, at least not until Easter. The more time and distance between us, the better. I still find it impossible to reconcile my past regard for Arthur with my current disapprobation. Each time I encounter him, the effort to do so leaves me more miserably perplexed than the last. No, complete separation is the only safe solution.

~~*~~

With Arthur and Tom now gone, life at Fairfield settles into a quiet routine. I keep mostly to home to avoid the curiosity of my neighbors who, whenever they do see me, are sure to inquire about the wedding date or when my "young man" will be visiting Wallerton. Perhaps it is my imagination, but it seems to me, from their pointed questions, that a general suspicion of my trouble has already been aroused. Since the whole story will come out eventually, I would prefer to publish the truth of the matter at once – declare it in the town square and have done – rather than be left perpetually at the mercy of rumor and innuendo. Yet, since we have been advised to postpone any such announcement as long as possible, I must keep up the pretense that all is well.

I quite deliberately submerge my own troubles beneath the work of ministering to Agnes, making it my first project to see to it that she is weaned from the mind-numbing laudanum which Mr. Trask has prescribed to calm her. In its place, I supply liberal quantities of my own companionship, along with any other diversion I can contrive for her amusement. I read aloud to her from Mrs. Radcliffe's new novel and whatever book of poetry takes her fancy. We go for long walks in the garden when the winter weather permits. And I eventually manage to get Agnes interested in netting a new reticule. Frederick, who has postponed his return to Millwalk indefinitely, often accompanies me on these visits, contributing what he can to Agnes's entertainment. Her improvement is steady but painfully slow.

With Arthur safely away at Oxford, I resume calling on Mrs. Evensong as well. And all through January we continue to hope that the Grahams will come to add variety to our confined society. However, in the end, a letter arrives instead. In it Mrs. Graham confers the family's warmest regards along with their regrets at not being able to stop at Fairfield, their unwillingness to be separated longer from their younger daughters being sited as their reason for returning directly into Kent. A week later I receive a missive of my own from Susan.

My Dearest Jo,

Not a day goes by that I do not remember my friends in Hampshire with the greatest fondness. I wonder how you do, and how you are managing your cruel disappointment. I believe you to possess a particularly courageous character. So, I console myself by imagining that you rise above it all, refusing to give in to any serious despair. Am I right to think so sanguinely of you? Perhaps it is unfair to hold you to such a standard. You have as much claim to feel sorrow and as much justification to self-pity as anyone, I daresay.

Parting from you was trial enough, but there were more hardships to come. Mr. Ramsey and his mother followed you out of town immediately after Christmas. I wish I could report that the season stirred up the spirit of charity and goodwill in Mrs. Ramsey's heart, causing her to look with a friendlier eye upon a match between her son and myself. Alas, no such miracle took place and we are left with little hope that it ever shall. Yet George assures me that he will never give me up. He is so good, Jo. I cannot think what I have done to inspire or deserve such devotion. At all events, he has great plans for the future that do not depend upon his mother for success. He asks me to entrust my happiness to him, and of course I do with all my soul.

Our journey to Kent was a bit of a nightmare, what with the continuous rain, dirty roads, and not one, but two carriage breakdowns. You can imagine how glad we were to finally be at home. I was very pleased to see my sisters, who fairly squealed with delight upon our return. I do not doubt their affection, but I suspect their cause for rejoicing was somewhat selfish at the core. They longed for news of the outside world after so many weeks in comparative isolation. The late hour of our arrival notwithstanding, they could not be persuaded to retire until I related to them all my experiences in Bath. Mama and Papa have promised to take each of them thither in turn, when they are older. In the meantime, they are desperately envious of me.

Oh, how I miss you and our shared adventures in Bath. Despite the way things have turned out, I cannot look back on that time with any serious regret. I am certain that I was never so happy in all my life as in those short weeks there with you and our mutual friends. What excitement we had! It has taught me to be dissatisfied with the relative dullness of my life in Kent. Papa says that I may come to you for a visit before Easter, however. That and Mr. Ramsey's faithful promises give me much to anticipate with felicity.

Let me hear from you very soon. You must write to reassure me that you are well, and to inform me when I

*may come to you with the most convenience. My best re-
gards to all your excellent family.*

Devotedly, Susan

*P.S. - I thought you would wish to know that, before I left
Bath, Mr. Cox called on me to inquire after you and Miss
Pittman. Apparently, he had been round to your house in
Pultney Street first, but found you all gone away. He asked
to be remembered to you, should I have opportunity to
make such a communication on his behalf. And, judging
from the earnest desire he expressed to see you both again,
I should be surprised if Mr. Cox does not find some pretext
for visiting Hampshire before many weeks have elapsed.*

About the middle of February, another correspondence arrives,
this one not nearly so pleasant. Addressed to my father, it is from
Mr. Randolph Pierce. He therein outlines his grievances in the
most outspoken language imaginable. He writes in part, *"On
behalf of my son, it is incumbent upon me to remonstrate against
your daughter's outrageous conduct."* He goes on to describe his
complaint against me in these terms: desertion… unaccountable
dereliction of duty… calculated cruelty… trifling with a true and
loyal heart… the young man's emotional devastation… potentially
blighted future… insulted honor… etc., etc. *"Unless Miss Walker
is prepared to complete her marriage contract as planned, my son
will be left no alternative to taking proceedings against her in his
own vindication. Should the wedding date pass unconsummated,
you may be assured that the matter will be turned over to our
solicitor for prosecution,"* and so on and so forth.

Thus dies my hope that Richard would reign in his father's
thirst for litigation.

Papa puts the matter into perspective. "It is precisely what our
solicitor in Bath told me to expect. The demands, the rhetoric, and
the self-righteous posturing are designed to intimidate us. No one,
including Mr. Pierce, really wants the expense and notoriety of a
court case if it can be avoided. Still, now that the first salvo has
been fired, it behooves us to seek some professional advice in the
matter. There is no need to panic, but we must take all prudent
precautions, I think. I shall go to London myself and consult the
man who was recommended to us; I believe his name is Gerber.
Then we shall see what is best to be done."

The same as any sensible person wrongly accused, I feel the pressing need to defend myself, to clear my name, yet there is no way to confront my enemy at present. I find the only release for my resulting frustration in sharing it first with Agnes, and then with Susan in a letter. I write…

…Could you have imagined that it would come to this? I could not. It is inconceivable to me that I should be put in this compromised position by the scheming of persons whom we called our friends, by the collusion of the man who still claims to be in love with me. Papa soon leaves for London to seek out a solicitor who can advise us in the matter, and I hope to persuade him to take me along. We shall not be away more than a few days, however, so do come as soon as you can, Susan. I need my true friends about me now more than ever.

26

In London

My father at first objects to the idea that I should accompany him on his London undertaking, sighting the difficulties of travel and the disagreeable nature of the mission as reasons to spare me that inconvenience. "You had much better stay at home and let me handle this," he says.

"No, sir, I strongly disagree. I got myself into this muddle; it is my responsibility to discover the best way out. As you said before, it is my decision to make since I am of age. And you cannot dispute the fact that I am the only person in a position to give the solicitor a full account of what transpired in Bath. Besides, I had much rather be doing something useful than idly waiting at home. I am quite determined to go, Papa, and I promise I can bear whatever unpleasantness it entails."

Allowing the justice of my arguments, Papa ultimately relents.

I have been to London several times before to see my great aunt Augusta, a very formidable woman. This trip promises to be no more a pleasure scheme than those visits. It will be strictly business – no social calls, shopping, or excursions. We are to consult on our legal affairs with Mr. Gerber in Freeman Court, and then return home directly, which suits me perfectly well. I am in no humor for frivolity, and I do not care to be very long away from Agnes, whose spirits are still occasionally depressed. Fred's offer to look in on her whilst I am gone has relieved my mind considerably on that score, however.

It is my father's idea that Mr. Pittman should accompany us, in the hope that our solicitor might be able to help him as well, or recommend someone else who can. So we three travel together, and it is a comfortable if not lively party.

We arrive in London quite late and are met by Mr. Ramsey, to whom we sent word of our plans. Due to his familiarity with the part of town which concerns us, he engaged to arrange suitable lodgings for us there. After being introduced to Mr. Pittman and escorting us to the inn, he joins us for a light repast. It is very good to see him again, and I say so.

"I only wish we could have been brought together by more pleasant circumstances," he tells us in response. "The need for legal services is rarely a happy event, but you will be in good hands with Mr. Gerber."

"You know the man, then?" I ask.

"Oh, yes. He was my father's solicitor briefly, and he has proved himself a great friend and mentor to me since I began my study of the law. I believe you will find him an honorable as well as a clever man."

"Excellent. Yes, this is most encouraging," says my father. "Two recommendations are always more reassuring than one, especially where matters of consequence are concerned."

"I venture to say that Mr. Gerber will be able to advise you on any manner of problem."

"You have come to our aid as well, Mr. Ramsey," I say. "We are so grateful."

Papa adds, "Yes, do allow me to show my appreciation, Mr. Ramsey. Join us here for dinner tomorrow, if you will."

"Thank you, sir. You are very kind, but regrettably, I must decline. I keep terms at Lincoln's Inn, and I am required to dine there nearly every day. My holiday in Bath has put me somewhat in arrears with my studies as it is. I must keep my shoulder to the wheel from now on, for I am determined to make a success of it – for myself and for the sake of another who depends on me."

Before he takes leave, Mr. Ramsey wishes us success in our discussions with Mr. Gerber and promises to look in on us again in a day or two.

That night in my bed, as I wait for sleep to overtake me, I consider what the morrow may bring. From what we have been told, I have no doubt that Mr. Gerber is a highly competent man. But will he be sympathetic to my cause? My father has cautioned that there may be unpleasantness involved in the interview. Yet, in an odd sort of way, I look forward to the meeting since it will offer me the first chance to take a positive step in my own defense. The novel prospect of having a look inside the legal system appeals to me as well, although I believe I would much rather learn about judicial process in a less personal way.

~*~

Freeman Court stands not far from our temporary lodgings. When Papa, Mr. Pittman, and I present ourselves at the offices of Messrs. Gerber and Cobb the next morning at the appointed time, the clerk ushers us into Mr. Gerber's chamber.

"Thaddeus James Gerber at your service," announces the well-dressed gentleman rising from behind a desk piled with musty books of every description.

As introductions and opening pleasantries are passed all round, I eye the solicitor with uncommon interest. He is a spare man not yet in the prime of life – in his early thirties, I estimate – with a premature hint of silver distinguishing his temples. In contrast to my nervousness, he is completely at his ease, which immediately inspires confidence. His manner bespeaks a serious, business-like attitude, yet his face is not devoid of warmth, I note. Watching him, I soon believe that if I must reveal my most personal thoughts and actions to a stranger, I can trust them to Mr. Gerber with more security than to most anyone else.

"Now, Mr. Pittman, follow me next door and allow me to introduce you to my associate, Mr. Cobb," he says. "I have arranged for you to meet with him whilst I confer with the Walkers. He is a capital fellow and precisely the one to best advise a man in your situation. Will you excuse me a moment, Mr. Walker, Miss Walker?"

Once by ourselves, Papa whispers, "Well, what do you think of Mr. Gerber, my dear?"

"Not that first impressions are always reliable, but I am already disposed to think well of him. There is a certain wisdom and dignity in his countenance, and he speaks with appealing straightforwardness."

"Just so. I believe we are in good hands, as Mr. Ramsey said."

Mr. Gerber returns. "Now then, your friend is settled with Mr. Cobb, so let us begin. I understand this concerns a threatened breach-of-marriage-contract suit, an area of the law in which I have considerable experience. Miss Walker, if you are comfortable, I should like to hear your story from the beginning. Tell me how you met your betrothed, how your engagement was formed, and why you wish to break it off. I also need to know about your financial situation, which has apparently made you an attractive target for a lawsuit. Please make your account as complete and accurate as possible – no editorializing or demurrers. If I am to help you, I must know all the facts."

After a few moments to collect my thoughts, I start by telling him about my inheritance, which seems both the most logical and least perilous place to begin, since I know I can speak on that topic without excessive emotion. My father then presses my hand as if to give me courage to move on to the more sensitive subject of Richard. As I do so, Mr. Gerber listens attentively but unobtrusively, jotting down a few notes, nodding in understanding, and only occasionally asking for a point of clarification before bidding me to continue. When I am at last finished, I blot the dampness from my eyes and look up. "I believe that is all, sir, except that I think it grossly unfair that the law may choose to punish me when I am not the one who behaved dishonorably in this business. Pardon me if I am too blunt."

"You must forgive my daughter's outspokenness, Mr. Gerber. Naturally, she is a little overwrought by circumstances."

"No apology is necessary. I like the fact that you speak your mind, Miss Walker; you may certainly feel free to do so with me. I quite agree with you, by the way. The law can be an ill-mannered beast at times, but we must do the best we can with it. It is my job to see that, in the end, it does you no harm."

"Then, sir, you do agree to advise us?" my father inquires.

"Yes, for as long as you desire of my services. I must tell you, though, my style is very direct. I find it saves time, and it is the only way I know to go about my business. I hope that will be agreeable to you, Miss Walker." I nod. "Good. I felt sure that you would neither appreciate nor require coddling. I suggest we continue our discussion here tomorrow at this same time. I wish to give the matter more thorough study before I render an opinion on how we should proceed."

"Very good, sir. Until tomorrow, then," says Papa.

We take our leave of Mr. Gerber and find our friend waiting in the outer office, his business with Mr. Cobb already concluded. Mr. Pittman looks more cheerful than he has since his financial woes began. On the ride back to the lodging house, he speaks with guarded optimism about what the solicitor said of the possibility of recovering his property.

"...The upshot is that Mr. Cobb has promised to look into the matter for me. He says I must not let my hopes soar too high, but he thinks there is a reasonable chance that the villains who cheated me can be forced to make some restitution."

"That is good news indeed, old friend," Papa agrees. "I was sure there must be some legal recourse available to you. The culprits should not be allowed to get away with their booty un-contested. Let us hope Mr. Cobb is the man to give them a proper run for their money."

~~*~~

The next day, my father and I return to Freeman Court to hear Mr. Gerber's considered opinion. He wastes very little time coming to the point.

"To begin, Miss Walker, I must say that I believe sufficient grounds exist for bringing a suit of non-performance of a marriage contract against you. Or, I should say, they will exist if you fail to appear for your wedding on the appointed date. There is abundant evidence to show that a valid engagement was established between you and Mr. Richard Pierce, so that aspect of the case cannot reasonably be contested."

This comes as no surprise to me. I nod and he continues.

"However, there are mitigating circumstances which your barrister will argue should the suit ever come to court. For example, the brief duration of the affair weighs in your favor; Mr. Pierce can claim neither excessive monetary investment to be reimbursed, nor substantial hardship for a protracted restriction of his ability to find affection elsewhere. We can also assert that Mr. Pierce committed a fraud by deliberately concealing the true state of his finances from you, which goes to his presumed respon-sibility to provide for you and your future children.

"In my view, the plaintiff's barrister will have a ticklish situation on his hands. Should he argue that Mr. Pierce deserves compensation for being disappointed in his expectation of bene-fitting financially by his marriage to you, then he runs the risk of his client being deemed an unchivalrous cad at best and a calcu-lating fortune hunter at worst. On the other hand, should he claim that the damage is primarily emotional in nature, the danger is that the jury will judge his client weak and unmanly, and a large financial settlement inappropriate. Neither strategy alone guaran-tees meeting the burden of proof, and the two can hardly be argued together since they tend to contradict each other, if you see what I mean."

"That makes a deal of sense," I eagerly agree. "Surely any reasonable person would see the weakness of either argument, as you described."

"Yes, any *reasonable* person," Mr. Gerber says. "No doubt Mr. Pierce's solicitor, if he be a competent man, will acquaint his client with these facts. In addition, it behooves him to remind Mr. Pierce, as I do you," he says with particular emphasis and a solemn look, "that going to court is to be avoided for two very good reasons.

"First, juries are notoriously unpredictable. They are as likely as not to wholly disregard the logic of the arguments presented, ignore the judge's directions, and side with the barrister who puts on the best show, awarding either nothing or an excessively large judgment according to their collective whim." He pauses a moment for that news to make its impression. "And second, win or lose, one who is a party to this sort of suit may well come away dissatisfied. It can be a long, grueling process with costs counted not only in pounds, but in a heavy toll on one's dignity and peace of mind."

I shudder at the thought of such a dismal outlook. Seeing my distress, my father takes upon himself the trouble of responding. "Thank you for being so very direct on this point, Mr. Gerber, just as you promised you would be. It is for our benefit that we know these harsh realities in advance, I'm sure. Yet, that being the situation, what can we do about it, sir?"

"I did not say these things to discourage you. On the contrary, these 'harsh realities,' as you so aptly termed them, Mr. Walker, may be your strongest allies since they apply in at least equal measure to your adversary. He has as much to lose by a court trial as you do – less in monetary terms, perhaps, but more risk of damaging his family name. Consequently, I am convinced that, should Mr. Pierce continue to pursue the matter, his true goal will be to achieve an acceptable settlement without the pain, expense, and publicity of a trial. Our advantage is that we know it and can plan accordingly.

"At this point, I would advise you against making any response to the threatening letter you have shown me. It would seem that the senior Mr. Pierce is the driving force behind the idea of taking legal action. Yet you are free to ignore his tirades. He has no legal standing in the case. Only his son, as the allegedly injured party, has the right to file a suit. Should he refuse to do so, it will all come to nothing."

"If only that were possible," I interject, "but I cannot be so optimistic. I find it difficult to imagine that Richard will have the fortitude to oppose his father in this."

"Well then, we must be prepared for the alternative. With a sound plan in place beforehand, there will be no temptation to panic if and when you are served with notice of Mr. Pierce's definite intention to sue. His solicitor's letter will state his client's claims and stipulate a specific amount in damages. That is when the real negotiations begin. There can be a lot of wrangling back and forth before a mutually agreeable settlement is found. I will, of course, handle all of that for you, according to your instructions. Unless the two parties arrive at a complete impasse, the case need never come to trial."

"What do you recommend?" Papa asks. "I suppose Jo must be prepared to offer Mr. Pierce something."

"Yes, I believe that is the wisest path if you wish to keep out of court. It needn't be a huge sum. As little as a thousand pounds might well do the trick. After all, if he takes the matter to trial, he will have ten times the trouble and perhaps clear no more than that in the end."

I cannot help interrupting. "Excuse me, Mr. Gerber. May I be frank?"

"By all means."

I rise from my chair and pace the confines of the small room like a caged tiger. "You speak of claims, damages and settlements as if it is simply a matter of course. Perhaps for you it is, but not for me. In fact, it strikes me that the whole scheme is little better than a form of legalized extortion! Do not misunderstand me; the money is of minimal importance to me. It is the principle involved that is impossible to surrender. Mr. Pierce's bad conduct is responsible for placing me in this dreadful position. And now, on top of what I have already suffered, he threatens to drag me into court. Does such barbarous behavior deserve to be rewarded?"

"I understand your repugnance for the notion, Miss Walker. Obviously, you are a woman of high ideals, and I admire you for it. My own personal sympathies tend in much the same direction, I assure you. However, years of experience have taught me that survival often demands compromise. In the judicial system, taking an unyielding stand for one's principles can prove exceedingly hazardous... and enormously expensive. That is the plain truth. As your solicitor, it is my sworn duty to steer you away from such peril." He pauses and sighs thoughtfully. "Nevertheless, should you be firmly of that mind, there is another course of action you may wish to consider – a very effective but extreme measure. I hesitate even to mention it."

"Tell me," I demand. Mr. Gerber looks dubious. "You promised to be straightforward with us, sir. Now, tell me your idea."

"As you wish, Miss Walker. But let me first remind you that this is *not* a recommendation, only one possibility, and that I advise very careful reflection before taking such a drastic step. In the end, however, you must be the judge of whether or not it is the best solution. I am entirely at your service; I will do as you instruct me regardless of what you decide."

"Yes, yes, I quite understand, Mr. Gerber. Now what is it?"

"Well, Miss Walker, the surest way to prevent Mr. Pierce getting his hands on any of your fortune is to dispose of it before he has the chance. You can divest yourself preemptively. Whilst the money is still yours to do with as you like, you can give it away."

27

Home Again

Give away my fortune? What an idea! Such a strategy would never have occurred to me, yet I must acknowledge it has a certain appeal. The money has never brought me any joy, and the thought of Richard's father finding the cupboard bare after dreaming about its contents so long makes me laugh aloud. "Oh, to see the look on his face... It might almost be worth it, Mr. Gerber. You say it has been done successfully before?"

"Oh, yes. People go to great lengths to avoid paying a judgment, especially when they believe, as you do, that the plaintiff deserves nothing. I have known defendants in such cases to go so far as to emigrate, or even submit to imprisonment rather than give in. Although it is more common to hide or actually dispose of assets in order to keep them out of reach – a large bequest to a near relation, for example. However, I must state again that I consider such radical measures completely unwarranted in your case, Miss Walker, at least from a practical standpoint. In my opinion, Mr. Pierce's claim is not strong enough to endanger the bulk of your fortune."

"Yet you have also said that juries are unpredictable, and, as I have told you, it is the principle as much as the practical that interests me."

The discussion continues some twenty minutes more, the solicitor explaining various details concerning the legal process and the likely sequence of events in order that I should be fully prepared for every eventuality. No immediate decision will be required of me, as the wheels of legal process grind exceedingly slow. For now, Mr. Gerber charges me to give very earnest consideration as to how I wish the situation handled, to keep him apprised of any new developments, and to take no serious action without first consulting him.

That evening, Mr. Ramsey calls again, spending most of his visit in quiet conversation with me. "So, your business is finished here?" he asks.

"Yes, for now."

"And are you satisfied with Mr. Gerber?"

"I am satisfied that his counsel is wise and well-founded, yes. It is not the most pleasant news to hear, but I would not have thanked him for giving me anything less than the truth. He told us at the outset he would be direct, and he has kept his word."

"I am pleased to hear it."

"The quality of Mr. Gerber's advice notwithstanding, I come away from my first encounter with the legal system scarcely less ignorant than when I began. The little which I could understand, however, appears to contradict the very few notions I had entertained on the matter before. It seems the law has only a nodding acquaintance with justice and an even more tenuous association with common sense. I find it sadly disillusioning. Are you certain you can be happy pursuing a career as a barrister, Mr. Ramsey?"

"The law is a flawed institution, I grant you. Still, I believe reform is coming, and perhaps I shall be able to do my part. At any rate, it is an honorable profession and genteel enough to suit my mother. Of course, she does not intend that I should ever make a living at it. I can, though, if I am obliged to, and that gives me hope for the future."

"As we are speaking of Miss Graham ..." I say mischievously.

"Oh, were we?"

"Perhaps not, but I felt certain we were both thinking of her just then. Be that as it may, I had an idea you might like to know she is to come to me in Hampshire soon. So, should any chance occurrence or errand of business coincidentally take you in that direction, you may have the pleasure of meeting with her again sooner than you expected."

"Thank you, Miss Walker," he says with a warm glint in his eye. "I shall certainly bear that in mind."

~~*~~

I return to Wallerton with thoughts of everything I have lately learnt about my situation stirring round in my head. Thankfully, I have weeks to sort it all out, since the event that will seal my fate – the scheduled wedding date – is still three months off.

A letter from Richard has arrived whilst I was away, insisting on a more expeditious response. It says in part, *"I know you asked not to be disturbed, but you leave me no choice. I can tolerate this silence no longer. It is still my earnest desire that, in the end, you will agree to marry me in May as planned. Yet every day that passes without word from you eats away at that hope a little more. I beg you, Jo, put an end to this awful suspense. Have I not been punished enough? Come back to me and let us be happy together as we were before."*

Richard's words tug at my heartstrings. I find myself softening toward him despite my efforts to resist. He has done wrong, certainly. Still that does not mean that he is entirely without redeeming qualities, without any proper feeling. Perhaps he really does love me, just as he has claimed all along. In some ways, I should like to think so. Alas, I will never know for sure. Strictly speaking, his professions only establish that he would rather have the whole twenty thousand pounds by marriage than whatever fraction thereof he might realize in a settlement.

~~*~~

The next morning, I prepare to visit Agnes after my absence. Although I ordinarily prefer to walk the distance or ride horseback, today's persistent, unseasonably late fall of sleet demands that I commit myself to the carriage instead. On my way, I remember that Mr. Gerber has cautioned me against discussing my legal situation with anyone beyond my own family. However, I have little need to be evasive with Agnes, as she proves remarkably disinterested in the subject. Once she hears that the trip to London has been a success, she is satisfied and ready to move on to more interesting topics.

"I am glad to see you, Jo, but I have hardly had a moment to miss you, what with all my other visitors," she says with considerable animation, looking much like her old self again. "Your good brother has come every day, and Miss Ainsworth was here on Monday. And then, who do you think came calling Tuesday?"

"I haven't a clue."

"Mr. Cox!" she says, laughing. "Well, you needn't look so surprised. Miss Graham wrote you that he might come, and so he did. He claimed some business brought him as near here as Guildford, but I cannot help suspecting it was just an excuse. He sat and talked with Mama and me for nearly an hour. Then, at his insistence, we took a turn in the garden together before he went away. Mr. Cox asked after you as well, Jo. Perhaps you shall see him when next he comes, for he said he will call again that he might be introduced to my father."

"Well, I must say his visit seems to have done you a world of good, my dear. I did not realize that you cared for his company so very much."

"I am not certain that I do, but does that mean I cannot enjoy the fact that he apparently cares a great deal for mine? It is flattering to be liked so much, you know, especially after everything that has happened."

"Yes, of course, but take care, Agnes. The poor man may be falling in love with you. You would not want his broken heart on your conscience."

"I'm sure I should be very sorry to break his heart. Still, I never asked him to fall in love with me, did I?"

However, invited or not, Mr. Cox declared his passionate ardor for my fair friend when he called on her again a week later, according to Agnes's spirited report to me the next day. Apparently, after doing his best to ingratiate himself with her father, the young gentleman had once again taken her for a stroll in the garden. There he sought to recommend himself to her by expounding on the considerable scope of his worldly resources, and by elaborating on the extent of his love for her, which he allowed to be of equally prodigious proportions. Whilst the eloquent recital of his adoration did not fail to gratify, judging from the glow of Agnes's cheeks as she retold it, neither did it succeed in winning for him the object of that affection. Agnes turned down his offer.

Surprised, Mr. Cox wondered if she could be perfectly serious in her refusal.

She was.

Would she like to take a little time to reflect before answering?

Not necessary.

Could she at least give him leave to hope for a more favorable response at some future point in time?

No, she could give him no such encouragement, but would he like to stay to tea?

Not likely. Apparently the unfortunate fellow left the place at once, entirely forgetting to visit his other friends in Wallerton, of whom he always claimed to be excessively fond.

159

"Poor Mr. Cox," I lament after hearing the whole story. "I was afraid he had become too attached to you, Agnes. Were you not at all tempted to consider his offer? With Arthur out of the way, I suppose you are perfectly free to accept someone else."

"I am free, but I shan't accept the first offer that comes my way. Still, Mr. Cox has done me a great service. His proposal has taught me that I needn't despair about my fortune being now so small. As he generously pointed out, I have other assets which more than make up for it. If Mr. Cox is eager to take me, with or without a dowry, surely there will be other men of consequence who feel the same. I am bound to like one of them well enough to marry. Therefore, I am through being downcast over Arthur Evensong. I shall never forgive him for what he has done…"

"Nor shall I."

"…but henceforth I shall set my sights somewhat higher."

I cannot help wondering if Agnes's bravado is sincere or a mask for a heart still aching over Arthur's abandonment. Either way, her new optimistic outlook is a refreshing change from the low morale under which she has suffered these many weeks. "Yes, I am sure there are any number of fine gentlemen who would be proud to have you, Agnes."

~~*~~

When I return to Fairfield, I find Frederick in the parlor, reading the newspaper. He glances up as I enter. "Ah, there you are." Presently, he continues in an off-handed way, "How did you find Miss Pittman today?"

"In tolerably good spirits, I am happy to report. I believe she has turned a corner in her recovery. She begins to seem much more like her old self again."

"I am pleased to hear it."

He returns to his paper, and I take up my needlework. We sit together quietly several minutes until Frederick makes another casual attempt at conversation.

"Your friend took this financial setback very hard, I think. I have done what I can to cheer her, but I daresay she would much rather it was Arthur who came calling. I am a poor substitute, to be sure."

Since Agnes still keeps the change in Arthur's standing to herself, I take care in my answer. "I would hardly characterize the situation in that way, Fred. I know your visits have been greatly appreciated, and I believe they deserve at least a small part of the credit for Agnes's improvement."

"Well, if I have been of any service, then I am gratified."

We fall silent again, each of us attending to our own pursuits.

Finally, Frederick adds, "As you judge that my visits to the Pittmans have been of some little use after all, perhaps I should trot round tomorrow before I return to Millwalk. It is two days since I was last there, and I should hate to be remiss. What do you think, Jo? You know them better than I do."

"By all means. In such cases, it is far better to err on the side of giving too much consideration rather than too little. Besides, I truly believe the Pittmans would be very glad to see you again."

"Just as you say, then. I shall stop there on my way."

28
Visitors

Mama does not have an easy time parting with her firstborn all over again, having grown quite accustomed to him being back in the nest during his protracted stay at Fairfield. The renewed separation leaves her prone to fits of melancholy for the next week. Each meal during that same period invariably begins with a deep sigh as she observes his empty place at table. Indeed, I am sorry to see him go as well, more than I expected. The same stolid manner that renders him difficult to know intimately has made Frederick a reliable rock in the storm of recent events.

With him gone, I revert to making my visits to Agnes alone. Though the trend is definitely for the better, her moods still vacillate between her former despondency and her new-found confidence. Whenever her spirits are low, as they are this particular day, I cannot help remembering that Arthur is principally to blame. Still, since revisiting that subject can do neither of us any good, I direct the conversation along more positive lines.

"What a fine day it is, Agnes. I believe spring is nearly upon us at last. Shall we not walk into Wallerton? I need to stop at Colby's to buy some ribbon to trim out my new bonnet, and I could use your help. You know very well that your understanding of finery is far superior to mine."

"No, I could not possibly go into the village. Not yet. We had much better keep to the garden."

"Soon, then. We cannot stay at home forever, hiding as if we have something to be ashamed of. Let us not give the gossips that satisfaction; they mustn't be allowed to think they have beaten us."

"I suppose not," Agnes agrees half-heartedly. "Perhaps by next week I may feel up to it. Or someone else might assist you with your shopping. Your friend Miss Graham will be here shortly, will she not?"

"Yes, and you will like to see Susan again too, I'm sure. She arrives in a fortnight and is to stay through the whole of April. You shan't mind if she joins us on our outing to Millwalk, shall you?"

"Not at all. But there is another member of the proposed party whom I should very much like to see excluded."

"Arthur."

"Yes; Arthur."

"Well, perhaps he will choose not to come, to spare everyone that discomfort. Or you may be strong enough to bear it by then, Agnes. It is still a few weeks off, and you are improving every day. What a triumph it would be for you to show him exactly how little you care what he does."

~~*~~

The first three months of the new year slip away quietly with very few social engagements to disturb our routine at Fairfield. Our style of life is now decidedly retired. We entertain no company – a hardship for my mother – and what few dinner or card parties we hear of, we do not attend, either for want of inclination or want of invitation.

Unfortunately, this withdrawal from local society tends to lend credence to the rumors circulating about some trouble with my engagement to Mr. Pierce. My evasive responses to such civil inquiries as, "Have you purchased your wedding clothes yet?" or, "When shall we meet your young man?" no doubt contribute to the general curiosity. Gradually my neighbors stop expecting answers from me and begin supplying their own. That there has been a rupture is soon considered an established fact. So I am told by reliable sources. It seems the only question that remains in people's minds is which of us has made it; who is the jilt and who the jilted?

In due course, March makes way for April with its brighter weather and wildflowers blooming in the park. The advent of Spring also brings the promise of Miss Graham's arrival and the much-anticipated excursion to Millwalk. Yet the outlook is not entirely sunny. The weeks ahead hold at least two causes for concern as well. I will likely have to face Arthur at Easter with my feelings for him still in a state of considerable ambivalence. And what has been heretofore only a threat of legal action might well become a reality requiring a difficult decision on my part.

That issue has never been far from my thoughts since my trip to London. Whilst I busy my other faculties with purposeful activity, my mind wrestles with the all-consuming questions day after day. Dare I hope that Richard will defy his father, preventing the suit altogether? If not, how far should I go to avoid paying any claim? Should I trust my fate to a jury or take matters into my own hands? Is the money worth the trouble it will cause to keep it? In the end, might I not be just as happy without it? And, if I am honest with myself, I will admit there is still a small voice inside my heart that favors a yielding to Richard's request, not for money but for my return to his arms.

Meanwhile, Susan comes as expected, and a poignant reunion ensues. After a separation of over three months with only written correspondence to sustain our friendship, the first two days of her visit are necessarily given over to recanvassing in person all the events, thoughts, and feelings that the weeks apart have supplied.

"We have barely touched on your trip to London as yet, Jo," Susan remarks the second day.

"I am really not at liberty to discuss any of the particulars. At all events, you are doubtless more interested in my consultation with Mr. Ramsey than the one with Mr. Gerber."

"In point of fact, I have heard all about it in a letter from the gentleman himself. Still, I would be more than happy to listen to your report as well, especially if you take care to praise Mr. Ramsey a great deal."

"So you correspond with an unmarried man, Miss Graham? This is quite shocking," I tease. "Many a young woman has lost her character for less."

"As you know perfectly well, there is nothing improper about an engaged couple writing letters, and that is what we consider ourselves to be. Only Mrs. Ramsey would be shocked by that, and she needn't ever know."

"What about your parents?"

"They are far more understanding. I believe they like George nearly as much as I do myself. They will be delighted to see us married whenever circumstances allow."

"By which you mean overcoming Mrs. Ramsey's objections?"

"Yes, or failing that, we will risk her wrath and be married without her consent when Mr. Ramsey is established in his own right. Either way, it is bound to be a long engagement."

"Ah, but he is well worth waiting for, is he not? Shall I remind you of all his admirable qualities? You did suggest that I praise him a great deal."

But it is Susan who takes up the office of elucidating Mr. Ramsey's perfections, with which she is the one more intimately acquainted. According to her, his character has no rival for loyalty and integrity; his temper is mild as a lamb's; his nimble mind navigates the mechanics of the law and the subtleties of poetic verse with equal dexterity; and in the countenance and person of no other man does the ideal of understated male beauty more comfortably reside.

"And yet, to all this you must add one more enormously important quality, Susan: his excellent taste. For without it, where would you be? Had he not shown the wisdom to prefer you to every other woman of his acquaintance, none of his merits would signify in the least."

"True." We both laugh. "He is a prince among men, Jo. That is my honest opinion, and I make no apologies for it. Oh, if there were but such another man for you, someone worthy of you this time."

"Well, never mind that. I have sworn off men for the time being. After all, I had my chance. Mr. Ramsey was *my* dance partner first, as you will recall. Perhaps I should not have been so quick to give him up to you."

On the third day of Miss Graham's visit, we call on Miss Pittman together. After spending a pleasant hour renewing and improving the acquaintance, Susan and I announce our intention of continuing on into the village. Although every enticement available is brought to bear in the case, Agnes cannot be persuaded to join us.

"Are you sure that you are robust enough for such a perilous expedition?" I ask Susan in mock concern as we go on our way. "Consider carefully. By accompanying me, you risk being censured as soon as you are known in Wallerton. Although most of my neighbors can now behold me without severe agitation, likely as not I will give offence wherever I go."

"I am relieved to hear you joke about it, my dear. It is exactly as I expected; you have risen above your misfortunes. But really, is the rumor of a broken engagement the best this town can do for scandal?"

"I'm afraid so – no murder or mayhem to relieve the monotony. The Pittmans and I have done what we can, but it is meager fare at best for the true connoisseur. I shall have to conjure up something more substantial for the next course. A breach-of-promise suit… with a twist, perhaps; that should satisfy everyone's appetite. What do you say, Susan?"

"I say, God forbid you should be so accommodating! Let the gossip mongers find their next entertainment elsewhere."

Susan credits me with rising above my circumstances when, in truth, it is partly due to her encouragement that I have the confidence to do so. Together, we freely move about the town, making calls of charity and business. Somehow, I can better bear the looks and the whispered remarks of others with her by my side. Agnes, who has no strength, thought, or courage to spare from herself, is incapable of doing me that valuable service.

True adventures are more difficult for us to come by in Wallerton than in Bath; that is to be expected and not very much regretted. What amusement we can find, Susan and I are glad to share with Agnes. The real excitement, however, arrives late one morning in the form of an unannounced visitor: Mr. George Ramsey.

Upon being informed of the gentleman's presence, Susan and I are the first to join him in the drawing room. Mr. Ramsey has just enough presence of mind to greet me before turning his full attention to my friend. I am thrilled to see the couple reunited so happily – and by my means too – but I cannot help feeling myself an intruder almost immediately. As the hand-holding and whispering of endearments commences between the lovers, I wander across the room to the window, affording them a few minutes to themselves.

Their privacy does not last long; my parents soon enter. "Why, Mr. Ramsey," begins Mama, "what a fine surprise this is. We did not expect you. At least *I* did not. Perhaps Miss Graham… That is to say… Well, we are all very pleased to see you, I'm sure."

"Have you come on business or otherwise, Mr. Ramsey?" Papa asks pointedly, glancing between the young man and his lady.

"Business mostly, sir. I am here on a commission from our mutual friend Mr. Gerber. He asked me to give you this," he explains, handing over the portfolio he has brought with him.

Papa opens the parcel and takes a cursory look inside. "These papers must be important, requiring early attention, if delivery by a messenger rather than the post was called for. What were your instructions, Mr. Ramsey? Are you to wait for an immediate reply?"

Mr. Ramsey goes quite red in the face. "Nothing so urgent, sir. I confess I was rather looking for an excuse to get out of London for a few days. I let Mr. Gerber know that if he should have an errand or anything wanting delivery, especially to Hampshire, he should call on me."

"I see. Yes, of course. I understand precisely what you mean, Mr. Ramsey. So we may examine this material at our leisure?"

"Yes. If there *is* a return message, I shall be happy to carry it back to London in a day or two. I am completely at your service, Mr. Walker. I have taken a room at the Red Bull for the next two nights."

"So, we shall be seeing a lot of you in the meantime, I gather," Mama says eagerly. "You will join us for dinner, I hope. We have been sadly lacking in company at Fairfield since we returned from Bath, Mr. Ramsey. With both you and Miss Graham here, it will seem like a real party."

29

Anticipation

The agreeable Mr. Ramsey consents to stay to dinner and beyond, much to everybody's delight. No one could be more gratified than Susan, but Mama is also very well pleased – pleased with having a full table again and pleased with herself for her foresight in ordering such a fine meal even before she knew the young gentleman would be at hand to eat it.

Shortly after dinner, my father summons me to his library, whereupon Mama announces that she has household duties requiring her urgent attention. Susan and Mr. Ramsey, being well able to bear the solitude, are kind enough to excuse us all.

"You should study these papers for yourself, my dear," Papa begins when we are alone, "but in short, Mr. Gerber is asking for your decision. These documents will authorize him to carry out your wishes if and when he receives notice from Mr. Pierce's solicitor. As you will see in the letter attached, he does not require your reply immediately. However, if you are prepared, we can take advantage of Mr. Ramsey's offer to carry it back to London."

"I still have not yet made a final decision, Papa. I need a little more time."

"Of course. Such a weighty matter mustn't be rushed. A fortnight from now will do as well." He stands quietly by whilst I read through Mr. Gerber's correspondence, and then he remarks, "I collect that you have at least a tolerable grasp of this legal jargon, Jo, so I trust you are not overwhelmed by what you find there."

"Not exactly overwhelmed. The responsibility is sobering all the same."

"Well, you have already had benefit of my opinion on the subject. Still, if you wish to discuss it further…"

"Thank you, Papa. I have very nearly made up my mind. I only want to let the idea rest for a while, to allow it to settle into a firm resolve, to be certain I can live at peace with it."

"Then, my dear, since we can do no more about it at present, we had best get back to our guests. No doubt they have been very lonely without us," he says satirically.

When we rejoin the couple in the drawing room, my father seems unable to resist the temptation to have a little sport at Mr. Ramsey's expense. "Good news, Mr. Ramsey," he says. "There is no need to delay your return to London. My daughter and I have made quick work of the documents you so obligingly brought to us. They are signed and ready to go back to Mr. Gerber at once. So you will want to be off at first light, I should think."

The suddenly crestfallen young man is too bewildered for words. I come quickly to his rescue. "Never mind, Mr. Ramsey; Papa is only teasing. The papers are by no means completed, and you are to remain at Fairfield as long as you wish."

Mr. Ramsey breaks into a wide smile. "I am relieved to hear it, for I have already discovered a great fondness for this place. I should be sorry indeed to leave it so abruptly," he says glancing at Susan.

Mr. Ramsey spends the whole of the next day with us, and every effort is made for his comfort. I believe we secure his highest appreciation, though, not by attentiveness but by neglect, our chief accommodation being the way we find other occupations for ourselves to afford him as much privacy with Miss Graham as proper decorum will allow.

Unfortunately, Mr. Ramsey's commitments in London will not allow him to extend his stay. After a farewell call the following morning, he takes himself off as planned, leaving his dear Susan refreshed for his visit but desolate anew at having to part with him again so soon.

~~*~~

By now, weeks have elapsed since I received Mr. Randolph Pierce's threatening letter. I can picture his vexation at being so long ignored, and imagine the resulting arguments between father and son over what to do about it. My somewhat-better opinion of the younger Mr. Pierce leads me to believe he will offer at least nominal resistance to filing suit when the time comes. He implied as much when we last spoke in Bath and in his letter. Yet Richard is no match for his father, I fear. I have little doubt that he will ultimately relent.

In the meantime, I do my best not to dwell on that unhappy prospect. Susan is here to keep me busy and to prevent me taking my troubles too seriously. With her support, I venture farther and more frequently from home. We traipse everywhere together – calling on the Pittmans and Mrs. Evensong, shopping at Colby's, placing orders for Mama with the butcher and the baker in the village, and taking the air on the roads and footpaths round about. We even induce Agnes to break her seclusion at long last and join us on some of these outings.

Whereas it is too soon to expect a letter from Mr. Pierce's solicitor, we do hear from both Frederick and Tom concerning the forthcoming outing to Millwalk. They have settled the particulars between them and determined that it will be as well for the two from Oxford to travel directly into Surrey rather than first making a lengthy detour to Wallerton. Mama approves the plan, proposing herself as chaperone to accompany Agnes, Susan, and myself on the trip.

I relay the information to Agnes. "…So it appears that Arthur does intend to come after all. Shall you mind so very much?"

"No, not in the least," she declares haughtily. "My confidence grows day by day. It no longer signifies what Arthur Evensong says or does. I care no more for his presence or his opinions than for an indifferent acquaintance's. To object to the notion of seeing him would be to pay him too high a compliment."

"Bravo! I must say I shall be proud to see you put him in his place. As for me, I admit I would rather avoid him altogether. However, if you can abide his presence, surely I can. Your behavior shall be my guide. Do you still wish to conceal the fact that there has been a break between the two of you? I do not know what Arthur may have told Tom, but Mama and Frederick could have no idea of it, I suppose."

"I confess I did drop a hint about the alteration to your eldest brother last time he visited. Yet for your mother's sake and for the geniality of the gathering, I shan't make an issue of it."

"Then nor shall I. I can exert myself to be cordial to Mr. Evensong if I must. Let us hope he will make an effort to keep up appearances as well."

"If he is any kind of a gentleman, he will let it seem as though it is my idea that we go our separate ways. When the time comes, that is what I intend to say. That is what I told your brother, in fact."

The more we discuss the excursion to Millwalk, the more my anticipation increases for going. Agnes's excitement for seeing Frederick's estate, and her sanguine attitude toward Arthur, are contagious. Listening to her talk, my own expectations for success improve likewise.

I have pleasant memories of Millwalk going back to when I was a small child. My uncle always made such a fuss over me when we came to visit, calling me his "little princess" and giving me a bedchamber done up in keeping with the title. He stabled a pony especially for my use, which I rode near the house until I was old enough to keep up with my brothers on the bridle paths throughout the park. Millwalk is something of a second home to me, so much time have I spent there over the years. It will be good to see the place again, yet strange that my uncle will not be there to greet us on this occasion, or indeed ever again.

Two days before the trip to Millwalk, Mama orders the carriage and drives into Wallerton to discharge her errands. She returns just an hour later. "Jo, dear, get your things. I desire you should accompany me to call on Mrs. Evensong. I have just heard in town that she is unwell. Miss Graham will excuse you for an hour or two, or she may join us if she likes."

Susan, having just received a letter from London in a gentleman's handwriting, is perfectly content to remain on her own at Fairfield for the rest of the morning. So Mama and I set off without her. We find Mrs. Evensong in her cozy parlor, wrapped up warm near the fire with her maid Annette fussing over her comfort. She does indeed look very poorly compared to when I saw her Sunday at church.

"My dear Martha," begins Mama, "How distressed I was to learn you are unwell. When we heard, we came straight away. What ails you, old friend?"

"'Tis nothing alarming – just another bout of my usual complaint, Doris. The apothecary has been here and prescribed the standard physic, but I believe a visit from such friends as you will do me more good." A coughing spell interrupts her conversation. As we wait for it to pass, the maid offers a dose of medicine, which her mistress waves off. When Mrs. Evensong has recovered herself, she goes on. "I am especially pleased to see you, Jo. One likes to have the liveliness of young people always about the house."

"You have two of your sons with you. They must be good company for you, Mrs. Evensong," I suggest.

"Yes, I shall always have little John with me; he will remain a child forever. Robert, though, is very much occupied with business since his father died. He has grown so severe!" she says in good humor. "I declare, he is become quite an old man in his manner now. Still, I cannot fault him for that. The mantle of responsibility fell upon him so unexpectedly. Arthur would make me the best companion if he were not away so much of the time. I know it is necessary, but I cannot help feeling the loss most acutely each time he leaves."

"I often think," says my mother, "that there is nothing so bad as parting with one's children. One seems so forlorn without them. I miss my sons dreadfully, but a sensible daughter is a great main-stay. Jo is a real comfort to me. It looked as though I might lose her to Surrey, but she has changed her mind about that, thank heavens."

"Mama! The less said about that misadventure, the better. Besides, nothing has been officially announced yet."

"Never mind, dear; I will tell no tales," Mrs. Evensong assures me. "Although I daresay it is very selfish of me, I am glad to hear you will be staying in Wallerton. You are the nearest thing I have to a daughter of my own, and I should have been very sorry indeed to see you go away."

30
To Millwalk

On the Thursday before Easter, the carriage is brought round to the door at half past nine in the morning to receive Mama, Susan, and myself. We set off for Surrey in short order, collecting Agnes along the way.

Of the four of us, my mother may be the most enthusiastic about the much-anticipated excursion to Millwalk. For someone of her sociable disposition, being cooped up at home for three months together has been a severe trial. This outing constitutes not only her release from an unnatural isolation, but also a chance to see both her sons again. However, the real prize – the reason she most wishes to go, according to her own admission – is to behold her eldest comfortably established as lord of the manor. Her chance to witness that glorious spectacle lies only four hours and some thirty-five miles hence.

Having traveled the route many times before, I serve as guide to my two friends, pointing out anything noteworthy along the way. Yet nothing captures Agnes's particular interest until we are within a few miles of the estate. Then everything related to Millwalk takes on extra significance: the nearest serviceable market town, which she pronounces "adequate"; the tumbling river that parallels the road over the course of the last mile or two; and especially the parsonage, for the closer inspection of which the carriage must be brought to a complete stop by her command.

"So, this is destined to be your brother Tom's home," she says to me. "I must say, it seems exceptionally fine for a parsonage. I should not have imagined anything half this size. Indeed, I think with six or seven well-trained servants, one might be tolerably comfortable here. Do not you think so, Jo?"

"I quite agree, although I think the place could hardly support so large a staff as that. As for me, I have always been extremely partial to the house. It is too substantial to be called a cottage, and yet it has that sort of appeal, the way it is done up with window boxes and shutters all round, and the walls thick with ivy."

"The garden is delightful," adds Susan, casting an eye over the neat lawn and tidy surrounding shrubberies. "And listen... you can hear the river in the distance."

"A curate lives here now, since the death of the former incumbent," my mother informs them. "He serves as temporary vicar, holding the place for Tom. I daresay he will be very sorry to leave this house when the time comes."

"Yes, yes," I say, becoming impatient at the thought of Mr. Summeride. "Let us be on our way before we disturb the man. We are not here to call upon *him*."

Mama signals the driver to go on.

"I am glad to have seen the place at last," says Agnes. "Now, how soon shall we reach the Great House?"

"Just a few more minutes," I answer. "You will observe it on the left as soon as we round the bend and clear this fine grove of birch trees." All eyes strain for the first glimpse. "Wait a moment. ...There! Is it not an excellent prospect?"

Although the parsonage has been approved as charming, it cannot compare to Millwalk Hall itself, which far exceeds it in size and grandeur. The sight of the house across the expansive park immediately draws appreciative gasps and expressions of admiration from the two uninitiated on-lookers. Susan declares it "a very stately house" and Agnes swears it is "even more handsomely situated" than she had pictured from Frederick's description.

I am moved as well. It is a sweet view – sweet to the eye and the mind. Indeed, the elements combine to show the place to uncommon advantage as we arrive. A shaft of sunlight graces the façade, causing it to stand out nicely against the dark backdrop of a glowering sky. The white-fleeced sheep, scattered in random pattern on the surrounding hills, play up the pastoral setting to perfection. And, as the comfortable end to our long journey, we weary travelers cannot help but be pleased with the place.

Movement near the stables catches my attention as we approach; a groom is leading two saddled horses in. Tom and Arthur have just arrived, I surmise. My stomach begins to churn uncontrollably at the thought. I knew all along that Arthur would be here, and I prepared myself for seeing him. Why should I now be so disconcerted? Agnes has better reason for anxiety, yet she seems perfectly calm.

Upon alighting from the carriage, the others bustle up the steps. But I hold back, taking a deep breath to steady my nerves before following.

Susan waits for me on the porch. "Are you quite well, Jo? You look a little pale."

"Oh, yes. I am very well, thank you. Standing up suddenly after such a long sit has made me a little light-headed. That is all. I shall be perfectly fit in a moment."

Frederick greets each of us as we enter, his countenance clearly bespeaking both pleasure and pride at playing host. Tom soon joins in the welcoming party, whilst Mr. Evensong waits to one side. Agnes does not shy away from the inevitable. To my amazement, she walks straight up to Arthur, addresses him with dignified ease, and moves on. As I have pledged, I do my best to follow her lead. I only hope the prodigious awkwardness I feel is perceptible to no one else.

"Hello, Arthur. I trust you are in health."

"Yes, thank you, and I am gratified to see you looking so well, Jo. How are you?" he asks, studying my face.

"Never better!" I answer more blithely than I intend. Susan is at my elbow. "Mr. Evensong, you remember meeting my good friend Miss Graham in Bath."

"Yes, of course. Miss Graham, how nice to see you again ..."

With that, I abandon them. I am anxious to speak to Agnes, to be reassured that she endures Arthur's presence with composure, and to be reminded myself how I should behave. Yet it seems that Agnes needs none of my consoling; she had taken Frederick's arm.

"Miss Pittman has asked for a tour of the house," he explains. "Would anyone else care to join us? Miss Graham?" Susan is more than willing, and Mama goes as well, though she hardly needs to be made acquainted with a place she has spent so many weeks visiting before. No doubt on this occasion the novelty is to be found in the new proprietor's giving of the tour.

Only Tom, Arthur, and I remain behind, and I am already wishing I had gone with the others. But, remembering Agnes's example, I quiet the voice of doubt in my head and move with my companions to the drawing room. Having already established the fact of our mutual good health, a discussion of the weather and the state of the roads naturally succeeds. The men have made a dry but difficult ride from Oxford. Tom fears his horse may come up lame as a result. I likewise give an account of the trip from Hampshire,

and greet both Arthur and Tom from my father. With all the effort-
less subjects thus dispatched, a dreadful silence ensues until at last
I hit upon a new topic.

"Mama and I called upon your mother two days ago, Arthur."

"That was very good of you."

"Not at all. When we heard she was ill, we went straight
away." Seeing his troubled expression, I quickly go on. "She is in
no danger; only her 'usual complaint' she says. The apothecary
had been to see her and was satisfied. He left her some medicine
and told her to rest. Annette is taking very good care of her, I
believe."

"My mother's constitution is not robust, and I do not think she
has ever fully recovered from my father's death. So I cannot help
worrying about her when I am away. I have charged my brother
Robert with keeping me informed of her health, but no letter
concerning this latest turn reached me before I left Oxford. How
did she seem to you, Jo? Did she have much of a cough?"

"She did cough a good deal, but there was no menacing sound
to it. She was a little tired, perhaps, but in good spirits. We had
quite a cheerful visit."

"I am certain your company was a great encouragement to her.
She has a very high regard for you, you know."

"As do I for her, Arthur."

Talking about his mother just now, everything has reverted to
our previous pattern – two old friends completely at ease with one
another. It is our first normal exchange in months. But as I recall
more recent events, I immediately draw back and fall silent again.
The moment is lost, and the insurmountable barrier between us
reinstated. I read in Arthur's expression his disappointment.

Our attention is then drawn by the sound of laughter echoing
down the corridor from the east wing.

"If you will excuse me," Arthur says, rising, "I think I shall
join the tour after all."

When he has gone, Tom resurrects the conversation. "So,
Sister dear, I see you are still determined to hold on to your grudge
against poor Arthur. I thought perhaps you might have got over it
by now."

"What makes you think I hold anything against him? Has he
accused me of some injustice in that regard?"

"Of course not, but anyone can see…" He sighs impatiently. "Look here, Jo, I know Arthur has inadvertently offended Agnes and you have taken her part."

"You make it sound so trivial! Had you seen, as I have, how much Agnes has suffered as a result, you might judge differently. But he is your friend; I suppose I cannot expect you to side against him," I concede with annoyance. "You have had the story from him, and I suppose in his telling, Agnes is the one at fault."

"Arthur never uttered one word in disparagement of Miss Pittman, I assure you. In fact, he would not tell me a thing at first. Only after I badgered the unfortunate fellow with outlandish scenarios of my own invention did he finally think it best to set me straight. He told me that, seeing Miss Pittman apparently preferred another, he had attempted to free her from obligation to himself. She took it amiss. That is all I know for fact." He pauses. "However, the rest I may deduce easily enough."

"What might that be, Tom? By all means, do give me benefit of your vast wisdom and experience in these matters."

"Is it not obvious?"

I respond only with a blank stare.

"Goodness, how slow you are, Jo. Why, it is perfectly clear that he also prefers another."

"Of course," I say with disdain. "*That* is why he was so quick to break it off with Agnes. It makes perfect sense. Who is she, pray? Someone with her dowry still in tact, no doubt."

In contrast to my sharp tone, Tom adopts a teasing manner. "You have guessed it, Sister. I believe the young lady has quite a sizable fortune, although I doubt it much influenced our friend."

"Forgive me, but I find that impossible to believe."

"Nay, I daresay it is true, for the lady of whom I speak has many other attractive qualities capable of engaging a man's affection – to name them, wit, tolerable good looks, a generous disposition, and an excellent family."

"You sound as if you know her personally."

"Oh, I do. I have been closely acquainted with her for years, and it is inconceivable that she could have escaped *your* notice. Can you not guess who I mean?"

"Honestly, Tom, why you think I should be interested, I haven't the least idea," I say, affecting nonchalance. In truth, I can barely contain my curiosity. If Tom has known the lady for years, she must be someone from our home county, I decide. But

177

heiresses in the vicinity of Wallerton are scarce as hen's teeth. I study my brother's inscrutable face, and suddenly the light begins to dawn. "Oh, good lord! You do not mean me, do you? You cannot possibly think… No, Tom; I am wise to your game. You are up to your old tricks again, making mischief, as usual. Now, tell the truth. Arthur has never mentioned anything of the kind, has he?"

"Not one word. Still, I have eyes, haven't I? I see the way he looks at you, and I know in what high esteem he holds you. I doubt he would admit the depth of his attachment, even to himself, but he cannot disguise it from his closest friend. I know him too well."

"Oh, but it would be a disaster!" I cry, rising to my feet. "I pray you are wrong."

"Really, Jo, I am surprised at you. I rather thought you might be pleased about it."

"Pleased? I'm horrified!" I say, bringing my hands to my cheeks, which are hot with embarrassment. "Is it not bad enough that Arthur has most grievously injured dear Agnes? If it was in any way on my account, that only increases the crime, for it makes me an unwilling party to it. How could I ever reconcile myself to that?"

31

The Evening's Entertainments

Tom's speculation about Arthur's true sentiments shocks me. I hastily excuse myself to my room – the same lovely bedchamber I used as a child – ostensibly to dress for dinner, my real purpose being to find composure in solitude.

Arthur in love with me: an alarming thought! But is it possible? I do not wish to believe it. Yet, now that Tom has suggested the idea, my instincts tell me it may be true. His unfailing benevolence to me, even in the face of my deliberate coldness, I supposed to be evidence of nothing more than friendship and a generous nature. However, looking back, perhaps there have been subtle clues suggesting special affection – an expressive look, a meaningful word, a tender clasp of the hand – but nothing overt, nothing that cannot be explained by some other circumstance. And I would much prefer to attribute it to anything other than love.

"What an infernal nuisance!" I complain aloud to the empty room. It seems we digress from bad to worse by degrees. Still, no need to panic. After all, there is no definite proof. Until there is, I plan to behave as if I do not suspect a thing, despite what Tom has said.

Although I advocate calm, I cannot entertain the notion of going down to dinner with any equanimity. If seeing Arthur has been awkward before, it seems utterly insupportable now. Yet there is no evading it; I must face him. My consolation is that he knows nothing of what Tom told me. Nothing has changed according to his view. Therefore, I have no more reason to be self-conscious in his presence than I had an hour ago. At least that is what I tell myself as I make my way to the dining room.

There is Arthur, standing near the head of the table with Frederick and Tom. The three of them turn when I enter; all eyes upon me. I stop short, feel my face flush, and retreat with a stammered excuse about helping Susan and Agnes find their way through Millwalk's maze of stairways and halls. Only when I have these friendly reinforcements on either side of me do I return.

Frederick makes good on his pledge from six months prior. A fine meal – fit for nobility if not royalty – is spread before us. He has even remembered the promised fatted calf; the main course is indeed veal. With cordial conversation flowing freely round the table, I begin to be more at ease. Clearly, I am the only one who feels any constraint. I marvel at Agnes's unruffled demeanor. To see her now, one would never guess she had so recently suffered a broken heart at the hands of the very man who sits opposite, sharing with her a sumptuous repast and polite banter.

Mama revels in the party atmosphere, liberally contributing her own discourse to the liveliness of the affair. I, on the other hand, keep my thoughts mostly to myself, being primarily occupied with watching Arthur's behavior for any symptom of peculiar regard. Now that my senses are alert to it, the evidence seems everywhere apparent. Or is it only my imagination that whilst I discretely observe him, he studies me even more intently?

After dinner, when we reconvene in the drawing room, Arthur introduces a serious note into the dialogue. "Mrs. Walker, I understand from Jo that you visited my mother two days ago. I would be much obliged if you would give me your opinion of her health. If she is truly unwell, I should not linger here in Surrey for my own pleasure."

"My dear boy, your concern does you credit," she answers. "However, I truly believe there is no cause for alarm. Your mother is brought a little low, but no more so than on other occasions. I am confident that she will rally again as before. Her strength of spirit will carry her through this."

"I trust you are right, Mrs. Walker. Still, my presence might be of some comfort, and I shall not be quite easy until I see her for myself. Frederick, as much as I appreciate your superb hospitality, I think I must cut short my visit. If you will give me leave to go, I shall ride for Hampshire at first light."

"Of course, if you wish it," says Frederick, "but it will be a sad loss to our party, old boy."

Others join in expressing regret. Only Agnes and I remain silent on the subject.

"Well then, we must make merry tonight," says Tom, "whilst you are still with us – hold nothing back. I think a little dancing would be the very thing if we can persuade Mama to play for us.

We have just enough here to form a set of three couples. What do you say, Miss Pittman?"

"Oh, yes! Do let us have dancing, by all means," she cries. "It wouldn't be a proper house party without dancing. You will play for us, Mrs. Walker, will you not?"

"My skills are meager at best. But if you insist..."

"Then it is settled," Tom concludes, rising to escort his mother to the instrument.

"Capital idea," adds Frederick. "Arthur, give me a hand with this rug."

Just that quickly the plan is resolved upon and set into motion. Being as fond of dancing as most of my sex, I have no initial disinclination for the idea – not until, in a flash of enlightenment, I realize what will happen next.

As Mama begins to play, Frederick leads Susan to the floor. Agnes, taking Tom's arm, instructs Arthur, "You must be Jo's partner tonight, for she cannot possibly dance with either of her brothers. It wouldn't be at all suitable."

"Of course. It will be my pleasure," he says. Before I can do anything to avert it, Arthur advances toward me, hand outstretched.

"Thank you," I tell him, "but... I really do not care to dance."

"Come, come, Josephine!" exclaims Agnes. "You must join us for we cannot attempt a dance with less than three couples. You know very well that such a thing is quite impossible."

"You see our desperate situation, sister dear," says Frederick. "I am afraid we simply cannot spare you. You must relent or we shall be obliged to give up the scheme entirely."

I direct a pleading look at Tom, but help comes from a completely different quarter.

Arthur declares, "It is not fair to urge her in this manner. Let her choose for herself as well as the rest of us. If Jo is opposed to dancing tonight, surely we are capable of finding some other source of diversion."

"No, Arthur," I interrupt. "Thank you, but it's all right. I have no serious objection, and it would be selfish of me to spoil everyone's pleasure."

"Well, if you are quite certain..." He offers his hand again. This time I take it.

I have accepted that same steady hand dozens of times before, but always in friendship. Everything is irrevocably altered now.

For me, Arthur has changed over the course of the last three months from friend to foe, and as of tonight, unwelcome admirer. No wonder, then, that I sense an unfamiliar charge when our fingers meet this time. It gives me an odd, unsettled feeling in the hollow of my being as I rise to take my place opposite him. Fortunately, with only three couples, there will be little standing about or opportunity for conversation; the less time I have to stare across at Arthur, the better.

The first dance is a lively reel, and the one that succeeds it, nearly as demanding. Tom and Frederick then switch partners. For me, no change is possible; I dutifully carry on with Arthur when we resume, continuing thus until I am quite exhausted. Frederick, who looks rather done in himself, diplomatically calls for an intermission "that the ladies might receive benefit of rest and refreshments."

"I remember well the last time I had the pleasure of dancing with you, Jo," Arthur comments in a low voice.

"In Bath. Yes, how different things were then."

"Indeed. That night you thought *me* the reluctant partner. Tonight it is you yourself who does not care to dance. I am sorry you have been placed in such an uncomfortable position. Still, it is good of you to put up with my company for the sake of the others."

"I do it for Agnes, of course. She loves to dance, and I would endure anything, no matter how disagreeable, for her sake."

My cutting words take immediate and devastating effect. Although I fully meant to wound him, the pain I see in his eyes gives me no satisfaction. For a moment, we stand mutely staring at one another before Arthur brakes away. "Excuse me," he says quietly.

"Wait, Arthur…" But it is too late; he is already addressing the others.

"I need to make an early start of it in the morning, so I must leave you all now, which is likely to be regretted by no one so much as by myself. Although I suppose it means that the dancing is at an end. For that, I do apologize. Mrs. Walker, I am much obliged to you. Frederick, thank you once again for your hospitality. Good night everyone." With a curt bow, he turns to go, despite the protestations of his friends.

Although I suffer lingering qualms over the manner of our parting, the rest of the company recovers from the disappointment of Arthur's early departure soon enough. Tom calls for more music. He cannot persuade me, but both Susan and Agnes consent to play. Later, Mama proposes that the card table be set out for loo, the pursuit of which constitutes the balance of the evening's entertainments.

After we at last part company for the night, I steal to Agnes's room and tap lightly on the door. She lets me in. "Why, Jo, what do you do here?" she asks.

"I could not rest without speaking to you. I need to be convinced that you are well. You bore Arthur's presence bravely, but it must have been a great strain on you to keep your countenance under such admirable control."

"My dear, I told you I no longer care what he says or does."

"I know that is what you claimed, but I confess I doubted your sincerity. I believed it no more than a boast to keep up your courage. Now then, tell me honestly, are you as indifferent to him as you evinced tonight?"

"'Tis not so much that I am indifferent to what has passed between us. That can never be. What is more to the point, I refuse to let him triumph over me." There is a lilt in her voice as she continues. "Besides, I found everything else today so much to my liking that I could almost forget he existed. This house is divine; your mother and Susan so affable; and as for the kind attentions of your brothers… Well, let me just say that I do not think I could ever be miserable in such pleasant surroundings." She begins to dance across the room. "So, what care I for Arthur Evensong?"

"Extraordinary. It seems I might have spared myself a great deal of worry on your account."

"Yes, you might have done, had you only believed me before! Now you may at least sleep easy tonight, and Arthur will be gone in the morning."

"So much the better."

32
Plans for Improvements

How I wish that I could more speedily adopt Agnes's philosophy for dealing with my feelings about Arthur. Whereas my friend has successfully resolved that what he has done will spoil neither her current enjoyment nor future plans, I can boast no such emotional detachment. Had he not seemed such an icon of uprightness to me in the past, perhaps Arthur's downfall would not continue to grieve me so. As it is, I remain sorely disconsolate on the subject with no remedy in sight.

Such reflections as these keep my mind occupied until sleep at last overtakes me. I awake quite early the next day to take up the same chain of thought again. Upon hearing some noise outdoors, I slip from my bed, cross to the window, and draw the heavy damask drapery aside a few inches. Every room on the west front looks across a lawn to the beginning of the avenue immediately beyond tall iron palisades and gates, although these are indistinct at present. It has rained during the night, and a heavy morning mist blankets the ground rendering every distant article in ghostly guise.

The objects close at hand I can discern clearly enough. A horse and two figures – Mr. Evensong and a stable boy – converge on the drive. Arthur mounts up and takes one last look at the house. For a moment, I think he might see me, though if he does he betrays no sign of it. After a parting word to the lad, he sets off and is soon swallowed up by the fog.

As I watch him disappear, I remind myself what a relief it will be to have Arthur – and the inner turmoil he creates for me – gone from Millwalk. Yet the way we parted last night continues to trouble me. My conscience accuses me of deliberate cruelty. With the subsequent assurance of Agnes's well-being in view, my rudeness to him now seems unnecessarily harsh. Still, if it serves to discourage him from cherishing any unrealistic hopes about me, perhaps insolence has been the wisest, and ultimately kindest, course. In any case, it is over and done – no sense in beating the thing dead when it cannot be changed.

I go about my morning toilet slowly. There is no need to hurry downstairs; the others, in all likelihood, are not yet stirring. A faint rap on my door soon gives evidence of at least one exception. I open to find Susan standing there in her dressing gown.

"May I come in?" she asks in little more than a whisper. "I could not sleep, so I thought I would take a chance that you might be awake as well."

"Of course. Come in, by all means. I hope you are not ill or that you find your accommodations uncomfortable."

"No, not at all. I rarely sleep well the first night in a new place. That cannot be the origin of *your* restlessness though; you have been here countless times before."

"True, and yet never under these peculiar circumstances. Ah, well, the cause of the variance is now gone, so we may all be more at our ease today."

"A peculiar variance? Is that how you think of Mr. Evensong? I might call him many things, but never that. Still, if his presence upsets you, then I am glad he is gone."

"Oh, Susan, you are only aware of half the story. You know that I cannot forgive him for abandoning Agnes. Now the plot has taken another turn, and for the worse, I'm afraid. I have to tell somebody, but my dear, you must not breathe a word of this, especially not to Agnes."

"What on earth…"

I pull Susan over to sit beside me on the bed. "My brother Tom believes Arthur – oh, I can scarcely bring myself to say the words – that Arthur has thrown Agnes over because he cares for me!"

"Is that what he told you? No wonder, then, that you have been so little like yourself."

"So you can appreciate my vexation."

"…and the awkwardness of your situation, yes. The assertion that Mr. Evensong cares for you, I can well believe. I suspected as much myself. As for the rest, I should not hazard an opinion. In my experience, venturing to ascribe motives to another person's behavior is a singularly perilous undertaking. I believe we have both fallen victim to that sort of error."

"How do you mean?"

"In my case, Mrs. Ramsey accused me of wishing to marry her son to improve my financial and social position. When in truth, I would gladly take him if he were as poor and insignificant as a church mouse."

"And in my case, the reverse is true," I continued for her. "I believed Mr. Pierce pursued me out of love, and his true purpose turned out to be avarice. I see what you mean."

"Yes. I am sorry, Jo. Perhaps I should not have reminded you."

"It does not signify. Although it still pains me to think of him, I am quite reconciled to the loss of Mr. Pierce. Yet how can you compare that gross error in judgment to this business with Arthur? The situations are so dissimilar."

"I only mean that it is just as likely you are mistaken in this case as in the other. Then you assessed a gentleman's motives too charitably and now, perhaps…"

"…too severely? You must think me a blind fool and a dreadful judge of character."

"No, indeed I do not. Yet we, none of us, can be objective where our hearts are involved. I simply fear yours has become too much entangled in this quarrel between your friends for clarity. I doubt that the case is as straightforward as it was represented to you, for rarely is one person solely to blame in a dispute and the other completely innocent. Mr. Evensong is probably no more a black-hearted villain than Miss Pittman is a saint."

~~*~~

At breakfast, Mama reminds us that the day is Good Friday. "In light of that fact, I propose that we should have a small service tonight. You remember that it was always your uncle's custom to assemble everyone in the chapel for evening prayers. It would please me very much to honor that tradition. Tom, I would be obliged if you would lead us."

"I am not prepared," he protests.

"It needn't be anything elaborate – a hymn or two, an appropriate scripture reading, a few thoughts from you on the text, and a prayer. That will do nicely. It shall be only we six plus those servants who might wish to join us. Such a trifling thing can hold no terror for you, surely. After all, not many months hence you will be responsible for much more than that every Sunday."

Further remonstrations fall on deaf ears; Mama's mind seems quite made up.

To his brother's suggestion that he reveal his plans for the proposed improvements at Millwalk, Tom responds with far more enthusiasm. After we finish our meal, he brings out his drawings, proudly spreading them on the table in the library for all interested eyes to behold. With the young squire at his side and the rest of us looking on as well as we might, Tom explains the carefully prepared illustrations.

"Here are the two tenant cottages. I think you will find the design consistent with your specifications, Fred. As you see, all the main living spaces are on the ground floor with a central staircase to the sleeping quarters above. Now, my idea is this. Why not build them both together – not just side by side, but attached? If one is made the mirror image of the other, they can share this main wall and chimney. The savings to you would be substantial and the tenants would stay warmer in winter for losing less heat to the outside. By the same principle, you could add more cottages on to either end as needed in future."

Tom next reveals his innovative ideas for the landscape transformation and the conservatory addition, the plans for which are likewise beautifully drawn.

"Very good. I like what I see," says Frederick. "Your designs prove you have vision and an artist's eye, Tom. But are the buildings structurally sound? Can we be certain they will stand the test of time and weather?"

"Oh, yes. I have done my research and made exact calculations. You needn't be uneasy, dear brother. I am not really such a great dunce after all. My failure to distinguish myself at Oxford owes more to want of inspiration than lack of ability. When I find a project that I can sink my teeth into, such as this one, I am quite capable of producing work of high quality."

"Well, I think your plans are wonderful, my dear," declares our mother. We all voice our approbation and questions, the further discussion of which occupies much of the morning. By noon, the sun has chased away the dampness, so we embark upon a pleasant walk in the gardens near the house, to take the air and to examine the sites for the proposed changes.

After tea, when at last the topic of improvements has been canvassed in and out of doors to the point of exhaustion, other occupations must be found. Whilst Tom closets himself in the library to prepare for the evening's religious observances, Frederick orders a phaeton and horses to drive the ladies all round the park. Mama excuses herself from this second airing of the day in favor of a little rest before dinner, but we three younger ladies are keen to go. Agnes, especially, takes in everything she sees along the way with interest and admiration.

Immediately following dinner, the whole party proceeds to the chapel, which is appointed in copious quantities of mahogany and crimson velvet. The sinking sun shines through the lofty stained-glass window, scattering red, blue and gold beams about the room, on the furnishings and occupants alike. Once we have taken our places, half a dozen servants file in behind.

Tom puts us through our paces exactly according to the formula laid out by our mother. We begin with an old standard hymn appropriate to the day, followed by Tom reading the account of the crucifixion from the twenty-seventh chapter of St. Matthew's gospel. He then adds a few awkward words of his own on the subject, and closes with a brief prayer. I know I should be focused on Christ's sacrifice, but through it all I'm thinking of poor Tom. I cannot help noticing that, despite his training, he wears the mantle of presiding minister with very little ease or natural grace.

The service having reminded us what the solemn occasion signifies, the rest of the evening takes on a more serious tone than the one previous. Gaiety seems out of place and dancing, impossible. Instead, quiet conversation fills the remaining hours before bed.

I seek out my younger brother's society. "What a triumph for you, Tom. It is not often that one has the chance to establish ability in both one's vocation and avocation in the same day. Well done."

"You are too kind, Jo. Although I did my best, my performance tonight could hardly be called a triumph. I fear I shall do little justice to the sacred office for which I am destined. I have no talent for it. Still, where the heart is sincere, I trust the service must be acceptable in God's sight."

"That is precisely what I believe."

"It is unfortunate that Arthur had to leave us this morning. He would have done a more creditable job at chapel, given the chance."

"Well I, for one, am glad he is gone. You did very well tonight, Tom. You needn't disparage yourself by an unfavorable comparison to anyone, least of all to Arthur Evensong."

33

Easter

Although the visit to Millwalk has been, for the most part, enjoyable, when it is time to leave the next morning after breakfast, I do not regret it. Mama comes into my room just as I finish packing.

"My dear, the footman is here to take your trunk if it is ready," she says.

I close and latch the lid. "Yes, all ready. What about Agnes and Susan? I wonder if they need any assistance."

"Susan's trunk has just gone down and Agnes finished long ago. Yours is the last one. We shall soon be off."

Going to the window, I observe, "We have a fine day for traveling. Apparently, Agnes could not wait to be out in it," I add upon noticing my friend strolling on the lawn with Frederick. "How well she looks compared to only a few weeks ago! It does my heart good to see it."

"Yes, you ought to be pleased with her improvement, for you have a good share of the credit."

"Nonsense. I have done very little – only what any true friend would under the same circumstances."

"You have a very high standard for friendship in that case. Nevertheless, I wish you to know that your charity has not gone unnoticed. I, at least, have seen it. It is all the more laudable since this service to your friend was demanded at a time when you were in want of sympathy yourself."

"Dear, Mama! You see only the good in me, but I am a very selfish creature. What I needed far more than pity was to be doing something useful, something to distract me from my own problems. Caring for Agnes was the best medicine for what ailed me, and to see her fully restored will be reward enough."

Mama and I proceed downstairs to thank our host and take our leave. Tom is already seated atop his horse, which, contrary to his earlier fears, appears perfectly sound. Frederick helps each of us into the carriage, and we set off.

"What an exceedingly pleasant visit we have had," sighs Agnes, taking one last look out the window before Millwalk is lost from view. "It is over far too soon."

"Take heart, Miss Pittman," says Mama. "It is a pleasure we can expect to have oft repeated in future, I should think."

"Yes, I depend on it," she replies.

~~*~~

Easter morning in Wallerton dawns in dreary shades of gray, thanks to the impenetrable clouds aloft delivering an unrelenting precipitation below. The spirits of those filling Wallerton church are dampened but little, however. Sitting with Susan, my parents, and my brother Tom, I look about myself at the crowd of familiar faces.

The full complement of Pittmans are present, I observe with satisfaction, but the Evensongs are lacking one of their usual number. Since Mrs. Evensong rarely misses Sunday worship, least of all on a high holy day such as Easter, her absence gives me real cause for concern. Accordingly, after the service, I determine to set aside my personal reluctance in order to ask Arthur about the condition of his mother's health.

The cramped quarters of the little church, filled to overflowing, offer scant opportunity for socializing within its walls. So, despite the inclement weather, the congregation begins spilling out of doors directly. Being nearer the exit from the start, the Evensong brothers preceded us thither. I have no choice but to throw myself into the current and wait for it to carry me out as well.

Once free of the press of people on all sides, I make straight for Arthur. He sees me approaching and hesitates, with the uncertain look of an injured creature wishing to avoid further abuse.

"Arthur, please wait," I call. "I promise I will not keep you standing out in this rain long. I only wish to inquire after your mother. How is she?"

"She is still quite unwell."

"Happy Easter, Miss Jo," interrupts little John. "Do you have a new story for me?"

"Good morning, my dear boy. No new stories today, I'm afraid. What should you like for me to write about next?"

"A cow! Make it about a brown cow... one who goes to school," he says laughing.

"Just as you like, John. And since it is your idea, you must name the cow, if you please. It must be a girl's name, you know, for all cows are ladies." John rolls his eyes. "Well, you think about it and tell me her name next time I see you. All right?"

"Yes, Miss Jo."

John runs off and I return my attention to Arthur. "I am exceedingly sorry to hear about your mother. Has Mr. Trask been to see her again?"

"Yes, he attends her every day, much good may it do her."

"Mr. Trask is a very clever man; he will surely see her through this. Please do give her my very best wishes."

"I know she would be far happier to hear them from your own lips. Call on her tomorrow if you will. I shall stay well out of your way, since you have made it clear how ill you can bear my company."

I drop my eyes. "That will not be necessary, Arthur, and I am sorry to have been so uncivil as to make you feel that it would. I will come tomorrow if I may, and I pray I shall find your mother a vast deal better by then."

"Yes, God grant that you shall." We linger in the rain until Arthur breaks the awkward silence. "Well, until tomorrow then?"

"Yes, until tomorrow."

~~*~~

At breakfast the following morning, I state my intention of calling on the ailing Mrs. Evensong without delay. Susan, who has no appetite today, elects to stay behind, feeling somewhat unwell herself. Mama says she will defer her visit until a later hour. So, with the weather agreeable and the distance involved – barely a mile and a half – no obstacle, I refuse my father's offer of the carriage, throw a light shawl about my shoulders, and set off on foot.

I see Arthur only briefly when I arrive and find his mother, to my very great relief, tolerably improved. She brightens when she sees me. "Josephine, come. Sit here beside me, my dear."

191

Going to her at once, I take her offered hand. "How are you, Mrs. Evensong?"

"I believe I am a little better, thank you. I ought to be for all the attention I have received. I fear I have made a great nuisance of myself lately."

"No indeed! It is only right that you should allow someone to take care of *you* for a change."

I encourage Mrs. Evensong to carry the conversation as much as possible. Not surprisingly, then, it tends very much to center on her three sons. She talks about her eldest, Robert, who is primarily occupied administering all manner of business for the estate, a source of both pride and regret to her. According to her report, he works hard to fill his father's shoes, yet his diligence leaves him little time to spare for his own mother and brother living under the same roof. Little John, who comes and goes throughout our visit, periodically commands our attention with his questions and needs. As for Arthur, Mrs. Evensong can scarcely say enough about him – his fine record at Oxford, his bright future, his attentiveness during her illness.

All these things I know already, and I bristle slightly at being forced to listen to a recitation of praises that I can no longer enter into with any enthusiasm. Still, allowances must be made for a mother's feelings, I remind myself. Mrs. Evensong's pride no doubt blinds her to her son's failings, and it is neither my intention nor my place to disillusion her. Fortunately, a nod or smile from me now and again seems to answer.

When I leave Mrs. Evensong, I decide to call on Agnes next. However, it is not only my friend, but the whole Pittman family I find assembled in the drawing room when I arrive. And although I am happy enough to make conversations with them all, Agnes soon grows restless and spirits me away into the garden.

"I have hardly ever had you to myself these few weeks," she complains. "And I am impatient to ask if you have any news concerning Mr. Pierce. Has he or his father made any attempt to contact you again, Jo?"

"No, I have had only the one letter from Richard and nothing more from his father, thank goodness. Nor do I expect to hear anything official until the end of May, when I shall be in violation of the marriage contract... unless I relent."

"Perhaps you should consider it. Nearly anything would be preferable to ending in court, I daresay. The scandal, the publicity: it is horrifying to consider!"

Agnes's latent curiosity takes me by surprise. This is the first time she has asked about my plans. "I quite agree with you there, and I will be at great pains to be sure that it never comes to that. Rather than suffer the indignity of having my private actions and character put on public trial, I would sooner part with every last farthing of my inheritance."

"Josephine, you mustn't even joke about such a disaster. Heaven forbid! How could you hope to make a good marriage with no fortune?"

I laugh. "I see you have no very high opinion of my other good qualities. I flatter myself that my prospects would not be quite as bleak as you represent them. Without my inheritance, I would be no worse off than I was a year ago. I shall still have my dowry and a little money from my mother as before. No honorable man will despise me for not possessing more."

Agnes shakes her head, sadly. "Poor naïve girl. Do you still expect men to behave honorably in financial affairs despite what has happened to you, to me, and to my father? Clearly, the last several months have taught you nothing."

"On the contrary. I have learnt to be more careful, but I have not yet been educated into a state of complete pessimism. You see, I am still unwilling to denounce the male sex entirely. And you? Surely you are not ready to give up on men so soon."

Agnes shrugs her shoulders and blushes becomingly.

"There, now. I suspected as much."

"You suspect a deal more than that, Jo, from the way you look at me. And I know what it is too. I daresay you have noticed your brother's kind attentions to me, and you think I might fancy myself the next mistress of Millwalk. Ah! You clever creature; that's very true. What a thinking brain you have!"

"You give me too much credit, Agnes. Although my thoughts did tend in that direction, they had not yet carried me so far down the path. But now you must tell me all! Is there an understanding of some kind between you and Frederick? Am I to wish you joy?"

"Not exactly, at least not yet," she says with a coy smile. "He did ask if he might see me when he next comes to Wallerton – to speak to me about something very particular, he said."

"Aha! That can mean only one thing. What did you say? How did you answer him?"

"I said that I should be only too pleased to hear whatever he had to say."

"Oh, Agnes, how heavenly. We would be sisters! Yet my own wishes are unimportant. What is more to the point, do you really care for Frederick? I trust you would not encourage him unless you are sure that you feel for him what you ought."

"I have not your romantic sensibilities, Jo, but I am convinced within myself that I like your brother quite well enough to be happy. So, should he make me an offer, I intend to accept him."

34

Engaging Miss Pittman

Mrs. Evensong rallies sufficiently that Arthur can return, along with Tom, to Oxford for the start of term, assured of her current safety. Shortly thereafter, I have a long, somewhat contentious discussion with my father concerning my wishes for managing the lawsuit, should it come to pass. Although we do not see eye to eye on the matter, he ultimately agrees not to oppose my decision. I pen my instructions to Mr. Gerber on the documents he provided and it is done. Now if the worst occurs, I am prepared.

Susan, who was originally scheduled to return to Kent at the end of April, successfully petitions her parents to extend her stay at Fairfield another month complete. We are by now accustomed to the regular correspondence she receives from Mr. Ramsey. One of these letters arrives on the first of May, and, although I am not privy to all its contents, my friend does share one portion of particular interest with me:

The most unexpected thing has occurred, Susan. You will never guess who has been visiting my mother in Mayfair: Mr. Randolph Pierce! I have it on the good authority of my youngest brother that the man has called on her several times over the course of the last two months. According to Kenneth, the two of them have become quite cozy. When I asked Mother about it myself, she was not very forthcoming. However, she did ultimately own that she began corresponding with Mr. Pierce on matters of mutual concern shortly after being introduced to him in Bath last winter. Apparently they share a common interest in politics, particularly church politics. I cannot help wondering what other interests may be drawing them together. Is it possible that my mother has a suitor? Good lord, what a thought! Miss Walker narrowly escaped

*having the man for her father-in-law. Now I could end
with Mr. Pierce as my step-father instead.*

"What do you think of that, Jo?" Susan asks when she finishes
reading this out to me. "Is it a good or a bad development? I cannot
decide."

"I hardly know. If love is truly in the air, I could see where it
might give both of them a more charitable view of others, which
could have a positive effect on both your situation and mine. On
the other hand, it is somehow unsettling to think of our common
enemies joining forces."

Another letter arrives, this one from Frederick, stating that he
plans to visit us at Fairfield shortly. Knowing what I do from
Agnes's confidential report, I doubt that it is his family that he
longs to see again so soon. My anticipation builds for the projected
outcome. How delighted I shall be to have my brother married to
my dear friend, and how much sweeter my visits to Millwalk
thereafter.

Frederick is every day expected. Then, before we have any
sign of him, Agnes calls one afternoon in quite a flutter of spirits.
Her countenance evincing a mixture of joy and trepidation, she
asks to speak to me alone.

"I have something to tell you, Jo," she says. "But first you
must promise you will not be angry. I couldn't bear it if you were
cross when I am so happy."

"Whatever makes you happy is certain to please me as well," I
assure her. I can see she is holding back some great mountain of
excitement. With a little more encouragement from me, it begins to
tumble out. She thrusts her left hand forward for my inspection.

"Look, Jo! Look!" she cries, displaying a sapphire ring of
stunning proportions. "It is an engagement present. Do you not
wish to know from whom?"

"I don't understand. Has Frederick already been to see you?"

"Oh, dear," she says with a pouting lip. "I suppose you *would*
think of your brother – a very natural mistake after our earlier
conversation."

"Mistake? What on earth do you mean, Agnes? Who else can
it to be from?"

"Now prepare yourself, Jo. You may indeed be surprised, but I
am going to marry dear Mr. Cox."

"Mr. Cox! What of my brother? He cares for you, and you led him to believe that you returned his regard."

"Your brother is very amiable, to be sure. And if he had been quicker to come to the point, I daresay I might well be engaged to him now instead. Still, with Mr. Cox being so very attentive... and so very persistent..."

"Oh, Poor Frederick. Did you have no thought for him at all, Agnes?" I ask in exasperation.

"See, now you *are* cross. I was afraid you would be. Yet consider my struggle. On your brother's account, I did try to resist Mr. Cox's offer. In fact, whilst he was proposing, I even pictured myself at Millwalk again, to give me strength. Until the last, I swear I had every intention of answering him the same as before."

"Then why didn't you?"

"Well... Mr. Cox can be extremely persuasive. If you had been there, Jo, you would understand my difficulty. Depend on it. He quite overwhelmed me with the violence of his affection. From the way he praised my character, I knew he was most sincere. He pointed out how well suited we are, and how he should make my happiness his life's work. He showed me this fine ring, saying it did not do justice to my beauty. Then he happened to mention that he will be a baronet one day. I believe that is when my determination to refuse him gave way. I was quite overcome, and before I knew what I was saying, I had accepted him!

"He wants us to be married right away, Jo!" she continues, "by a special license if necessary. And we shall live in his London townhouse until he comes into his other property and title... which may not be long because his uncle is exceedingly old, I understand. Think of it – Sir Phillip and Lady Cox! Oh, do say you will be happy for me. It really is for the best; I am certain of that now. Your brother will not regret me for long. Any young woman – well, almost any – will be proud to take him, I should say. He shall have very little difficulty finding another, someone to make him forget he ever entertained the notion of marrying me. Perhaps he never did! I might have been wrong about that all along. It would not be the first time my vanity led me astray, would it?" she finishes, laughing.

True enough. Yet, unfortunately for my brother, I know this is not one of those occasions.

I am too appalled to listen to any more. I get to my feet, plead a sudden headache, and leave Agnes without further comment. I fear my astonishment and displeasure over this development are not to be recovered from immediately. Indeed, I must own to feeling – somewhat irrationally, I suppose – a sense of betrayal as well. Not only has Agnes wronged my brother, but she has, apparently, also withheld from me the true nature of her interest in Mr. Cox these many weeks. For years I have considered myself to be her closest friend and confidant. How is it possible I have known Agnes so long and still understand her so little?

~~*~~

When Frederick arrives the very next day, I look for the first opportunity to disclose to him the news of Agnes's engagement. By taking on the unhappy task, I can at least spare him the embarrassment of finding out in some other fashion, such as from the lady herself.

Frederick never flies into a fit of wild emotion, regardless of the provocation. Instead, when I tell him, he falls completely silent. Only the change in his countenance betrays the battle within. I avert my eyes, giving him time to recover his composure. Finally he asks, "Had you any idea that Miss Pittman was about to take such a serious step, Jo? You are her friend; she must tell you these things."

"I never had the slightest suspicion. You may be very sure that if I had, I should have cautioned you accordingly."

"Cautioned me? I hardly see where there was any need for that. If Miss Pittman wishes to throw herself away on some... some... London dandy, it is clearly none of *my* affair."

"But I thought..." I stop short, understanding that he would rather save face than be comforted. "Yes, of course. I only meant that I should have prepared you against the shock of the thing, since you are such a close friend to the family. It has taken us all by surprise – no one more than myself, I daresay."

35

The Other Shoe Drops

Not surprisingly, Frederick's stay in Wallerton is brief. With his stoic demeanor, it is impossible to judge the extent of his injury, but I pray his pain will be of short duration. My acrimony on his account simmers just below the surface for the better part of a week. During this interval I think it best to avoid Agnes entirely lest further irritation should heat my anger to the boiling point, doing irreparable harm to us both.

The tincture of time ultimately does its work, teaching me to view the situation with more philosophy than was initially possible. Although I still cannot credit Agnes's explanation with any greater insight than the wisdom of self-interest, one of her statements does have the ring of truth to it. Her break with Frederick is most probably for the best. Far better that he should suffer a temporary disappointment than the permanent misfortune of an inconstant wife.

Upon further reflection, I also decide that my friendship with Agnes, though damaged by this episode, is worth salvaging. Little time remains to us. All too soon, the more tangible gulf of distance will divide. I will lose my life-long companion to London in a matter of weeks, and thence to Hertfordshire when old Sir Edmund Cox – the current baronet – passes on, leaving his coveted lands and title behind. Therefore, I resolve to set aside my wounded feelings and my misgivings about this engagement.

Agnes's head is awhirl with wedding plans, but I cannot enter into her frenzy, at least not with the pure enjoyment I had always imagined I would feel on the occasion. Still, the bride-to-be has more than enough enthusiasm for the both of us. When we are together – with Susan as an interested third – Agnes's incessant chatter centers on the specifics of the upcoming ceremony and the expected glories of her future life, its wealth and status comprising the chief elements of pleasure. I notice Mr. Cox is mentioned mostly as an afterthought, as the convenient means of providing her all these benefits. At least for that he will have his wife's gratitude if not her love. About the true depth of Agnes's affection for her future husband, I can only guess.

"I should think I love Mr. Cox well enough. I would never have agreed to marry him otherwise."

This, or some similar response, is her answer to my every attempt to examine her on the subject. My doubts do not signify, however. Agnes has made her choice, and I hope it will prove a happy one.

~~*~~

What was to have been my wedding day at last arrives. I have no desire to mark the occasion with an observance of any kind. Although one portion of my heart persists in keeping Richard's flame alive to torture me, his memory and the pain associated with it continue to subside. So short was our time together and so many weeks have elapsed since, that he begins to seem like a relative stranger to me. In truth, until the end, I never knew the real Richard, and yet I might have been made his wife today. The very idea shocks me.

Other than a few weak moments, briefly lapsing into sentimentality, I finish the day without much regret at still being single. My chief distress stems from the knowledge that the wheels of legal machinery will likely soon be set in motion against me, now that I am clearly in breach of my marriage contract.

A few days later, Susan and I pay a call on Mrs. Evensong and little John. When we return to Fairfield, my father is pacing the entry hall, wearing a frown and a deeply furrowed brow. "There you are," he says, his eyes settling upon me with a portentous weight.

"What is it, Papa?" I ask.

From his waistcoat pocket, he pulls a letter addressed in an unfamiliar hand. "Perhaps you would care to join me in the library, Jo."

So it did come, and exactly when it might be reasonably looked for. I know immediately what the ominous letter contains, of course. Its arrival forever extinguishes the small spark of hope, the frail, secret wish I had continued to nurture, that Richard might override his father's plans.

Susan gives me a sympathetic squeeze of the hand, and I reluctantly go to face my fate.

After closing the door, Papa answers my unspoken question.
"Yes, the letter is from Mr. Pierce's attorney. I have taken the
liberty of examining its contents. There is nothing that should
surprise you; it is exactly the kind of nonsense we were told to
expect. Sit down, Josephine, and have a look for yourself."

The letter reads as follows:

Freeman Court, Cornhill
Pierce against Walker
To Miss Josephine Walker
Madam,

*My client, Mr. Richard Pierce, has instructed me to
commence an action against you for the breach of your
promise to marry him, claiming damages in the amount of
twenty thousand pounds for the disappointment of his
expectations. A writ to that effect has been issued against
you in the Court of Common Pleas. Hence, it is incumbent
upon me to recommend that you retain the counsel of an
attorney directly and to then inform me, by return post,
who will accept service of the aforementioned writ on your
behalf.*

Your humble servant
Mr. Clarence Dewberry

"Twenty thousand pounds! So he wants the lot. He would
leave me without a penny of my uncle's money to my name," I
summarize.

"Now, Jo," says my father, "Mr. Gerber did warn us that the
initial demand would be high – just a starting point for negotiations."

"Yes, I know. Still, even though it is not altogether unexpected, it is astonishing to see such a sum in writing."

"I am truly sorry that it has come to this, my dear. I should
have done more to protect you, to prevent your falling into this
trap. As your father, it was my duty…"

"You are not to blame, Papa. We were all taken in by Mr.
Pierce, and he himself is little more than a pawn in his father's
hand. It is a miserable business all the way round."

"Indeed. Well, we must inform Mr. Gerber at once what has happened. There may be no absolute need for us to travel to London again; the whole thing could be handled through the post. However, it did occur to me that since Miss Graham is obliged to leave us in a few days and our carriage must, therefore, travel the distance in any case, you and I might just as well be in it. Perhaps we could prevail upon your brother to meet us there as well, if you like."

"Oh, yes. I would not lose Susan's company a day sooner than necessary. And I believe I shall be more confident that everything has been done properly if we are all assembled in Mr. Gerber's office together."

Accordingly, an express is sent off to the solicitor with the news of the recent development and our plan of coming to London. Another goes to Tom, stating that his attendance is also required. Papa takes it upon himself to break the news to my mother and leaves me to inform my friend.

"This is too cruel," exclaims Susan in response. "What have you ever done to deserve being treated in this fashion, I should like to know? Of all the ungentlemanly things of which a man might be capable, this is near the top of the list. To steal a woman's fortune just because she will not marry him? Abominable! I under-estimated Mr. Pierce, it seems. I never before believed he would go through with it. Well, I hope this London solicitor of yours will know how to deal with him."

"I have every confidence in Mr. Gerber, and Mr. Ramsey thinks very highly of him as well."

"I wish George had already made barrister. He would represent your interests in court as vigorously as anyone, I daresay, and make the jury see that there is no merit whatever in Mr. Pierce's claims."

"I am sure he would. I am sure he would indeed." Despite the circumstances, I smile at Susan's vehemence, which rings out in equal force in defense of my innocence and in praise of Mr. Ramsey's as-yet-unproven talents in the legal arena. "But, in any case, I do not expect to need a barrister; the matter will never come to trial."

"How can you be so certain, Jo? You do not intend to give in to these demands, I hope."

"No. That is the one thing I have sworn never to do."

36
The Decision

My father, Susan, and I set forth for London on Wednesday. Mr. Ramsey, by prior arrangement, meets us at the same lodging house we patronized on our previous visit. He serves as a welcoming committee of one and as a messenger from Mr. Gerber, delivering a note advising us at what time the solicitor will see us the next day.

"We are much obliged to you, Mr. Ramsey," says Papa. "Will you not stay and take supper with us? I know your commitments prevented you before, but there is an additional inducement this time," he finishes with a nod to Susan.

"As luck would have it, sir, I am currently between terms, so my time is my own. Nothing would please me more than to stop for a few hours in a place with such charming company."

It is a very congenial gathering. Having by now recovered from the shock of the letter's arrival, I set a cheerful tone and the others take their cue from me. We have only this one evening together, as the Graham's carriage will come to take Susan to Kent on the morrow.

Miss Graham's parting with Mr. Ramsey's that night is rendered more poignant by the fact that their separation is likely to be of some duration. Mr. Ramsey says he despairs of being able to elude his mother's watchful eye long enough to make a sojourn to Kent, and Susan has no expectation of returning into town in the foreseeable future. My farewell to her the next morning is likewise tinged with sadness.

"When do you suppose we shall see each other again?" Susan asks at the curb before boarding the carriage sent to fetch her home.

"Not these many months to come, I shouldn't wonder."

"It is your turn to visit me. Promise that you will."

"I promise to come to Kent for your wedding, dearest, and to be your faithful correspondent until then. Will that do?"

"You mustn't tease me so, Jo. My wedding is a long way off, as you are well aware."

"Perhaps it is and perhaps it isn't," I say lightly. Then, handing my friend a sealed letter, I continue, "At any rate, here is the first installment on my pledge of correspondence. You see how seriously I take my commitment; you are not yet gone and already I have written. I put a little surprise inside for you, but you must not open it until you reach your destination. Then it will be as if the letter arrives the very moment you do." We embrace, and then Susan climbs into the carriage. "Goodbye, my sweet friend," I say as the coach pulls away.

Not long after Miss Graham's departure, Tom arrives and I explain to him the situation. He reacts with predictable indignation, venturing to disparage Mr. Pierce in terms even more unflattering than Susan dared to employ. When he at last exhausts the preponderance of his ire, Tom asks what he might do for me. What service in defense of my honor would please me best? Would I give him leave to challenge the scoundrel to a contest in one of the manly arts, where he might expect to have the pleasure of bringing profound insult down upon both Mr. Pierce's person and reputation?

"Although you would no doubt prefer pugilism, I have something else in mind," I tell him. "The best service you can render me, my dear, impetuous brother, is to stand at my side whilst I do what must be done. Come to Mr. Gerber's office with me, Tom. If anybody can prevent me sinking into undue gravity over this business, it is you. But you must recover your good humor first, so that you can make me laugh at myself... and at this absurd situation."

"Are you quite certain you wish me to accompany you, Jo? This is rather a private matter. Of course you want Father there, but perhaps you would rather I wait in the carriage."

"No, there is no need for that. This business between me and Mr. Pierce is no longer an affair of the heart. It ceased to be that months ago. It is purely a legal question now, and as such, it concerns the whole family to one degree or another. I want you present, Tom; it is right that you should be there."

"As you wish, then."

Upon our arrival, the clerk, who is expecting us, ushers us into Mr. Gerber's chamber. "Ah, Mr. Walker, Miss Walker, I am glad to see you again but sorry for the need of it," the solicitor says. He shakes hands with each of us. "Please, do make yourselves comfortable."

"This is my brother Tom, Mr. Gerber," I inform him before taking a chair.

"Yes, yes. Young Mr. Walker, I am delighted to make your acquaintance at last."

"At last, sir? I had no idea that you knew of my existence. Whatever my sister has told you about me, you mustn't believe the half of it, you know," he says, returning Mr. Gerber's smile and firm grip.

"She has told me a deal about you, sir, but nothing to your discredit, I assure you. Well now, Miss Walker, may I see the letter?" I hand it over and he gives it a cursory perusal. "Yes, just as we expected. Are you still determined to proceed as planned? Remember, you have every right to change your mind; there would be no disgrace in it."

"No change, Mr. Gerber," I declare. "I have turned the matter over and over in my mind, and I am quite at peace with my decision. I have no doubt this is the right course, for myself and for the others involved."

"And you, Mr. Walker? Are you in agreement?"

"Let us just say that I am resigned to it," Papa grumbles. "My daughter may do as she wishes."

"Very well, then."

Tom breaks in. "Pardon me. Everybody else seems to know what is going on, but I haven't a clue. You wanted me here, Jo, so will you please let me in on the secret?"

"Be patient, Tom. Mr. Gerber will explain." I nod to the distinguished man across the desk, authorizing him to do so.

"Mr. Walker, your sister no doubt wanted you here because this matter concerns you very greatly. Rather than risk her fortune falling into the hands of the undeserving through this noxious law suit, she has decided to dispose of her inheritance as she sees fit. Therefore, this is a little like the reading of a will, except your benefactress is still living."

"My benefactress? I do not understand." He turns to me. "Jo?"

Knowing that what I am about to say will forever change my dear brother's future, I feel my chest swell with pride and excitement. "Tom, I mean to give Miss Graham and the Pittmans each a portion, but I want you to have the bulk of my money, so that you may pursue your ambitions in architecture. Talent and passion like yours should not be allowed to go to waste. Twelve thousand pounds should enable you to make your way – to travel, to study, to apprentice under the best men in the field – without worrying for your daily bread."

"Good lord! Have you completely lost your senses, little sister? Give away your inheritance? Why, it is ludicrous! Incredibly generous, but ludicrous all the same, and I will not allow you to do it."

"You mustn't argue, Tom; it is already done," I say, laughing with delight at his reaction. "Believe me when I tell you that the money has never given me a moment's happiness until now. It would satisfy me still less to see any of it go to Mr. Pierce. Instead, think how much joy I shall have using my fortune to benefit my dear friends – to restore some of what the Pittmans have lost; to give Susan and Mr. Ramsey the chance to marry early; and to put your dream within reach. What could possibly give me more pleasure than that?" My voice falters with emotion on the last few words, and my eyes fill with tears against my will.

"Mr. Gerber, can she do this?" questions Tom. The solicitor merely nods. "Father, cannot you dissuade her?"

"I assure you, I have tried, but your sister is quite determined. I fear you have no choice, my boy, but to bravely bear the consequences," he says wryly.

Tom shakes his head in bewilderment, mumbling, "Twelve thousand pounds. The chance at my dream? I cannot believe it." Abruptly, he turns back to me. "Wait, Jo, what about my duty to Millwalk parish? I am expected to take up my post there shortly. Have you forgotten about that? "

"No, but I thought perhaps Mr. Summeride could be persuaded to manage things a little longer whilst you take your training in architecture. Then, when you are ready to assume your place as rector, you can keep him on as curate if you wish, to allow you more time to pursue your other interests."

"I see you have given this a great deal of thought."

"I have. That is how I know I am doing the right thing. You may depend on it."

Tom presents no more arguments. He leans back in his chair, agape, as if in disbelief.

"Ahem. Well then," says Mr. Gerber, "if that is settled, I have a few papers that need to be signed. Then I can manage everything else for you. Once the disbursements have been made, I shall respond to this letter from Mr. Dewberry informing him that you haven't the resources to pay the damages claimed, nor even a fraction thereof. It will come as a great disappointment to his client, no doubt, but there will be nothing whatever that he can do about it; he cannot legally sue any of your relations to recover the money. So I expect that will be an end to it, exactly as you wished, Miss Walker."

"Excellent. The sooner it is done, the better."

Ten minutes later, our business complete, I thank Mr. Gerber sincerely and leave his offices quite elated. "It is over! It is over!" I repeat to myself again and again in nervous gratitude. The worst is over. The money is gone and I am free of the burden it has been to carry it. Had I not been perfectly content before without it? Now I shall be even happier to have rid myself of it in such a way as to benefit people I love most in the world.

I will not see Susan's face when she discovers my gift in her letter, but I anticipate the pleasure of witnessing Agnes's excitement. Tom's reaction continues to evolve minute to minute – from his questioning disbelief, to a stunned silence, and finally a bright-eyed animation as he begins to talk about his new future.

"You dear, sweet, generous girl!" he exclaims as we travel back to our lodgings. "I still cannot believe my luck in having such a sister. I hope you are absolutely certain this is what you want, for I warn you, once I have the money, I will not easily be persuaded to give it back again. I intend to put it to good use without delay. I shall embark on the grand tour immediately, taking in the finest architecture on the continent and seeking out the great minds in the field. Not that I need pattern myself after anyone else. I have more ideas of my own than I could possibly put into practice in a lifetime. The improvements at Millwalk will be just the beginning, thanks to you, Jo. I will do you proud, I swear. You shall have no cause to regret investing in my career, and, in future, you will find me your most loyal champion. You shall never be in want, danger, or despair so long as I can prevent it."

~~*~~

Mama welcomes us home the next day, her anxious eyes flitting from face to face. "Did everything go well in London?" she asks. "Has it all been settled according to Jo's plan?"

Tom cuts in. "I collect that everybody knew about my good fortune before I did."

"I trust you will forgive me that, Tom," I say. "Yes, Mama, it is just as I wished."

Papa adds, "For better or for worse, it is done. And I must say Tom appears happier with the money and Jo happier without it. So perhaps it has turned out as it should after all."

"That is very well then. There may yet be a complication, however," says Mama, producing a letter addressed to me and bearing the initials *RP,* denoting the sender. "This arrived whilst you were away."

"What can it mean, I wonder?" Taking the unexpected missive, I open and read it aloud.

My Dear Miss Walker,

I must begin by expressing my deep disappointment that I cannot yet address you by a different name, as should be the case by now if all had gone smoothly for us. Yet I am by no means discouraged. No, I believe I can interpret your reason for this delay. You intend it as a test of my constancy, and I flatter myself that I shall pass that test and win you in the end.

It is in testimony to my faithfulness that I write to you now. The necessity arises from my desire to prepare you for the imminent arrival of another communication, one from our solicitor Mr. Dewberry. I would not have it take you unawares. I wish with all my heart that I could spare you entirely, but I find I can only warn you of its coming and explain my actions.

As I feared, I have been unable, by any art or reason, to convince my father that he should give up seeking damages against you. To refuse his demands entirely would be impossible in my dependent state. His threats against you notwithstanding, my father will never pursue the matter into court for dread of the unfavorable publicity. He only means to intimidate you into offering a substantial settlement. He hopes for six or seven thousand pounds, but Mr. Dewberry has told him that is unlikely. For my part, I am determined that he shall accept as little as three. Should you tender an offer of that amount, I swear I will sign the papers, with or without his approval, and this business will be over.

I beg you would not think of me too meanly for my current powerlessness. I would do more if I could. And I must insist that you make no response by return post, lest the letter should fall into the wrong hands and my father be made aware of my collusion. He would consider my telling you these things a gross disloyalty. Instead, if I may be so bold, I intend to call upon you as soon as ever I can get away, to ascertain your reaction to this proposal. My hope is that you will be pleased to see me. I remain...

Yours ever,
Richard Pierce

"I do not understand," I continue. "Richard meant for me to receive this before the notice from Mr. Dewberry arrived."

"Look here at the date," my father tells me. "This letter must have been misdirected at first, so it has come too late. Had you known all this before, would it have made a difference?"

I consider the question a moment and then shake my head. "This changes nothing; I would do exactly the same all over again. It pleased me very much to put the money to better use than if I had kept it. Besides, despite what he says here, I could never be certain Richard would stand firm against his father, now any more than in the past. No, I was satisfied with my decision before, and I will not allow this letter to cast doubt over it. But, dear me! According to this, we must expect Mr. Pierce to turn up at any moment."

37

Telling Effects

When, a few days later, I deliver the news to Agnes of my bequest to her family, she exhibits far fewer scruples about it than did my brother. She accepts the gift at once with unabashed pleasure. However, the potential benefit to herself notwithstanding, Agnes can little appreciate my decision to divest myself of my fortune.

"I can understand your placing some of the money out of reach in the care of your friends, Jo, but how could you bear to part with all of it? I would not have believed you capable of such a rash act. Indeed, I thought you were only joking when you mentioned it before. Had I known you were serious, I should have counseled you very sternly against the idea."

"Never mind, Agnes; it would have made no difference. Others tried to dissuade me, and I would not listen. You and I have chosen different paths, and we must, each of us, wish the other contentment in her own way."

After I leave Agnes, I decide to call on Mrs. Evensong. The servant who answers the door shows me to the sitting room and goes to summon his mistress. When she enters, I am struck by how gaunt and pale, almost emaciated, she looks. The steady decline in Mrs. Evensong's health has been so gradual that I suppose I have become accustomed to it by degrees. Yet, compared to the picture in my mind from former years, the change in her is startling. I can hardly keep my countenance.

"Ah, my dear Jo, how good of you to stop," she says coming to me and taking both my hands with her thin ones. "I was hoping I would see you soon, for there is a delicate matter I wish to discuss with you." My concern and curiosity are immediately aroused. We take seats together and she continues. "It is about Miss Pittman's engagement."

"Miss Pittman's engagement?" I repeat stupidly.

"Yes, I was very much surprised to hear of it."

Her mild tone and placid aspect gives no hint of the annoyance she might be expected to feel at the event. Still, I answer cautiously. "Of course. It was quite unexpected, even by her closest friends. I did not know you had become aware of it though, Mrs. Evensong. It has not yet been announced."

"Your mama told me."

"Ah. No doubt she thought you had a right to be acquainted with the fact, since Agnes was for so long intended to be your daughter-in-law. I pray you will not think too uncharitably of Miss Pittman for changing her mind."

"I do not resent her for it, not in the least. I know she was perfectly free from any obligation to my son. Oh, you needn't be afraid of owning it to me; Arthur has told me as much himself. I was in favor of the match when I thought they would make each other happy, but it is a long time since I believed that possible. So I harbor no ill will whatever against Miss Pittman for choosing someone who suits her better. Will you allow the same for my Arthur, Jo? Will you grant that he is also justified in preferring another?"

I study my folded hands for a diplomatic response to this uncomfortable turn in the conversation, finally saying, "I do not know that he does prefer another."

"Of course he does, my dear." She reaches over and strokes a gentle finger across my cheek. "If you cannot see it, it is only because some unpleasantness has clouded your vision."

"It seems your son tells you everything."

"Far from it. A mother does not need to be told when her child is in pain ... or when he is in love either."

"Oh, no," I protest miserably. "You must not think he cares for me in that way, Mrs. Evensong. Arthur and I are friends ... we were, that is."

"Call it what you like, only tell me what has gone wrong between the two of you. Arthur will not speak of it, but you might if you choose. What can be so grave that you would turn your back on such a friend?" She draws a long, rasping breath and breaks into her now ever-present cough. "Come now, Jo," she says when sufficiently recovered. "I can see you are nearly as wretched about this muddle as Arthur is."

"Dear, dear Mrs. Evensong, I beg you would not concern yourself. You must save your strength."

"Pray, excuse my meddling, but my son's happiness is a matter of no small importance to me," she says quietly. "Under normal circumstances, I would be slow to interfere, but I feel constrained to do what I can for him... whilst I am able. I fear I have too little time to be patient."

I groan aloud, at the thought of losing this dear lady and also at her insistence that I should answer importunate questions about Arthur. Yet there is no help for it. The situation being what it is, I cannot deny her request. With tears now freely rolling down my cheeks, I abandon any further attempt to dissemble.

"Very well. If you must know, it is simply that I owe my first allegiance to Agnes. When Arthur cast her off, she was devastated. I mayn't forgive him without being disloyal to her. Can you not appreciate the difficulty of my position?"

"Certainly, I can." She is silent for a thoughtful moment. "Forgive me for saying so, my dear, but it seems to me that if Miss Pittman has put the matter behind her and is happy, you might consider yourself free to do the same. Holding on to resentment on her account will do no one, least of all yourself, any good service in the end."

"But there is a principle at stake. Agnes's current happiness does not change what Arthur has done."

"My dear Josephine, you know you are like a daughter to me. I only want what is best for you, the same as I do my other children. Although nothing would please me more, I do not require that you should fall in love with my son. However, I must insist that you be fair to him. Hear Arthur's side of the story before you condemn him. That is all I ask." She leans forward and lifts my chin, looking me earnestly in the face. "You must promise me that you will do this."

I answer without hesitation. "Yes, of course, Mrs. Evensong. For your sake, I will hear him out. I promise."

Her taut expression eases and she slowly settles back into her chair. "Thank you, Jo. That means a great deal to me."

~~*~~

Later, when I leave Mrs. Evensong, I come face to face with the subject of our discussion. He is coming in the door as I am preparing to go out. "Arthur! I... I did not expect to see you."

"No, I am only this minute arrived from Oxford."

I look away, but I can feel his eyes still resting upon me.

"How are you, Jo? You look well."

"I am, thank you. You must have had a wet ride," I say, noticing the condition of his greatcoat as he removes it.

"Yes." An awkward silence sets in. "Well then... I suppose I mustn't keep you standing here in the hall. Is your carriage coming for you? I did not see it without."

"No, I came on foot."

"I gather that the weather has been more obliging here; it does seem a fine day for a walk."

"Indeed it is." I feel as if I can bear his concentrated gaze no longer. "If will excuse me now..." I move toward the door.

"Please, one moment," he says, stretching his hand out as if to touch my arm, and then withdrawing it self-consciously. "Can you tell me, is your brother Tom at home?"

"I believe so."

"I wanted a word with him. Would you mind terribly if I escorted you back to Fairfield?"

"No, not at all." It is more than mere politeness that makes me answer him so; a particular purpose has just popped into my head.

"Thank you. Let me just look in on Mother first, and then we can be off."

As I wait for him, I plan my strategy. By way of an experiment, I think I shall see how Arthur takes the news that I am no longer a wealthy woman. He will find out about the business soon enough anyway, and to see his reaction for myself might be enlightening. If indeed he has any designs on me, which seems to be the developing consensus, I may well be able to observe his disappointment when I tell him.

We walk a little in silence before I bring the subject forward. "You have asked me nothing about the reason for our sudden trip to London, Arthur. Have you no curiosity why Tom was summoned to join us there?"

"I am sure it is none of my concern."

"Nor is it a secret. My brother will tell you if I do not. No doubt he has already apprised you of certain facts about the unfortunate outcome of my brief engagement to Mr. Pierce – the threat of a lawsuit arising from my putting an end to it."

"Yes," Arthur says uncomfortably.

"Well, a few days ago I had a letter from his attorney confirming it. We went to London to finalize some arrangements prepared for that contingency. You see, I had already decided that rather than allow the courts to take my fortune, I would prefer give it away. So that is precisely what I have done. I have given most of it to Tom, and the rest to other worthy friends." I watch for some sign that Arthur understands the import of the information, but his pensive expression reveals nothing remarkable. Receiving no reply, I prompt him further. "So the money is gone... all of it."

After a moment, Arthur asks, "What do you intend that Tom should do with this generous windfall?"

"I intend that he should use it to pursue his ambitions in architecture."

"Then the money is not gone to waste. I should say instead that you have invested it well, and I am very happy for your brother."

In amazement, I confess, "This is hardly the reaction I expected from you, Arthur."

"I am sorry to disappoint you, Jo. What did you wish me to say? That I am shocked? Well, I am not. I know you never cared about the money, that it was in many ways a burden to you. It seems the most reasonable thing in the world that you should put your inheritance to better use than..." He breaks off mid-sentence.

"Better use than what?"

"Never mind. It is not my place to say."

"I have asked for your opinion, Arthur. I invite you to give it freely and honestly."

"It is only that... well... most people would probably advise you to hang on to your fortune with all your might, in hopes that it would soon secure for you a brilliant marriage. Yet it has always struck me that, with money for bait, what a young lady is most likely to catch is a greedy husband. You understand that as well, or you would never have attempted to keep your inheritance from becoming common knowledge when you went to Bath. That is why what you have done does not surprise me in the least."

"You presume to know me very well, Mr. Evensong."

"I hope that I do."

I consider what he has said as we walk on. "So, you think I was right to do as I have?" I ask after some minutes.

"It matters very little what I think, but yes, I do."

Suddenly, I become conscious of someone on horseback approaching from behind. I glance round to find that it is Richard Pierce.

~~*~~

The sight of Richard gives me a momentary start, but nothing more. Although I half anticipate being overtaken by a resurgence of the powerful feelings he once inspired, to my relief, it never comes.

At the same time that I see Richard, he recognizes me. "Miss Walker! How fortunate," he says, dismounting at once and coming to my side. "I was just now on my way to Fairfield."

"Yes, we have been expecting you, Mr. Pierce," I respond guardedly. "You remember Mr. Evensong."

"Of course. How do you do?" he says with a scowl. Arthur acknowledges Mr. Pierce with a small bow, and Richard goes on. "Now that I am come, sir, perhaps I may relieve you. It would be my honor to escort the lady the rest of the way. We have personal business to discuss which does not concern you."

Arthur gives not an inch of ground. "That is an honor I had hoped to reserve for myself, Mr. Pierce."

"But surely, you will yield to the lady's wishes," Richard counters.

"Naturally. What is your command, Miss Walker? Shall I stay or go? I am completely at your service."

Looking about myself, I discover that Arthur and Richard are not the only ones awaiting my answer. Our little gathering has drawn the notice of several passersby. Any stranger in town attracts a degree of interested speculation, but a gentleman overheard to be called Mr. Pierce – the known identity of my reportedly jilted lover – must arouse particular curiosity.

"We all have the same destination in mind," I say with feigned cheerfulness. "Let us walk on together." We do so, mostly in a tense silence, until we reach the grounds of Fairfield. Once safely away from prying eyes, I stop. "Arthur, would you mind ...?" He takes my meaning and moves off a little to stand his watch at a discrete distance. With a measure of privacy established, I continue, "Mr. Pierce, there is no need for you to go any farther. I can tell you now that you have wasted your time in coming."

"That cannot be true. Did you not receive my letter?"

"I did."

"Then you know the measures I have undertaken on your behalf, how I am prepared to intervene with my father to protect you. You shall be spared the embarrassment of appearing in court, and your fortune will remain nearly intact. All this I have done for you. Surely you cannot fail to perceive it."

What I perceive in that moment is that he presumes himself heroic for offering to rescue me from the peril into which he himself has placed me! I can hardly keep my indignation in check. "Do you desire my thanks for your trouble? Is that why you are here, sir?"

"I do not require your thanks, but I did expect you to be pleased. I hoped to learn that you think better of me now than you did before, that you take my efforts as clear evidence of my steadfast regard for you."

"So you still profess to be in love with me, do you? To want me back? With my carefully preserved inheritance into the bargain, I suppose."

"I would marry you tomorrow, Josephine, fortune or no fortune."

"Fine words, Mr. Pierce. It is interesting that you should put your offer – and it was a renewed offer of marriage, was it not? – in those terms. For, as it happens, I no longer have any fortune. It is gone. I instructed my solicitor only a few days ago to dispose of it because of this tiresome lawsuit."

He starts noticeably. "The money is gone?"

"Yes, *all* of it."

"You must be joking. Only a fool would give up twenty thousand pounds to avoid paying three!"

"Then I am such a fool for that is precisely what I have done," I say without flinching. Richard stares at me askance for half a minute, as if taking my measure. "What is the matter, sir? Are you no longer in such a hurry to marry me?"

"I... I am astonished by what you tell me. What am I to make of this outlandish story? Can it be true, or is this another test of my constancy?"

"Where is the difference? If it is true, then, by your own declaration, I am a penniless fool. If it is not, then I have lied to you most cruelly. Either way, I suspect you will find it extremely inconvenient to marry me. In fact, I suggest that a hasty withdrawal of your proposal might be the wisest move, Mr. Pierce. I have some experience in these matters, and I would advise you not to lay yourself open to a nasty breach-of-promise suit by involving yourself any deeper."

"Well... since you put it that way... I ... I," he stammers.

I see that he needs one more little push to assist him, to make his course clear, to warm him to action. "Go home, Richard. It is over," I say with solemn finality.

This does the trick. His practiced mask of affability begins to crumble; his eyes narrow; his mouth tightens into a hard line; and, for the first time, I remark in his handsome countenance a decided resemblance to his father.

"Very well; I will not plague you any more," he says. "I see you have quite made up your mind, and I refuse to demean myself by begging you to reconsider. It seems that I have been completely mistaken in your character, Miss Walker. You are far from the prudent, amiable woman I believed you to be. You may consider this interview, and any interest I had in our continued association, at an end. I bid you good day." He bows stiffly and returns to his horse, muttering under his breath as he goes.

Arthur promptly steps forward. "Leaving so soon, Mr. Pierce? What a pity. Here, do allow me to give you a leg up." He does so and receives a sharp glare for his trouble. Mr. Pierce then administers the crop to his mount and rides away with nary a backward glance.

My mind is composed, but outwardly I am trembling from the confrontation. Arthur immediately draws my hand through to rest on his steadying arm, securing it with his own. To my surprise, I do not recoil from his unexpected touch. Instead, I tell myself that there is no harm in accepting the support of a gentleman's arm when it is needed, and that the small but unmistakable flutter of pleasure it excites is only a manifestation of gratitude for his kindness.

After strolling on in this manner for several minutes, he ventures, "Will you be seeing Mr. Pierce again?"

"Not if I can help it."

"That's the spirit, Jo." He presses my arm and his deep voice quavers with intensity. "Though you may despise me all the more for saying it, you are well rid of the scoundrel. He was unworthy of you."

I neither despise Arthur for saying so, nor do I feel the need to challenge his characterization of Mr. Pierce. Although I do think it strange that, of the two of us, I can view Richard with the most charity. I cannot hate him as an enemy for he no longer has the capacity to do me harm. I almost pity him his impotence. He never had the strength to stand up to his father, and now he has lost his ability to influence me. I begin to wonder that he ever could.

38
Aftermath

Tom loses no time making good on his plan to take the grand tour of the continent, his version of which will heavily feature the architectural wonders of each destination. Before setting sail from Ramsgate, however, he will for the last time accompany Arthur back to Oxford, in order to conclude his affairs there. After only two weeks at home, he takes his leave of us amidst a torrent of tears from Mama – proportional to the increased time and distance of the upcoming separation – and a flood of advice from Papa about the perils of travel, prudent money management, upholding the family honor, and so forth.

"I swear I will make you all proud," he declares. "Jo, I owe you everything. How can I thank you enough?"

"This is all the thanks I require: learn what there is to know about architecture; write to your mother once a week – a proper letter, mind, not the few scant lines with which she usually has to make do – and when you return, be prepared to entertain us nightly with stories of your travels. Oh, and pity us not a little for remaining behind whilst you go adventuring."

All this Tom faithfully promises to do.

Shortly after my brother departs, I receive a letter from Susan overflowing with gratitude and incredulity at the gift she received from me. Her continuing comments confirm the results I had hoped for:

> *"I have written to Mr. Ramsey, explaining our good fortune and who we have to thank for it. He agrees that our lovely new nest egg will allow us to marry far earlier than we could otherwise have expected. There will be no long delay in order to scrimp and save enough to set up housekeeping, thanks to you. As soon as ever George is called to the bar and secures a position, we intend to go ahead, with or without Mrs. Ramsey's blessing."*

This response, from the last of the three beneficiaries, utterly validates my decision to divest myself. To know that I have put the money to good use, that I have helped my friends in a tangible way... What could be better?

Others are less well pleased than Susan. A correspondence containing copious quantities of vinegar, tempered with not so much as a trace of sugar, arrives from Mr. Randolph Pierce. Considering the size of his perceived loss, his outrage at my action is completely predictable and nearly as rewarding to me as the reactions of those who gained by it. However, the final satisfaction springs from Mr. Gerber's advice that the lawsuit against me has been officially vacated. The end to the whole unfortunate affair with Richard seems at last within sight.

Only one more chore remains before I can put it behind me completely. With the need for secrecy over, it is time to announce the change in my situation to the world, or at least to the good citizens of Wallerton. After much consideration of how best to do it, I decide to call on Mrs. Oddbody, to make her a present of the information that I have broken off my engagement.

"You don't say?" she exclaims, feigning surprise at the news. "Why, Miss Walker, I never had the least idea that there was any trouble of the kind. Certainly there have been rumors, but I assure you I am not one to listen to the tittle-tattle of every servant and tradesperson I meet with.

"It is a pity things have turned out so badly for you, my dear. Still you mustn't sink into despair; you will only lose your bloom if you do. This unfortunate affair will blow over eventually, without so *very* much harm done to your reputation, I trust. Nowadays the scandal of a broken engagement is not considered completely fatal to a girl's chances, not so much as it once was in any case. I daresay, given enough time, another gentleman will come along to claim you. Was there not a curate from Surrey who liked you before? Perhaps you should encourage him to renew his addresses. Or you might look to an older man to secure your future; they are often far less particular, especially where there is fortune to sweeten the pot."

At this point, I impart the short, sanitized version of the disposal of my inheritance and the reason for it. I believe the old lady's surprise is now genuine. At all events, it is done. With the pertinent facts imparted to Mrs. Oddbody, I am confident she will spare me the trouble of explaining the state of affairs to everyone else in the surrounding community.

~~*~~

Although I am aware of a renewed hum about Wallerton, I am by now accustomed to ignoring the sound. If I have brought shame upon my family name, I am sorry for it. Otherwise, the idle talk of my neighbors will not much distress me. I am already assured of the loyalty of those persons whose opinions I value most. As for the rest? Well, let them be careful of casting stones lest their own behavior be found less than perfect when subjected to close scrutiny.

My original wish – that other sensational events would occur to distract attention from my situation – is nearly granted. Recent proceedings at the Pittman household have run a strong competition with those of my own. First, there was the news that a portion of Mr. Pittman's wealth had been recovered through the efforts of Mr. Gerber's associate in the law, Mr. Cobb. And Agnes, nearly simultaneously, put out the information that the much-touted understanding between herself and Arthur Evensong was at an end. Now, after only a minimal delay, she has announced her engagement to Mr. Cox.

The nuptials are to take place next month in London, so thither go Agnes and her mother, to meet the groom's family and purchase the wedding clothes. When they return, I receive a most animated report from Agnes.

"My dearest friend, I was never so happy in all my life! I flatter myself that I was quite a success in London society. That is where I truly belong, Jo. I only wish you had been there to witness my triumph. And nothing could be more gratifying than Mrs. Cox's way of treating me. You know how I dreaded the thought of seeing her. But the very moment I was introduced, there was such an affability in her behavior as really should seem to say, she had quite taken a fancy to me. Now I know whence Phillip takes his good looks; I would have recognized Mrs. Cox for his mother anywhere."

She goes on to praise, with equal enthusiasm, the beauty of Mr. Cox's sister Lucille, the style of his house in Berkeley Square, the fashionable wares to be found in the shops on Bond Street, and the grandeur of the church where the wedding will take place. "It reminds me very much of the Abbey in Bath, although by no means with so many fine stained-glass windows…"

As I listen to these effusions, everything I hear seems to confirm what Mrs. Evensong suggested before. Agnes is vastly contented, with no thought of Arthur to spoil her pleasure. But if she will not remember his sin against her, it seems somehow the more important that I should, as if I must dutifully carry on the task in her place. Although the idea sounds unreasonable, even to me, it explains the way I feel and why I am bound to continue suffering over the incident when, by all indications, Agnes has long since forgotten it.

The whole tangle is never far from my mind. I am dissatisfied with all of us: with Arthur for obvious reasons; with Agnes for accepting Mr. Cox; with myself for not being able to get past it; and with poor Mrs. Evensong for stirring up importunate questions in my mind.

Even my mother notices my discontent. "Something is troubling you, Jo," she says one day as we are joggling along in the carriage on our way to Wallerton. "It is useless to deny it. For weeks now, you have been gloomy and distracted. I thought once this lawsuit business was finally settled, your outlook would improve. Yet I must say, if anything, you seem the worse for it. Is it the loss of your fortune you mourn? For I trust you cannot be sorry for sending Mr. Pierce away."

"No. I harbor no regret on either count."

"I am relieved to hear it. But what then?"

"How can I explain it to you when I cannot quite put my finger on it myself? It is to do with Arthur mostly, I think." There, I had admitted it. It was not Agnes I suffered over, not really; she no longer needed my solicitude. It was Arthur and my confused feelings for him that tormented me daily.

"I suppose you know that he is in love with you," Mama says matter-of-factly.

"Why must everybody keep saying that? First Tom, then Susan, Mrs. Evensong, and now you, Mama. If it is so, let the man speak for himself. Until such time, I wish never to hear it mentioned again!"

"All right, but I cannot help being curious what you will say when he does declare himself, which I feel certain he will in due time. Do you care for him, Jo?"

"I have seen him only as the admirer of my friend. In no other light could I have even imagined him... until recently. Since he deserted Agnes, I have been more angry with him than anything. And yet now..."

"Now you hardly know what to think. Is that it? Do not worry, my dear. These things have a way of sorting themselves out by and by. What is meant to be will be, Jo, if only we allow it. Do you remember me telling you about my friend Maria?"

"Of course."

"Once again, your situation reminds me a great deal of her. It was a long while after she had got over her Mr. Goring before she was able to see that her happiness lay with Mr. March."

"Are you implying that Arthur is my 'Mr. March'?"

"'Tis possible. Only time will tell. However, to my way of thinking, I see a deal of similarity between the two – both respected gentlemen of good character and longstanding association with the family, both patient and loyal to the core."

"You may be able to vouch for Mr. March, but I am no longer so certain of Arthur's character."

"Not one of us is without fault, my dear. If you start by setting a man up too high – which I daresay may be the case here – you are likely to feel the disappointment all the more keenly when he fails you."

Is that what I have done, I wonder? Have I predestined Arthur for failure – and thereby myself for disappointment – by placing unreasonable expectations upon him from the start? That would be unfair. Still, if I have set the standard exceptionally high for him, it is no more than what I believe he has always demanded of himself. Then what of how he treated Agnes? How can he possibly justify it? To relieve my own perplexity, as well as to satisfy my promise to Mrs. Evensong, I want Arthur's explanation... and the sooner the better.

39

A Joining and a Parting

On an unseasonably damp Tuesday morning in July, Miss Agnes Pittman comes to a London cathedral to be united to Mr. Phillip Cox in the bonds of holy matrimony. The bride is in her best looks and the groom in finest humor as they say their vows and join their hands at the altar. It is all carried out with the utmost taste and decorum. In my office as bridesmaid, I witness the event at close proximity. To all appearances, the couple is launching onto the connubial sea under very favorable skies. Good health, considerable wealth, compatible temperaments, and the satisfaction of significant social consequence: all these signs bode well. I wish them smooth sailing.

My friend's eyes are bright with excitement as she comes to say farewell to me at the close of the wedding breakfast following. "Well, Jo, I am a married woman now. What do you think of that? Do not you envy me my good fortune?"

"I may be pleased for you without envying you, I trust, Mrs. Cox."

"'Mrs. Cox!' I shall have to get used to that, shan't I?" she says, laughing. "It is a fine-sounding name though, with a certain air to it, I believe."

"Yes, very distinguished, I daresay. Oh, Agnes, I *shall* miss you. Will you write to me when you return from your wedding trip?"

"I shall do what I can, Jo. But you know married women have never much time for writing, or so I have often heard it said. Well, we must be off. Say you wish us joy."

"Of course, I do! I am delighted for you both."

And I mean it. Over the past weeks, my doubts about the match have crumbled away, bit by bit, until Agnes completely won me over. I am now firmly of the opinion that the two of them will do very well together. Mr. Cox is not the sort of man that would appeal to me. But then, as has been brought into sharper relief by recent events, Agnes and I are very different, in this and in many other ways.

~~*~~

In early August, Mrs. Evensong's health takes a decisive turn for the worse, confining her to bed with a fever and a racking cough. As soon as we hear of it, Mama and I hurry to see her. Upon our arrival, Mr. Robert Evensong dolefully informs us that, based on Mr. Trask's gloomy prognosis for his mother, he has sent to summon Arthur home from Oxford.

My heart sinks at the news. Though I would feel the loss of the dear lady exceedingly myself, it is her sons I pity. Apparently they are to be dealt another dreadful blow not two years after losing their father. It seems so unfair.

In the hallway, we meet Mr. Trask, who is just leaving Mrs. Evensong's bedchamber.

"How does she do?" Mama inquires.

Mr. Trask shakes his head, looking very grim indeed. "She is in God's hands now. I fear I can do nothing more for her."

"But sir, you cannot give up hope," I insist. "Surely there must be something..." Feeling Mama's restraining hand on my arm, I reluctantly leave off.

"As you have stated, Mr. Trask," she says composedly, "it is out of our hands. If it pleases God, He will see to our friend's recovery. If not, He will carry her home safe."

"Exactly so, Mrs. Walker. You may visit your friend if you wish, but one at a time only, please. And I would not stay long; she is quite weak."

My mother goes in first and I wait in the parlor. Little John finds me there and hurries to retrieve one of my stories. He sidles up next to me on the divan. "Mama will not read to me," he explains, handing me the well-worn pages.

"You mustn't blame her, John. It is only because she is especially tired today that she cannot. I shall be more than happy to stand in her place this once. So, you wish to hear about the adventures of Percival Pig again, do you?"

"If you please, Miss Jo. I wanted Mr. Pondwaddle, but he has gone missing."

"I daresay he will turn up again soon. In the meantime, Percival will do just as well."

I am glad for this useful occupation whilst I await my turn in the sick room. I feel entirely unequal to the task of easing the mind of a dying woman. At least in this way, by entertaining her son, I can be of some small service to her.

I am just finishing John's story when Mama returns. She draws me aside, trying to hide her obvious distress from the boy. Toward that same end, I tell him, "John, let us have another story. Go take one more look for Mr. Pondwaddle, will you?" With him safely out of the room, I turn to my mother. "Is she as bad as that?" I ask with my heart in my throat.

"Yes, my dear. You must steel yourself; you will find Mrs. Evensong much altered. Still, she is coherent. We had a little heart-to-heart talk before she became too tired to continue. She is sleeping now."

"Shall I go in?"

"Certainly. Someone should sit with her. Then if she wakes, you will be there to... to cheer her. You are a great favorite with her, and she will want to see you. In fact, she asked for you most particularly."

"Very well, then. Will you take my place reading to John?"

She nods, blotting away her tears.

I slip into Mrs. Evensong's apartment noiselessly. Her faithful maid, Annette, gives way for me, vacating the chair at the bedside for my use and leaving the room. Even in the dim light, I can see that Mama is right. I hardly know my friend; the ravages of illness have taken such a heavy toll on her. She has grown even more gaunt in the short span of days since I last saw her, and every trace of color seems to have fled from her cheeks and lips. No doubt my own countenance betrays my shock at these changes. It is a blessing that Mrs. Evensong is not awake to see it.

For a long while I sit with her, listening to her labored breathing and silently praying – praying for her recovery, God willing, and for myself, that I might be of some comfort to her. At length, she wakes and becomes aware of my presence.

"Jo, dear, you have come." It is little more than a whisper.

"Yes, I am here. I am here, Mrs. Evensong," I say, taking her frail hand in mine. "Tell me what I may do for you. Mama said you asked for me."

"I only wanted to see you once more, to say good-bye."

"You mustn't talk like that, dear lady. You may yet come through this."

"It's quite all right, Jo. I have no fear for what lies ahead; I only regret what I leave behind."

I nod in understanding. "Your sons."

"Yes, and others that I love, and things I should have said or done differently."

"Your life has been very well spent, ma'am. I cannot imagine that you have much for which to beg anyone's pardon."

"I wish *you* would forgive me for how I spoke to you a while ago. I fear I was a little harsh, extracting promises from you under duress and so forth. I should have trusted to God and to your own sweet spirit to do right by Arthur. I know you will return his regard if you can, and you will treat him kindly if you cannot. Either way, I hope you have a family of your own one day. Seeing how patient you are with little John, I know you will make a good mother."

"You are kind to say so, and you needn't apologize, Mrs. Evensong. I have thought a lot about what you said that day. It was sound advice." She is looking at me very intently. "Is there something else you wish to say to me?"

"Yes, something my mother told me long ago. I will pass it along to you if I might."

"Please do."

She pauses to gather her strength. "Even as young as you are, you have learnt that life is full of trials. Yet I pray you never allow bitterness to take root in your soul. It is a deadly poison, Jo, and life is too fleeting to waste a moment on resentment or recriminations. Try always to remember that."

"I shall, Mrs. Evensong. I shall remember, always."

She sighs deeply, and I hear what I fear may be the precursor to a death rattle in her exhalation. "And now, I will rest if I might," she whispers.

"Yes, of course. I have tired you by staying so long. Goodbye, my dear friend." Her eyes are already closed. I place her hand back by her side, giving it a gentle squeeze before releasing it. Studying her face in repose for a moment, I wonder if I shall ever see her again.

40

Letting Go

My mother goes to attend our sick friend once more the following day. I do not have to ask; I know by her expression upon returning that Mrs. Evensong is gone. Mama falls into my arms and we attempt to console each other.

When we have both had our cry out, she explains, "She passed early this morning according to Mr. Trask. He assures me it was peaceful; she was in no pain."

"That is some comfort, I suppose." I hesitate before continuing. "Do you know... did Arthur arrive in time?"

"Yes. He was with her at the last, I understand."

"Oh, thank God; I am so grateful for that. He would have taken it badly had he missed the chance to say good-bye. What am I saying? As if being there makes losing his mother more acceptable. He must be devastated in any case. And poor little John! What is to become of him?"

"The child needs a woman's care, without a doubt," says Mama. "What a shame it is that Robert has no wife. I daresay he will hire a nurse or governess of some sort to look after the boy now his mother is gone."

The funeral is a small, private affair, just as the modest Mrs. Evensong would have wanted it. Afterward, the family retreats into seclusion, so I hear little and see less of them in the three weeks that follow. Then one day Arthur calls at Fairfield. His black arm-band of bereavement and his melancholy aspect remind me to receive him with compassion.

"Your visit is very kind, Arthur, but perhaps ill-timed. My mother and father are gone into the village," I explain as we settle in the drawing room.

"I am not sorry to see you alone," he replies, "for I have a good deal to say to you."

"Oh?" I respond with curiosity and some alarm for what he might mean.

"A great favor to ask, actually. You see, I must return to Oxford tomorrow."

"So soon?"

He nods. "Would that I could stay longer, but it is out of my hands. Still, my own preference is unimportant; my concern is for John. He is, naturally, very hard hit by what has happened. I am not sure he fully comprehends it either. All he knows is that his mother has been most cruelly taken from him. Now I must leave him as well. So I wondered... what I came here to ask is... would you be so kind as to look out for John whilst I am away, Jo? Whatever *our* differences..."

"That does not enter into it. I will do what I can for John, willingly... out of my fondness for him and respect for your dear mother's memory."

"I am most exceedingly obliged to you. I will be easier knowing he is safe in your care."

"I am more than glad to do it, but what of your brother Robert? Surely John will be more inclined to look to him than to me for reassurance at such a time."

"No doubt Robert will be a very... competent guardian," he says with a sigh. "And Mrs. Jones will spare what time she can from her housekeeping duties to attend to John's practical needs. But I fear he will require more in the way of – shall we call it maternal affection? – than either of them is capable of supplying. I thought you – you and your mother perhaps – might be willing to fill the void."

"I am sure no one should presume to step into your mother's shoes, and I would be a poor substitute indeed. Still, it will be no hardship for me to show John affection. I love him as if he were my own brother as it is."

"Yes, you are quite right. No doubt you understand these things far better than I do. An affectionate older sister, not a substitute mother, is what John wants. A sister in spirit if not in actual fact." he says with a long, pensive look at me. Then he rises abruptly. "Well, I needn't take any more of your time today. Would it be too much to ask you to come tomorrow though? To be with the boy when I take my leave?"

"If you think it will make John more comfortable."

"I do."

"Then I will come." After agreeing on a time for the following day, I see him to the door. However, my conscience will not allow me to let him go away with pressing questions still unanswered between us. On the porch, I stop him. "Arthur, a moment, if you please."

"Yes?"

I nearly lose my nerve. So instead of attacking the thing head on, I come at it awkwardly from the flank. "I... I am suddenly reminded of another conversation we had on these very steps."

"I well remember. It was nearly eight months ago, on the fifth of January."

He waits expectantly whilst I try to find the words. "You said that day you would be patient, and you have been. I will grant you that much to start. Now, if you are willing, I am asking for the explanation you were not prepared to give then. I promised your mother I would hear you out, and I mean to keep my word. But perhaps this is not the most appropriate time."

"I appreciate your scruples, but the sooner we clear the air between us the better. I believe my mother would have agreed."

"Very well, then. You must forgive me if I seem impertinent, but I shall put it to you straight. Tell me if you can, Arthur, how you pretend to justify what you did. How could you cast Agnes off in that cruel fashion?"

I see a sad smile cross his face. He shakes his head once and looks away, far into the distance. "I never meant to cast her off," he says quietly, almost as if speaking only to himself. "I considered myself honor-bound for as long as she wanted me. This I told Miss Pittman – for so she was then. I only meant to free *her* to accept another, if she so chose. But it all went very wrong somehow." He turns back to me again. "I daresay it was my fault, Jo; I must have put it badly. At all events, as soon as I broached the subject, she flew into hysterics and refused to hear anything more. I told her again and again, 'You are free and I am still bound by honor.' It was to no purpose, though; she had closed her mind to reason. I hoped to try again another day, but she flatly refused to see me. You know her disposition. Once Agnes takes an idea into her head..."

"...it is very hard to dislodge it, yes."

A thoughtful silence follows. The most pressing question now out in the open, the tension between us eases somewhat. As of one accord, Arthur and I stroll into the garden, allowing me time to digest what I have learnt thus far. His plausible explanation, though weighing significantly in his favor, falls far short of ex-onerating him completely.

"Still," I continue at length, "even if your intentions were essentially honorable, your timing could not have been worse. To deal Agnes another blow when she was already despairing over her family's financial losses... It was too unkind."

"Perhaps I am guilty of poor judgment, but *not* deliberate cruelty." He pauses. "As for the unfortunate timing, I did attempt to tell Agnes earlier, that night in Bath, as soon as I perceived her preference for Mr. Cox. She would not give me a private audience, as you will doubtless remember. When I next saw her, here in Wallerton, after her set-back, I debated with myself what would be the best course. By going ahead, I knew I risked distressing her further. Yet I reasoned that, with her dowry gone, she might be even more pleased than before to be at liberty to admit the serious addresses of a wealthy man like Mr. Cox. I had no fortune to offer her, and she is not the sort of woman who can be expected to suffer poverty for long."

I had to admit the logic of his argument. "Why did you not tell me all this before?"

"Would you have listened if I had? Your outrage was so powerfully engaged in Agnes's defense that I thought you would only hate me the more for attempting to defend myself, especially at her expense. You would not have thought any better of me for accusing her of willfully misconstruing my intentions, or so I believed at the time. I rather hoped Agnes would clear things up herself when she recovered her objectivity, that she would tell you the truth about what had happened or show you my letter."

"Your letter?"

"Because she would not see me again, I had no other recourse. I wrote down in a letter everything I have been telling you – everything I tried to explain to Agnes that first day. I sent it to her from Oxford a few weeks later, when I hoped she would be calm enough to study and understand it."

"Oh!" My hands fly to my face. "She never read it; she threw it straight into the fire."

"She told you this?"

"I was there when she did it! How I wish now I had attempted to stop her. Her suffering might have been over much sooner if I had. To this day, I believe she still regards herself as grossly ill-used, and you a villain."

"Well, she is happy now, and I am glad for it. It no longer signifies what she thinks of me. Have I redeemed myself in *your* eyes, Jo? That is what I wish to know."

I hesitate. Tom's theory of Arthur's ulterior motive still haunts me; it must be settled before I can be at peace.

"A point of clarification first, if you please. According to your telling of the story, your desire to 'free' Agnes from her obligation to you was driven solely by benevolent intentions. Was there no self-interest involved at all? No thought for making a more advantageous match yourself?" Although Arthur says nothing, a wave of scarlet floods up from his neck to overspread his face. With that evidence and his guilty look, I have my answer. "Yes, I suspected as much. Perhaps Agnes was not so very far off the mark in saying that you would not take her because she had no dowry. Thank you, Mr. Evensong. I believe I now have the full picture, and I must beg to return to the house. Good day, sir."

As I turn away, he restrains me with a firm hand on my shoulder.

"Wait, Jo," he says in a commanding tone. "Remember your promise to hear me out. You do have the full picture before you, yes, but you refuse to see it! I admit, I did hope for a more advantageous match, but in the way of *affection*. It was never about money. As I have already told you, I attempted to release Agnes in Bath, *before* she lost her dowry." He pauses to compose himself, then continues more calmly, "She did not love me anymore than I did her; I am still convinced of that. The feelings that bound us together were ones of habit... duty... and the expectation of others. I wanted a better fate for myself and for her. I rejoice that she has found her happiness with Mr. Cox."

"As do I." I take a moment to consider all that he has said. Much to my surprise, Arthur has answered my every objection and, in doing so, acquitted himself of any serious dishonor in the case.

He continues, saying gently, "Likewise, I hope one day to be so fortunate as to marry the woman that I love... if she will have me."

His vivid, blue eyes seek some sign of encouragement in mine. This time I am the one to blush. I take his meaning without resentment, being now at liberty to accept the compliment with no question of disloyalty to Agnes.

"I see that you understand me, Jo," he says. "That is enough for now; I will not press you further."

With considerable difficulty, I force myself to speak. "You have given me a great deal to think about, sir."

"I am pleased to hear it," he says with a diffident grin. "A fine mind like yours should not be left idle." He turns to go, calling back behind him, "Until tomorrow then?"

"Yes, Arthur, until tomorrow."

41

Food for Thought

So I go to the Evensongs' next morning as promised, feeling very conscious of everything Arthur said yesterday and my thoughts derivative to all the waking hours since. Robert is not immediately present, but both his brothers are there to receive me. From the way John is brooding, however, curled up in his favorite chair by the window at the far side of the room, I surmise he has not taken the news of Arthur's departure well.

"Miss Jo is come to visit you, John," Arthur says. "You must exert yourself and be a bit more cheerful, so she will know how glad you are to see her." His words having little effect on his brother, he then turns to me. "I'm afraid John is quite put out by my going. It seems I leave you with a challenging charge."

From the earnestness of his gaze, I suspect Arthur has more than his brother's welfare on his mind. I try to lighten the mood. "Not at all. I daresay John and I will get on splendidly once you are out of the way. Do not flatter yourself, sir, that you will be so very much missed by either one of us."

He smiles. "I shall flatter myself a little further still by presuming you are only teasing. I should be sorry indeed to think my absence shan't be at all regretted."

"Of what duration is your absence expected to be this time, Mr. Evensong? You will not stay long away from your friends, I trust, not unless you wish us to forget you entirely."

"Oh, your tongue is sharp today, Jo. Still, I intend to bear it with philosophy. It is worth everything to hear you include yourself amongst my friends again." A passage of silence rests comfortably between us. Through it we can only stare into each other's faces, as if for the first time. Then Arthur continues solemnly, "Yesterday you said I had given you much to think about. With your permission, I would now give you one more question to consider."

"I scarcely know if you should," I say with trepidation. "I'm not sure I am prepared for any questions of a serious nature."

"You needn't be alarmed. I will not distress you by renewing the subject I alluded to before. You may regard this as a totally unrelated matter, which indeed it may prove to be in the end. I only want your advice about my career."

"Your career?" I repeat in surprise. "Really, Arthur, I fail to see where I can be of any use to you there. I am not qualified to offer an opinion on that subject."

"Nevertheless, I will tell you my difficulty, if I may. You see, I have been offered a fellowship at Oxford, and I must decide whether or not to take it."

"A fellowship? Congratulations! That is quite an honor. Then I do not see your problem. I should think you would jump at it."

"Yes, it is an excellent opportunity. It would provide me a generous income whilst giving me a chance to teach and build up my professional reputation – all very agreeable. And, as it happens, I have no other viable prospects at present. Alongside all the benefits, however, the fellowship does carry with it certain inherent drawbacks. I would be obliged to continue living at Oxford, away from my home and family. That goes without saying. Also, as is traditionally the case, I would be required to remain a single man as long as I hold the position. I could perhaps resign myself to these conditions for a short time, but I have been asked to make a commitment of five years."

"Five years! That seems a bit unreasonable. How can you – indeed, how could anybody – predict the way your circumstances might change over such a lengthy period?"

"Exactly. So you see my difficulty. Still, I cannot justify turning down such a valuable offer without due cause. Perhaps you would be so good as to turn your mind to the question now and again. When I come back in a few weeks, I shall be most interested to know if you can give me any compelling reason why I should not accept the position." His look, no doubt intended to be innocuous, is full of latent significance.

So the question is there after all, suspended in the charged air between us. Yet Arthur has phrased it so gracefully that we can both pretend, for the time being, that it has not been asked. It is much like the elephant in the room that everybody has tacitly agreed not to talk about; the weighty item must perforce be dealt with eventually, but as long as it is well-behaved, we are free to act as if it is just another comfortably overstuffed chair.

A moment later, the spell breaks as Arthur says, "Well, I must be off."

I collect John to walk outside with us where Arthur's horse is saddled and ready. Robert Evensong appears in time to shake his brother's hand and see him ride away, but it is to me that little John looks for comfort. With Arthur gone and the boy clinging round my waist, I say apologetically, "I hope you will not find my presence here an imposition, Robert. Arthur asked me to come. I only wish to help. You must tell me if I begin to make a nuisance of myself."

"I hardly expect it will come to that, Miss Walker," he says in an oddly detached manner. "You are welcome to visit as often as you like. John is sure to be glad of your company since I have neither the time nor the talent for entertaining children."

Arthur was right; it is good that I am here. I can see that now.

~~*~~

With my duty clear, I fall into the habit of spending a portion of nearly every day with John, either at his house or mine or somewhere in between. Mama does her part, yet it quickly becomes apparent that it is to me that John has become most attached. I read to him; I help him with his simple lessons; we play games; he accompanies me on my errands of business – anything to divert his attention from the grave misfortune that has befallen him. Alas, none of my contrivances distracts him for long. I am searching for a more substantial diversion when one day inspiration strikes.

"John, I need your help with something," I tell him. "I am having a great deal of difficulty with my new story. You being so very fond of stories yourself, I thought you might advise me."

"You want *my* help?" he says with an expression of wonder.

I can see immediately that he is pleased and intrigued. "I do. You have given me first-rate suggestions before, so I make no doubt that you will know how to help me now. Perhaps we could even work on the story together. Would you like that?"

"Oh, yes! Is it another animal story? Those are my favorites."

"Mine too. But what kind of animal should I write about this time – dog, cat, mouse, or mule? I cannot choose. And what should be the creature's name, do you think? As for the sort of adventures that might come his way, I haven't a clue. So you see, I have barely begun and already I am in need of assistance. Come to Fairfield tomorrow, won't you? Bring all your best ideas and we shall write it together."

What starts as an entertainment develops into a highly thera-peutic exercise for us both. My young apprentice suggests that our hero should be a bear cub – one who is all alone in the world, both his father and mother having been taken by the circus. Our orphan's name will be John, we decide. The story develops bit by bit over the course of the next week. In the beginning, the cub hides in a cave, lonely and afraid after losing his parents. Then slowly, he finds the courage to explore the world and make new friends. John's imagination knows no bounds, and yet he is tract-able, allowing me to lead the way for how best to incorporate his ideas into his namesake's tale.

"Well, John, I think you and I make rather a good team," I tell him after a productive session. "In fact, I believe our book is nearly finished. But perhaps John Bear should have one last, grand adventure before we leave him. What do you say?"

"Yes, Miss Jo. I think he might wish to travel to town to look for his parents."

"To the city? Hmm, it would be a long journey for a little bear. Do you really believe he could undertake such a thing all by himself?"

"He could! He... he could... if he heard the circus was going to be there... and if he thought he might see his Mama and Papa again. I am sure he would do it. He is grown very brave now. Is that not so?"

"Indeed. No doubt he would have been afraid before, but no longer. It certainly would be a great adventure and a fine way to end our story. Very well; you have convinced me. We shall write just what you suggest."

In the end, the intrepid cub not only travels to the city, he finds the circus and rescues his parents, this last turn in the plot also being John's idea. After some judicious editing and the addition of a dozen simple illustrations, my co-author and I are well pleased with our completed book. I sew a binding on and add it to John's collection.

~~*~~

237

Apart from the time spent with little John, my mind is much engaged with thoughts of his elder brother. Arthur made his sentiments plain before he went away whilst generously asking nothing of me in return, except that I reflect on what he said. He would no doubt be gratified to learn that I think of little else. What I so lately considered unimaginable – a match between us – seems now a perfectly reasonable possibility. The knowledge that Agnes is happy and Arthur innocent changes everything. Whereas before Arthur's rumored regard for me seemed in the poorest taste, the confirmed admiration of such a man now strikes me as the highest of compliments.

I am intrigued. I am flattered. And as to compatibility of temperament, there can be no reservation; he is exactly the man who, in disposition and talents, would most suit me. But that is not love, I remind myself. After all, such a revolution of sentiments cannot be accomplished overnight. It must be built up by degrees.

Construction, therefore, commences immediately with the prompt recovery of the profound respect I long felt for Arthur when he was my friend and Agnes's intended. To that not inconsiderable foundation is soon added the gratitude that he should love me above any other. Then, as I give myself permission to remember them, I count every tender thought and secret longing for such an outcome, every guilty thrill of pleasure as a look or touch passed between us. I am in the middle of the process before I know it has begun.

Giddy excitement nearly overtakes me as I become more and more convinced that I have, in some fashion or other, been in love with Arthur Evensong all my life. My feelings only wanted the fullness of time and circumstances to flower into romance, a romance of a more complex and mature flavor than I have known before. The affair with Richard seems but a pale shadow, and every comparison to him only serves to increase the favorable light in which Arthur now stands.

Before I can be completely run away with by my feelings, however, inconvenient voices intrude upon my otherwise pleasant reflections. The first nagging utterance comes from my father. In my mind, I hear him repeating how "no poor parson" will satisfy his marital ambitions for his daughter. The next irritating reminder points out that Arthur is indeed poor. Were we to marry, what could we hope to live on? Finally, I picture Agnes telling me once again that she will never forgive Mr. Evensong.

All this – Agnes's friendship, financial security, and my father's approval – I would be prepared to risk in order to gain an object of such superior worth. Yet how would Arthur profit by the bargain? He would have a wife who loved him, but who could do nothing to promote his interests by either fortune or connection, and even less to enhance his future prospects. In the realm of church politics, where reputation is everything, I could only hinder his chances of advancement, a point further emphasized by information I receive in a letter from Susan:

> *"... I know not how it happened, but Mrs. Ramsey has found out about our plans to marry without her per-mission. Mr. Ramsey and I were prepared to bear her disapproval when the time came, so it is of little consequence to us. What I am most sorry for is that she has placed a heavy portion of the blame for this 'unmitigated disaster' upon your shoulders, my sweet friend. By arranging rendezvous for us in Wallerton and London, and by your financial assistance, you have gained our eternal gratitude but also Mrs. Ramsey's implacable wrath. She and her fast friend, Mr. Randolph Pierce, have sworn to do everything in their power to sink your prospects and thwart your purposes. That your kindness should be thus rewarded, I regret extremely."*

And so do I. Mrs. Ramsey can do nothing to me personally. But, with her meddling fingers sunk deep into the pie of church policy, she might do incalculable damage to Arthur's career, were he to ally himself with me. I am fully acquainted with his professional ambitions, and likewise convinced of his claim to ultimate success; a man of ability, strong will, and character must rise to the top in the end. It would be selfish to ask Arthur to sacrifice it all – the fellowship at Oxford and the hope of high holy office – for the dubious honor of marrying me. Indeed, it would be unkind to allow him to make such a grave error.

42

Coming to Conclusions

I am not insensible to the irony of my current situation. Although I am relieved to be free of the wealth which made me an object of prey to fortune hunters, I am not so well pleased that my relative poverty renders it impractical for me to marry where I choose. And now that I realize I would choose Arthur, it seems morally wrong that I should accept him.

I acknowledge the paradox, but I cannot laugh at it. When I consider the last several months of my acquaintance with Arthur Evensong, all I can do is sigh at the perverseness of those feelings which would now have promoted its continuance and would formerly have rejoiced in its termination. Perhaps it might have been better for all concerned had I never suffered my sentiments to be so lately transformed.

It is the middle of September and Arthur's return is everyday expected. To keep myself busy and my mind from brooding, I once again solicit little John's company, this time for an outing on horseback. He shares my relish for the sport, and I prefer his society to the hovering presence of a servant, who would otherwise be assigned to escort me on my ride. Fresh air and a gallop through the shades of Fairfield have always served well to clear my head. I hope for the same efficacy today.

Before John arrives, the post comes with the latest installment from Tom. He has been gone nearly two months and written with remarkable regularity – from Paris, Lyon, Barcelona, and various points along the French Mediterranean coast en route to Italy. As always, the letter is addressed to Mama. She eagerly opens it and scans the first few lines.

"He has made it to Venice!" she informs my father and me. "*'It is a place of rare enchantment,'* he says, *'quite set apart from the everyday world. It is not only the famous canals that distinguish Venice, but the unique style of the buildings. Here one can clearly discern the blended influences of eastern and western* cultures. *This place is an architect's paradise. My sketch book is filling rapidly; at every turn, I find a prospect worth preserving on paper.'* And look, he has sent along some drawings for us."

Mama passes the pertinent page of the letter to me, which I share with Papa who is sitting by my side. There are three ink sketches. The first one, labeled *"Ponte's bridge across the Grand Canal at the Rialto,"* reminds me a little of the Pultney Street bridge in Bath. The next is a detail of *"typical Venetian style"* picturing ornately fashioned arched windows and roof cornices very foreign-looking to my eye. The last drawing shows the heavily columned, arched, and domed façade of *"Saint Mark's Basilica."*

"Imagine the hue and cry that would erupt if someone were to erect such an exotic structure in one of London's finer neighborhoods," Papa muses.

"I daresay it had best not be attempted there, but it might look quite at home in Brighton, next to the Prince Regent's outlandish Royal Pavilion," I joke. "What else does Tom have to report, Mama?"

"He says that the letters of introduction he carried with him from Oxford have opened many doors. Apparently they were instrumental in his making the acquaintance of an architect of some importance from London, a Mr. Meacham, who happened to be sojourning in Padua when Tom passed that way. He writes, *'After listening to some of my ideas and looking at my drawings, Mr. Meacham invited me to come see him when I return to England, in order that we may continue our discussions. He would be in a position – and I dare to hope inclined – to assist me in my career.'* Well, what do you think of that, Jo?"

"I think it nicely substantiates what I have always attested: Tom has talent. I am gratified that someone besides his sister has recognized it."

"Humph!" Papa exclaims. "'My career,' Tom says. I fear this scrap of encouragement has gone straight to his head, filling it with unrealistic expectations."

~~*~~

John and I embark upon our ride shortly after noon, I on Viola and he on an ancient gelding called Max. The plan is to make for the glade in order to gather some of the blackberries that grow in the brambles round its fringes. Viola is eager, as am I, to set a brisk pace; Max and John are not so well able to follow suit. So the refreshing gallop I had hoped for must come in fits and starts. I race off for a stretch and then wait for John to catch me up. Still and all, the cool air and the beauty of the wood, both tinged with the first hints of autumn, do not disappoint.

At our destination, we tether our horses and begin the task before us. My pail fills quickly. John's progress is slowed by his propensity to deposit at least half the berries into his mouth, the evidence of which stains his lips and fingers a rosy purple. As we work, the sun warms our backs and the laden vines alike, releasing the sweet scent of ripe fruit into the air.

"Arthur will be home soon," John remarks.

"I know. I read his letter out for you, remember? You will be very happy to see him, I expect."

"Oh, yes." Then his smile changes into a frown. "But I wish he would not always go away again."

Our employment and conversation are interrupted at this point by the sound of a horseman approaching. When he breaks into the sunlight of the clearing, we immediately recognize him. John nearly spills all the contents of his pail in his excitement, dropping it to the ground at once and breaking into a run to meet his brother. I am equally discomposed by the sight of Arthur, but for materially different reasons.

After a few minutes, the two brothers come, hand in hand, to where I have continued my work.

"Hello, Jo," says Arthur, the earnestness in his voice matching the look he gives me.

"Good afternoon, Arthur. I did not know that you were back."

"Yes, just. Mrs. Jones told me you and John were off after some berries, so I thought I might find you here."

John shades his eyes to peer up at his brother. "Cook says she will bake me a pie if I bring her enough."

"And how much have you collected thus far?" John retrieves his half-empty container and shows it to Arthur. "Hmm. I am no expert, of course, but I think it will be a very small pie unless you put more berries into your bucket... and fewer into your mouth," Arthur adds with a laugh, examining his brother's juice-stained face. "I will wait for you to finish, and then we can ride home together, all right?"

This seems to satisfy John, who hurries back to the brambles with his pail, leaving me alone with Arthur. I try to cover my embarrassment by initiating a stroll round the glade and something that I hope will pass for light-hearted banter. It is of no use, however. The tension between us is palpable; the very air crackles with the strain of anticipation.

When I think I can scarcely bear it another minute, Arthur breaks in. "My dearest Jo, forgive me for being so abrupt, but I must know my fate. Tell me then; have you considered the question I left with you before I went away?"

"I have," I say, my voice trembling despite my exertions to the contrary. "I have thought of little else over the last few weeks."

"And what is your answer, pray? Will you give me a reason not to accept the fellowship at Oxford?"

I am moved by his supplicating tone, but I force myself to answer according to my prior resolve. "No, Arthur, I cannot. I think you had best take the fellowship."

I glimpse his crestfallen face before he turns and takes a few steps away. In silent agony I await his reaction, praying he is not too badly hurt.

With his back still toward me, he presently says, "I understand... and I do not blame you, Jo. I probably had no right to hope. It was irrational of me to think that, once our friendship had been restored, you could easily make the leap to deeper feelings; that because I care for you so... so ardently, you must somehow feel the same for me." With a heavy sigh, he faces me again. "It was a foolish delusion, and now you have kindly awakened me from it."

"I *am* sorry, Arthur, more so than you can possibly imagine. But consider, you have other, more worthwhile goals to think of, dreams which you have held far longer and dearer than this one. Your career ambitions are more important than any passing regard you may feel for me. They must take precedence. You are destined to do great things in the church – of that I am thoroughly convinced – and I would not hold you back for the world. You will rise farther and much more quickly without me."

I see in his face that my words bring him no relief.

"That is small consolation. Even supposing it were true, success at such a cost would be an empty victory. High office can give no satisfaction if I am alone." We both fall silent. The birds, however, continue soaring and singing all about us, unconscious of the crisis playing out before them. At length Arthur continues. "So you are quite certain you shall never be persuaded to care for me."

It is a statement of resignation, yet Arthur says it with the air of a man grasping at the last straw of hope left to him. My heart is cut to the quick. I have neither the will to hide from his searching gaze nor the courage to reply. All I can do is allow my expression to entreat his understanding and forgiveness.

"What's this that I see in your countenance, Jo?" he says, coming toward me. "A battle waging? Perhaps you have spoken with more decidedness than you feel. Is it possible that I still have some chance with you?"

In my anguish, I begin pouring out all my much-debated doubts and reservations: the inevitable objections at home, the want of sufficient income, my damaged reputation and adversaries. "… It is no good, Arthur! You must see that. You cannot marry me. On top of everything else, I should completely ruin your future chances. The whole thing is quite impossible!"

Though I am crying as I speak, Arthur's mouth has unaccountably stretched into a broad grin. His eyes shining, he then takes my hands and kisses each one, front and back. "My sweet, sweet friend," he says with barely restrained fervor. "So you *do* care for me after all."

"I never said so," I complain with the last morsel of my melting resolve.

"I know, yet, if I may be so bold, your passionate protests have spoken for you. Now, my dear Josephine – for dear you will always be to me – let us have no more of these demurs and scruples. You must be completely honest with me this time. Say no if it must be, but I am praying you love me as I love you, body and soul."

I cry out, "Of course I do, Arthur, but…"

"Then no more objections! Agree to be my wife and all the rest we shall work out together. I know I have precious little to offer you at present. If you accept me, I'm afraid it must be for myself alone."

I stare at him in wonder, forcibly struck by his words. "For myself alone," I repeat. It is a sign. How can I fault his logic or reject a petition based on such a plea, when it is precisely the consideration *I* have so long yearned for? I suddenly realize he has already offered to take me on those terms, and I have no reasonable excuse for denying him the same mark of respect.

A great peace floods over me, a peace which I can only represent by the image of the jumbled bits of a puzzle all at once settling into their proper positions. My misgivings drop away, one by one, as the completed picture falls into place before my eyes. It is a predestined design of sublime order and beauty. Arthur and I belong together; it is as simple as that.

"Yes," I say, acknowledging the whole of it.

Without another word, he gathers me to himself where, I notice, the curve of my body fits perfectly next to his. I forget all else. With my eyes closed, I drink in the moment – the scent of Arthur's skin, the warmth of his breath in my hair, the texture of his coat against my cheek, and his heart booming in my ear. For minutes we remain in this attitude. We cleave together, silently basking in the afternoon sun and in all the pleasurable implications of our new understanding.

In Arthur's arms, I begin to comprehend what has been missing from my picture of connubial bliss. There is an intenseness of feeling in our embrace that is new to me – a unity of spirit, and a powerful longing for a deeper oneness in every other sense. It threatens to overwhelm me. I know Arthur is aware of it too, for all at once he releases me and puts a prudent distance between us again.

When we have both recovered our composure, he offers me his arm and we resume our stroll round the clearing. John continues at his occupation with no apparent awareness of the monumental changes taking place in the lives of the two people who hold his concerns most dear.

"Are you absolutely certain, Arthur?" I ask presently. "To sacrifice what might have been a brilliant career for..."

"My dear girl, you take far too much responsibility upon yourself. And I must protest against writing off my career so quickly. I am by no means convinced that such persons as you claim as your enemies hold my fate in their hands. Moreover, if anybody must have the credit for undermining my career prospects, it is I. For I made myself an adversary of Mr. Randolph Pierce long before you incurred his displeasure. Remember?"

"I suppose that is true. Why *did* you turn down his offer? I have always wondered."

"As well you might then, for you apparently guessed nothing of my true sentiments at the time. I hardly acknowledged them to myself. However, now you must see how insupportable it would

245

have been. The disadvantages of Mr. Pierce's questionable character aside, nothing could have tempted me to accept a position where I would have been forced to continually witness your devotion to another man, to see you at his side by day and know you lay in his arms..." He closes his eyes and shudders. "Forgive me, Jo, but I could not have endured it. I made my choice then and there that, come what may, my future would be guided by personal conviction rather than blind ambition. Now I have my reward," he says, pressing my arm with his own.

I smile at the compliment but remind him, "You do not have me yet, sir, nor shall you for some time to come, I fear. You are currently in no position to take a wife."

"But I soon shall be. In one respect, my luck has already changed. My professional fortunes are bound to follow." Pausing, Arthur raises my chin until our eyes meet. Then he brushes my lips with a tender kiss, a tantalizing sample of what is to come. "Say that you will wait for me, Jo."

"I will," I answer, strangely out of breath, "but I pray you will not keep me waiting long. I suddenly find I am quite impatient for you to make a married woman of me, Mr. Evensong."

"As am I, Miss Walker, I assure you. As am I."

43

Epilogue

I have just filled the last page of my diary, which is entirely fitting since I am closing one chapter of my life and beginning another. Months have passed since that glorious encounter in the glade where Arthur and I confessed our love. Never once from that time until this have I had reason to regret the choice I made then. Whilst it is true that the waiting is a source of daily torment, the suspense is almost over now.

Tomorrow Arthur and I will be married at the same little stone church in Wallerton where we were both christened, he two years before me; where we saw each other every Sunday of our lives growing up; and where our neighbors – and, indeed, we ourselves – had originally expected each of us to be united with someone entirely different. To be sure, the setting will be far less majestic than the London cathedral where Agnes and Mr. Cox took their vows over a year ago, and even modest by comparison to Susan's parish church in Kent where she will wed Mr. Ramsey in January. Still, despite the limited length of the nave and the unimpressive height of the vault, I expect to be quite thoroughly married at the end of the day, which is all I want.

To my mind, Wallerton church is precisely the right size to comfortably hold all our family and true friends. Susan will be my bridesmaid. Agnes, who did not take the news of my engagement to Arthur with as much philosophy as I had hoped, emphatically declined the office. Although I attempted to clear away the past difficulty, presenting her the same account of the misunderstanding that Arthur gave to me, she will not yet allow the justice of his explanation. Her implacable resentment has hurt me deeply, and perhaps one day she will repent of it. But for now, all intercourse between us is at an end. I am through making excuses for her bad behavior and allowances for the weaknesses of her character.

Dear little John is to stand up as groomsman and, after we return from our wedding trip to Ireland, he shall come to live with us. Robert raised no objection when we suggested the idea, and Arthur and I would have it no other way. The matter is thus settled to everybody's liking. I know Mrs. Evensong would have approved, both of our marriage and of the arrangements made for John. We continue to mourn her loss, yet I make no doubt that we shall feel her benevolent presence with us tomorrow all the same.

My father will walk me down the aisle and bestow my hand on Arthur. I warrant this will pain him far less than it once might have done. He has had a full year to accustom himself to the idea, during which time pressure was brought to bear on our behalf by my mother. One day, according to her telling of the story, she reminded Papa about Maria and Mr. March, pointing out that, despite their equally unpromising beginning, their marriage has been blessed with three fine children, unexpected prosperity, and a vast deal of contentment. My father, who I believe knows the couple in question every bit as intimately as does my mother, was apparently persuaded by this compelling illustration to give his consent, albeit begrudgingly.

"Upon my honor, Josephine, I had hoped to see you do better for yourself as to fortune," he said on the occasion. "A man of some little property would have suited my ambitions very well. Mr. Arthur Evensong may prove a great success in the end, but as of this moment, I have seen very little evidence of his genius. If it will be any satisfaction to you, however, to be told that I believe his character to be in other respects irreproachable, I am ready to confess it. Beyond that, all I can do is wish you – improbable as it may be – the same measure of happiness I have enjoyed with your excellent mother these many years."

My excellent mother – for indeed so she is – has given the match her more enthusiastic endorsement. She is neither troubled by disappointed past expectations nor misgivings for my future. And, having foreseen the outcome months before I myself thought it possible, she boasts the added gratification of having begun to be happy for me well in advance of everybody else.

Both my brothers are returned to Fairfield for the wedding. Frederick came from Millwalk two weeks ago claiming he wished the favor of extra time with his sister (as if we will not be meeting with the greatest frequency after I am married). His noble assertion notwithstanding, I notice that he takes his duty to our neighbors at least as seriously as his duty to me, for he has called upon the Pittmans almost every day since his arrival. I daresay the once-pined-for Agnes is quite forgot, and her sister Judith – now a blooming young lady of nineteen – is the likely cause of Frederick's liberal attentions.

Tom, who had planned to be away on the continent for at least a twelve-month, cut his trip short at the urging of Mr. Meacham. After meeting in Italy, they continued their exchange of ideas by correspondence until their mutual respect and like-minded purposes clearly demanded that the possibility of a more permanent professional relationship be explored. Hence, for the last several months, Tom has resided in London, flourishing under Mr. Meacham's tutelage. Having recently accepted the offer to purchase a share in the business, Tom's future solidly resides in that vocation now. He will give no more nervous sermons, I am happy to say.

The ramifications of that chance encounter between my brother and his benefactor have been surprisingly far reaching, impacting the lives of several others for good or for ill. For example, I would be willing to wager that Mr. Summeride had no notion that day in September that events had already been set into motion against him, that the fickle hand of fate would reach all the way from Padua to interrupt his comfortable life at Millwalk. Yet that is precisely the case. Henceforth Mr. Summeride will have to practice his profession elsewhere; he has spent his last night at the parsonage.

That fine house, which I have always admired exceedingly, will be *my* home now – mine and Arthur's – the generous living of Millwalk parish having been made over to Arthur as a result of Tom no longer wanting or needing it. Accordingly, as soon as Arthur completed the one-year fellowship he renegotiated at Oxford, he took orders for his new post. By then, he had other offers, but nothing that suited us both so well as Millwalk parish. Tom threw his considerable influence on that side as well when he proposed the idea to Arthur in my hearing:

"…You would be doing me a great favor, old man. For if you will not take the living, you will force me into the position of acting as one of those absentee clergymen we all disparage so freely. This way, my conscience and reputation are preserved, and we both get what we want. You must admit there is a beautiful logic to the arrangement. As for compensation, I will not hear of it. When you consider all you will save me by taking this dependent sister of mine off my hands, I should more likely end by owing *you* something."

So, thanks to Tom, Arthur will begin his clerical career as rector of Millwalk parish. His ambitions for higher office, although still with him, have mellowed somewhat. Should it be God's will, no doubt he will advance despite the efforts of our detractors. Yet I cannot say that I would much regret being destined to remain always at Millwalk. I never aspired to be the mistress of a grand house or the wife of an illustrious man. A kind, honest husband and the more modest proportions of a parsonage will suit me very well. To live in a place that is so dear to me, and to be married to the man I love and admire most in the world – this answers all my ideas of happiness.

I marvel when I think that such an auspicious outcome hinged on the unlikeliest string of circumstances, beginning with Papa's indisposition. Were it not for his gout, we would not have gone to Bath, and I would never have become engaged to Mr. Pierce, which led to the breach-of-promise suit, which in turn motivated me to give my inheritance money to Tom, allowing him to travel to Italy where he met Mr. Meacham. Indeed, had events not unfolded exactly as they have, my lot might have been quite different. As it is, all things have truly worked together for my good, and I do not regret any of what has transpired along the way.

How wondrous strange are the ways of God, for it is surely His guiding hand that has brought me through my troubles to this remarkable conclusion. Not that long ago, Arthur and I were each obligated to marry other people. Yet, according to the direction of providence, we are now both honorably free of our former encumbrances to be forever attached to one another. Of all the varied fates that might have been mine, this is the finest.

The End

About the Author

Author Shannon Winslow specializes in writing fiction (novels and short stories) for fans of Jane Austen. *The Darcys of Pemberley*, a sequel to *Pride and Prejudice*, was her debut novel in 2011. *For Myself Alone* – a standalone, Austen-inspired story – now follows. For her third, she chose something entirely different – a contemporary "what if" novel entitled *First of Second Chances* (date of publication yet to be announced). She is currently working on *Return to Longbourn,* the next installment of her *Pride and Prejudice* series.

Her two sons grown, Ms. Winslow lives with her husband in the log home they built in the countryside south of Seattle, where she writes and paints in her studio facing Mt. Rainier.

For more information, visit www.shannonwinslow.com.
Follow Shannon on Twitter (as JaneAustenSays) and on Facebook.

Appendix

Author's Note: Below you will find all the direct Jane Austen quotes used in this novel. In some cases, slight changes were made from the original text to allow the excerpted passages to fit more seamlessly into the manuscript. The reader may recognize other familiar phrases, too short and numerous to cite here, which also point to Miss Austen's work.

Prologue: "By heaven! A woman should never be trusted with money." (Robert Watson; *The Watsons*).
"A lady cannot be too much guarded in her behavior towards the undeserving of the other sex." (Mary Bennet; *Pride and Prejudice*, chapter 47).

Chapter 1: A woman especially, if she have the misfortune to know anything, should conceal it as well as she can. (narrative; *Northanger Abbey*, chapter 14).

Chapter 2: "Will you not shake hands with me?" (Marianne Dashwood; *Sense and Sensibility*, chapter 28).

Chapter 3: "Is there nothing you can take to give you present relief? A glass of wine; shall I get you one?" (Mr. Darcy; *Pride and Prejudice*, chapter 46).

Chapter 4: Husbands and wives generally understand when opposition will be in vain. (narrative; *Persuasion*, chapter 7).

Chapter 5: "A single woman of good fortune is always respectable." (Emma Woodhouse; *Emma*, chapter 10). "I have traveled so little that every fresh place would be interesting to me." (Anne Elliot; *Persuasion*, chapter 20).

Chapter 6: "I will get the Bath paper, and look over the arrivals." (Henry Tilney; *Northanger Abbey*, chapter 25).

Chapter 7: "Were I to fall in love, indeed, it would be a different thing! …And without love, I am sure I should be a fool to change such a situation as mine." (Emma Woodhouse; *Emma*, chapter 10).

Chapter 8: "Well, Miss [Morland]," said he, directly, "I hope you have had an agreeable ball." "Very agreeable indeed," [she] replied, vainly endeavoring to hide a great yawn. (Mr. Allen & Miss Morland; *Nothanger Abbey*, chapter 2).

Chapter 9: "Surry is the garden of England." (Mrs. Elton; *Emma*, chapter 32).

Chapter 10: "Of all horrid things, leave-taking is the worst." (Frank Churchill; *Emma*, chapter 30).

Chapter 11: "I am afraid that the pleasantness of an employment does not always evince its propriety." (Elinor Dashwood; *Sense and Sensibility*, chapter 13).

Chapter 12: "He is just what a young man ought to be." (Jane Bennet; *Pride and Prejudice*, chapter 4).

Chapter 13: "You can hardly doubt the purport of my discourse... My attentions have been too marked to be mistaken." (Mr. Collins; *Pride and Prejudice*, chapter 19). "Yes, I call it a very easy distance." (Mr. Darcy; *Pride and Prejudice*, chapter 32).

Chapter 15: "If it were admissible to contradict a lady..." (Mr. Elton; *Emma*, chapter 6)

Chapter 16: "[He] can have nothing to say to me that anybody need not hear." (Elizabeth Bennet; *Pride and Prejudice*, chapter 19).

Chapter 17: "[It] had been my doing – solely mine." (Cpt. Wentworth; *Persuasion*, chapter 20).

Chapter 18: "I could rather believe every creature of my acquaintance leagued together to ruin [me in his opinion] than believe his nature capable of such cruelty." (Marianne Dashwood; *Sense and Sensibility*, chapter 29).

Chapter 20: "Resignation is never so perfect as when the blessing denied begins to lose somewhat of its value in our estimation." (Mr. Collins; *Pride and Prejudice*, chapter 20).

Chapter 21: "I do not know when I have been more shocked." (Jane Bennet; *Pride and Prejudice*, chapter 40).

Chapter 22: "I have said no such thing. I am only resolved to act in that manner, which will, in my own opinion, constitute my happiness..." (Elizabeth Bennet; *Pride and Prejudice*, chapter 56).

Chapter 23: [And she] long[ed] to be able to say something more to the purpose. After and interval of silence... (narrative; *Mansfield Park*, chapter 10).

Chapter 24: "How long has she been such a favorite? And pray, when am I to wish you joy?" (Miss Bingley; *Pride and Prejudice*, chapter 6). "I have not the pleasure of understanding you ... Of what are you talking?" (Mr. Bennet; *Pride and Prejudice*, chapter 20).

Chapter 25: While he [stood], as if meaning to go, but not going..." (narrative; *Emma*, chapter 45).

Chapter 27: The little which [she] could understand, however, appear[ed] to contradict the very few notions [she] had entertained on the matter before. (narrative; *Northanger Abbey*, chapter 14).

Chapter28: "If there were but such another man for you!" (Jane Bennet; *Pride and Prejudice*, chapter 55).

Chapter 29: "I often think ... that there is nothing so bad as parting with one's [friends]. One seems so forlorn without them." (Mrs. Bennet; *Pride and Prejudice*, chapter 53).

Chapter 30: It [was] a sweet view – sweet to the eye and the mind. (narrative; *Emma*, chapter 42).

Chapter 31: "It is not fair to urge her in this manner... Let her choose for herself as well as the rest of us." (Edmund Bertram; *Mansfield Park*, chapter 15).

Chapter 32: Every room on the west front look[ed] across a lawn to the beginning of the avenue immediately beyond tall iron palisades and gates. (narrative; *Mansfield Park*, chapter 9).

Chapter 33: "Ah! You clever creature, that's very true. What a thinking brain you have!" (Mrs. Elton; *Emma*, chapter 52).

Chapter 34: "I never had the slightest suspicion... You may be very sure that if I had, I should have cautioned you accordingly." (Emma Woodhouse; *Emma*, chapter 47).

Chapter 35: It did come, and exactly when it might be reasonably looked for. (narrative; *Northanger Abbey*, chapter 26).

Chapter 36: "It is over! It is over!" [she] repeat[ed] to herself again, and again, in nervous gratitude. "The worst is over!" (Anne Elliot; *Persuasion*, chapter 7).

Chapter 37: "Very well; I will not plague you anymore." (Mr. Knightley; *Emma*, chapter 5).

Chapter 38: "You know how I dreaded the thought[s] of seeing her, but the very moment I was introduced, there was such an affability in her behavior as really should seem to say, she had quite [took] a fancy to me." (Lucy Steel; *Sense and Sensibility*, chapter 35). "I have seen [you] only as the admirer of my friend. In no other light could..." (Emma Woodhouse; *Emma*, chapter 15).

Chapter 39: "But you know married women have never much time for writing." (Lydia Bennet Wickham; *Pride and Prejudice*, chapter 53).

Chapter 40: "I am not sorry to see you alone," he replie[d], "for I have a good deal to say to you." (Mr. John Dashwood; *Sense and Sensibility*, chapter 41). "I must beg to return to the house." (Elizabeth Bennet; *Pride and Prejudice*, chapter 56).

Chapter 41: He [was] exactly the man, who, in disposition and talents, would most suit [her]. (narrative; *Pride and Prejudice*, chapter 50).

Chapter 42: ... at the perverseness of those feelings which would now have promoted its continuance, and would formerly have rejoiced in its termination. (narrative; *Pride and Prejudice*, chapter 46).

Chapter 43: "If it will be any satisfaction to you, however, to be told, that I believe his character to be in other respects irreproachable, I am ready to confess it." (Mr. Willoughby; *Sense and Sensibility*, chapter 10).